Also by Rabih Alameddine

Koolaids

I, The Divine

A Novel in First Chapters

Rabih Alameddine

Weidenfeld & Nicolson
LONDON

First published in Great Britain in 2002
by Weidenfeld & Nicolson.

© Rabih Alameddine 2001

The right of Rabih Alameddine to be identified as the author
of this work has been asserted by him in accordance with
the Copyright, Designs and Patents Act of 1988.

A CIP catalogue record for this book is available
from the British Library.

ISBN 0297 60794 4

Printed in Great Britain by
Clays Ltd, St Ives plc

Weidenfeld & Nicolson

The Orion Publishing Group Ltd
Orion House
5 Upper Saint Martin's Lane
London, WC2H 9EA

à Raya

I, the Divine

Chapter one

My grandfather named me for the great Sarah Bernhardt. He considered having met her in person the most important event of his life. He talked about her endlessly. By the age of five, I was able to repeat each of his stories verbatim. And I did.

My grandfather was a simple man

Chapter One

At the age of thirteen, the age of discovery, I was moved from an all-girl Catholic school to a boys' school. My father decided I needed to have English, not French, as my primary language, so he transferred me to the best school in the city. It was all boys until I showed up. They wanted to integrate it and I was the guinea pig. What a guinea pig.

I was not the only girl in the school, but I was the only one in my class, all five sections. The four other girls were in the upper classes. It was life-changing culture shock.

In October of 1973, I arrived for my first day of school

Chapter One

Nineteen seventy-three was a strange year. I cut my hair short, which drove my stepmother crazy. The Lebanese army went nuts and started bombing the PLO, a harbinger of things to come. I left those wacky Carmelite nuns and entered an American-bankrolled school where I was the only girl in the whole class. I also met Fadi, who changed my life forever.

I had always been a little odd, which people blamed on my mother, but she was not at fault. My sisters were normal. People could not blame my father. My half-sisters turned out to be more normal than normal. Except for being gay, my little brother was probably the most normal of us all. I was the strange one.

When I was little, we had a nanny from the Seychelles named Violet. I remember her showing us a picture of her family—her parents and all her sisters. I pointed out a white girl in the picture and asked Violet who she was. She said that was her sister. Surprised, I asked how that could be. She said, "My mother went astray." That sentence stuck with me. I had always thought my mother "went astray" when conceiving me.

I was different, but not nearly in Fadi's league. We met my first day in class. I arrived ready for battle in jeans and sweatshirt, prepared to fight any boy who dared make fun of me.

Fadi did. When I sat behind him, he turned and whispered, "If you're a lesbian, I know just the right bar for you." My mouth dropped. The boys were supposed to be the crème de la crème. How had this boy slipped through?

He was disarming. His face had a combination of mischief and innocence that to this day I find attractive. He was not handsome, but an unearthly intelligence shone in his eyes. Years later they would dull, and after the gendarmes beat him senseless, an eye patch would cover one of them. He became a shell of his former self, a walking shadow. I try to remember him as he was at fourteen, the boy who turned my world upside down.

Chapter 1

At the age of thirteen, the age of discovery, I was moved from an all-girls Catholic school to a boys' school. My parents had thought an English education would be better than a French one. It was the first year of integration for the school, and for the first couple of years, I was the only girl in my class. At the school, I met two people who were to become primary influences in my life: Fadi, my first boyfriend, and Dina, my best friend, who appeared at school two years later.

I met Fadi on my first day in class. I sat behind him, where his first question to me was "Are you a lesbian?" My response was swift: "Your mother's cunt, you brother of a whore." The Lebanese dialect is filled with delectable curses, a luscious language all its own, of which I was a true poet, trained by none other than my father. He thought children's use of adult curse words tremendously amusing and trained all his children in the art of insult. I grew up an avid practitioner.

Fadi's reaction was an ear-to-ear grin, hands coming together for one clap, and a look signaling welcome-to-my-world. We became fast friends, at first because he would not leave me alone. The first couple of days, I could not move anywhere without him tagging along, trying to involve me in some activity he was cooking up. We became friends and partners in crime.

Fadi was not a handsome boy, nor did he mature into a handsome man. He had a long, pale face, with medium-long black hair, eternally unkempt, slightly frizzy. Depending on how the sun hit it, you could see single hairs sprouting independently out of the mess. His nose was long, downward, not outward, like the noses in ancient Greek drawings. His chest, skinny and caved in, as if malnourished. He was cute; all in all, not a particularly erotic package, but I always had peculiar tastes, somewhat exotic. Of all the boys in class, and I could have had my pick, being the only girl, he caught my fancy. His smile was his best and most memorable feature. Appearing quite natural, it was actually meticulously studied, its apparent innocence perfected in an attempt to confuse anyone who might suspect him capable of any of the acts he committed. I fell for his façade early on. I assumed he was a gentle, amazingly intelligent, studious boy. He was all that in a way, but as Miss Nahhas, our science teacher, once said, he was also the devil incarnate.

Fadi's intelligence was remarkable. We were both the top of our class, but the difference between first, him, and second, me, was immeasurable. He had an understanding of mathematics that bordered on genius. I excelled at mathematics but I was not even in the same league. My grades were close to his in the nonsciences, English, Arabic, French, history, geography, and civics, simply because he did not care about these subjects. He winged it in all the exams, never studying, and still he got higher grades than I did most of the time. He was a mechanical wiz. The first contraption I saw him make was a motorized bicycle. He took a motor from a scooter, attached it to an old bicycle. I thought it was such a magnificent feat, only to be more impressed when he confessed to having stolen both the bike and the motor. We became soul mates.

I remember the first time I caught a glimpse of his Mephistophelian side, early October, the beginning of the school year. It was a hot day, the ceiling fan circulating stale air. The building was more than a hundred years old and had no air-conditioning. Fadi sat in front of me as usual. French class and Mr. Assiss drunk and trying desperately to control the class. Without looking back, Fadi told me, "Duck when I say *duck*."

"What?" I asked, confused. Assiss was rambling on about subjunctive something or other. Utterly bored, I was carving my name into the desk with a Bic pen. "What do you mean?"

"Just duck when I tell you." I noticed he was clasping something black between three fingers. It took me a while to figure out it was one of the rubber stabilizers used under each of the legs to keep the chair from sliding. The instant Assiss looked away, Fadi threw the rubber stabilizer up toward the fan, saying "Incoming," in English. Half the class ducked under their desks. When the rubber stabilizer hit the fan, it ricocheted with such force, I heard the *whoosh* followed by various other sounds as it hit desks and walls. Assiss looked around, wondering what had happened. We pretended nothing had happened, so he pretended with us. Assiss continued with his boring lesson.

The French teacher's incessant drinking made him an easy mark and therefore Fadi's favorite target. Assiss drove an older model Vauxhall, which Fadi habitually broke into. During free periods, Fadi and I would push the car out from the spot that Assiss parked it in, roll it down the hill, and park it all the way by the lower entrance. Assiss never figured out how his car got moved.

We had three free periods a week. To this day, I have no idea what would possess a school to give a bunch of teenagers the run of the school unsupervised for an hour. Having arrived from a strict Carmelite school, where the nuns made us account for every nanosecond, I found the new school nothing short of heaven. The free periods were the time when Fadi shone.

Fadi used to brag that there was no lock he could not pick. The easiest were the numbered locks. He taught me how to do it. I had to pull the lock down as hard as possible and then roll each number until I heard a certain click. It was incredibly easy. During free periods, one of our favorite activities was opening lockers to ferret out the best lunch. Neither one of us brought lunch on Wednesday when the free period was in the morning. We looked in every locker until we came across something appetizing. When he felt playful, Fadi switched contents of different lockers causing complete chaos.

Fadi and I were both middle kids from middle-class families, and we were envious of some of the really rich kids who came to school on brand-new bicycles. During our free periods, we got to ride any of the bicycles we wanted. One day, while riding a new-model, three-speed, shiny bike, Fadi was approached by Art Haddad, who, like me, was of mixed Lebanese and American parentage, but who, unlike me, had grown up in the United States. He had come to teach at our school and see if he could "recapture his heritage." He always treated the students as equals, his American education method, and since he could not have been more than twenty-four or so, the approach was not considered offensive by the kids.

"Great bike," Art told Fadi. "Must be the newest model."

"Yes," Fadi replied. "Would you like to try it?"

The last question was followed by words like *wow, sure, gee, golly, man, thanks, incredible, hey wow, amazing, guy,* but not in any comprehensible order. Fadi told him he had to get back to class, to lock the bike in the bike rack when he was done. We left for class only to hear later that the owner of the bike had come out to find Mr. Haddad riding it. The kid had a fit. Mr. Haddad had to see the headmaster, who, of course, asked to see Fadi. Fadi said the bike was unlocked and he could not help himself. When Mr. Haddad begged him to ride the bike, Fadi specifically asked him to lock the bike so no one would steal it.

I was not saintly by any means before I met Fadi, nor was I led unwillingly down a path of demonic trickery and shenanigans. I was always a mischievous child. Fadi simply inspired me to greater heights. My father had divorced my mother, sent her packing back to America, and married a younger Lebanese woman. I saw my stepmother as a family intruder and spent most of my childhood trying to make her life miserable. I was so effective that at ten, I was transferred, along with my sisters, to the strictest school in Lebanon, run by a pod of fiendish Carmelite nuns. They were so strict, the punishments so severe, even my stepmother, a firm believer in discipline, could not leave us there. My sisters and I were transferred to different schools three years later. I won the lottery. I ended up in the best school in Lebanon, one where there was absolutely no discipline, where no teacher could raise his voice when talking to a student.

The school I transferred to had an outstanding athletic program. Since it was a boys' school, and I was the only girl in class, the PE class was geared exclusively toward young males. They played soccer primarily. I fit right in. If there was one thing at which I was superior to Fadi, and, as it turned out, every other boy in class, it was the beautiful game of soccer. I had always been a tomboy and I was blessed with a soccer-playing ability which amazed even those who knew nothing about the game. I showed up with the rest of the class on the soccer field for the first PE class. I was wearing the school's athletic uniform, a green T-shirt with the school's logo in yellow, white shorts with the logo in green, white tube socks, and a pair of desert boots. The last was not part of the uniform, but since my stepmother refused to consider buying me athletic shoes, let alone actual soccer shoes, I had to make do. Our PE teacher, Mr. Najjar, could not believe his eyes. He ordered me off the field, screaming and hollering. In later years, I would have been able to describe Mr. Najjar as a male chauvinist pig with the intelligence of a four-year-old, but back then I did not have the vocabulary so I simply called him an ugly-dog-fornicating-son-of-a-whore. I left the field. Fadi followed me, saying we had to go see the headmaster. He took me aside, went to his locker, pulling out a sheet of paper. On it he wrote:

> To Whom It May Concern:
> I hereby authorize my daughter, Sarah Mustapha Nour el-Din, to participate fully in all physical education classes. I wish her to be treated exactly like the boys. I do not wish her to be traumatized by unfair exclusionary policies. I expect my wishes to be followed or I will take appropriate action.
>
> Sincerely,
> Mustapha Hammoud Nour el-Din

I was dumbfounded. I could not believe he would do that.
"Nobody would think this letter is real," I said.
"Yes, they will."
"It's badly written," I said, alternating my weight between one foot and another, fidgeting. "My father would have written it better."

"They will believe it," he replied. "Trust me. I've done this many times before. They always believe it."

"They might call him to check."

"Look," he said. "Do you want to play or not?" When I did not reply, he pulled me by the hand toward the headmaster's office. "It would help if you look traumatized."

Fadi walked into the headmaster's office with me. He told the headmaster he had to come because his conscience would not allow him to stand idly by as Mr. Najjar screamed insults at me. Not during his entire stay at the school had he witnessed such repulsive behavior from a teacher, behavior sure to damage a sensitive student like me. I was shocked at his audacity, which the headmaster must have interpreted as my being adequately traumatized. Fadi proceeded to show my faux father's letter. The headmaster was livid, telling me I was to show up at the next PE class and he would take care of everything. Mr. Najjar was forced to apologize to me publicly, and I became one of the boys. I also became a Fadi devotee.

The first cigarette. In the Lebanese dialect, the words associated with smoking, verbs in particular, are sui generis. You not only smoke a cigarette, you can drink it. The verb *to smoke* may stand on its own, but the verb *to drink* cannot, of course, since it implies the drinking of liquids. One must use the phrase *drink a cigarette*, which sounds ridiculous in any other language. That kind of idiosyncrasy fascinated my thirteen-year-old mind. However, the particular use of the Lebanese dialect which turned out to be an embarrassment was the word *inhale*. When it comes to cigarettes, one does not inhale in Lebanese, one swallows. So, on a November day, first rain of the season, taking cover in one of the many Turkish arches embedded in the walls along the school grounds, Fadi offered me a cigarette, Marlboro, and asked, "Do you swallow?"

I replied, "Yes, of course."

I took the cigarette from his pale, nail-bitten fingers, and he proceeded to light it for me. I had seen it done many times. Everyone smoked in Lebanon. I could fool him into thinking I had done this before. I took a drag, but instead of inhaling, I swallowed.

At first, he fell for it. "You've done this before," he said. "If this were your first time, you'd be coughing like crazy."

"Of course, I've done this before," I said haughtily. "I've been doing this since I was ten." I kept swallowing over and over, drunk on my own pride for not coughing or wheezing.

He noticed what I was doing, though. He smacked me on the side of the head. "When you swallow, you don't swallow, you baby." He shook his head, smirking. "I've been doing this since I was ten," he repeated sarcastically.

I could not for the life of me figure out swallowing without swallowing, so I stared at him intently, earnestly pretending not to look. "Well," I said between swallows, which were beginning to sound more like gulps, "this is how we do it in my family."

"Yeah, right. I believe that." He inhaled on his cigarette, took a long drag, and blew in my face. He laughed and I had to smile. Finally I figured out how to smoke, but it was too late. I might not have coughed hysterically from smoking my first, and what was to be my last, cigarette, but the smoke I had swallowed upset my stomach. I began to feel more and more queasy until I threw up, right there in front of him. He worried about me, asking if I was all right. I was so embarrassed. I lay on the ground and teared up.

I sat up and he moved closer to me, shoulder to shoulder, extinguished his cigarette saying, "I think smoking is overrated anyway. It tastes like shit."

"I have to drink something," I said. "I have to get rid of this taste in my mouth."

"Let's get a Seven-Up." Excited to be doing something helpful. "It's good for your stomach anyway." He helped me up, even though I was feeling better.

"I have a better idea," he said. He zipped his anorak, but did not pull the hood up, running out into the rain. He stood five feet away from me, all smiles, impish as usual, calling me with his hands and eyes. I walked out tentatively. He pulled me close to him and hugged me, still smiling, hair all wet. He tilted his head backward, opening his mouth to the sky. I did the same, rain falling on my face, drinking whatever drops fell in my mouth, quenching an unnamable thirst, laughing. We hugged closer and drank. We were sopping wet. I looked down to see a craned neck, elongated like a swan's, and my heart fluttered. He looked at me, mouth open, tongue distended to capture more. And then he kissed me. Two thirteen-year-olds who knew nothing about anything, French kissing in the rain. I wanted to swallow his tongue.

CHAPTER 1

I was in New York last week and saw two retrospectives, Pierre Bonnard's and Rothko's. Besides noting that Bonnard could not draw if his life depended on it and that Rothko did not even try, I was stunned by a major realization. When it came to a choice between a beautiful color and the correct color, Bonnard always picked the beautiful one, while Rothko, in his great paintings, picked the correct one. I realized when it came to men, I did not pick the beautiful or the correct. I picked the wrong one. I chose David.

I stared out of my window onto the bleak, leafless branches of the tree in front of my Victorian flat. The late afternoon light was fading to violet. Noisy sparrows appeared, a bustle of activity before they retired for the night. January of 1992.

My ex-husband Joe had called and asked if I would be willing to fly and attend a party in his honor. His company had just promoted and relocated him to Dallas. Both he and his wife wanted me to join them in celebration, to see their new house and so forth. Joe was in constant touch with my brother, Ramzi, in whom I confided, so they knew I was feeling blue.

I started to make tea, but decided against it. I took a walk to Duboce Park, a short distance from my flat. Every weekday, beginning at four in the afternoon, the park transformed into canine heaven. Barking, frolicking dogs of every breed, color, and shape raced around the grass. Owners stood in groups chatting while their pets played, sniffed, chased, and did group somersaults. I had been coming to the park every day for the last two weeks. I was dogless, but I came prepared.

The instant Sally, a collie, saw me, she bounded over, jumped with joy as I reached into my coat pocket for her biscuit. I tossed it and she caught it in midair. Mindy, a tan pug, began licking my jeans. In less than a minute, I had ten dogs to play with.

"When are you getting one?" Annette, Sally's owner, asked me. She towered over me, looking taller from my new position, flat on the ground with dogs all over me. "Get off there. You'll ruin your coat."

"It's cheap," I joked. The dogs disbursed in different directions, forgetting me as I stood up. Annette was popular with the other dog owners; a couple of women moseyed over. "Besides, you know I can't get a dog. I can barely take care of myself. I don't even have a job right now. Anyway, my cats would hate me."

"A dog does wonders."

In a couple of minutes, a thin, lanky woman showed up, a sprightly spring in her step. I recognized the leashed dog, but it took me a moment to realize it was Sandra. She released her cocker when she reached us.

"Jesus," Annette exclaimed. "You're looking wonderful."

"I'm dating." Sandra beamed. She looked as if only her heavy coat kept her grounded.

"That really works," Annette laughed.

"We just had sex," Sandra giggled. "I left him sleeping on

the bed." She looked ten years younger than she had the day before. Her appeased lust had softened her face, smoothed her miniscule wrinkles.

After polite time had passed, I excused myself and walked the six blocks back home, alone.

I locked myself in, clicked on the teakettle, and sat on the sofa in the big mess otherwise known as my living room. I picked up the phone and dialed Joe and Charlene.

"I would love to come," I said. "It'll be good to see you both."

"I'm so happy you're coming," Charlene cooed. "You might even find Mr. Right. You should think about moving to Dallas. San Francisco is so depressing and morbid."

I was actually thinking of Joe. I would go to Dallas to show my support and try to give him the approval he always sought from me.

I overbrewed my tea; drank it slightly bitter.

I called my hairdresser and made an appointment to cut and dye my hair.

I arrived in Dallas two days before the party and planned on leaving the day after. I hated the city as much as I thought I would. All anyone could talk about were the Cowboys and their chances in the playoffs. Charlene was happy. Joe was not, or so it seemed to me, in spite of the fact that he had finally gotten exactly what he thought he wanted from a wife: she gave him an adorable boy, she did everything in their home including laundry, and most important, she did not embarrass him.

Whenever I was alone with Joe during the two days I was there, Charlene would send her son into the room with us.

The first time I carried him, Charlene made sure to mention how surprised she was that I had motherly instincts. She probably used the pronoun *we* more in one day than I have in my whole life. I did not blame her. Most plain women stake their claims clumsily.

———————

I decided on a short, fitted black Chanel for the reception, scoop neck, a tad risqué, but I figured one can never go wrong with black, and this dress in particular highlighted my best feature, my legs.

"I wish I had the nerve to wear something like that," Charlene said. She wore a long pink gown with white chenille daisies. She scrunched whatever was left of her eyebrows, lifted her dress, showing a purulent cyst on her upper right thigh. "Look, I can't wear anything above the knee until this is gone."

Joe watched the exchange, a puzzled look on his face. I saw him shudder and put his right hand in his pocket. He looked skinnier.

———————

The reception was at a downtown hotel. As usual, the first thing I noticed was how badly most women wore evening dresses. There are a few places on the East Coast, and maybe Los Angeles, where women understand evening gowns. The rest of the country still has far to go. That night most of the women wore expensive prom dresses in all kinds of pastels. The second thing I noticed was that, other than the help, there was not one nonwhite person in the room. These were the company executives and their clients. I began to see why

Joe would want me there. I had always been his defense against American gentiles, the country club set.

David stood in the center of the room surrounded by four people, holding their attention. He was unlike any of the men who usually caught my eye. He was a little over six feet, dark blond hair graying at the temples, not in very good shape, big-boned, with a slight belly. He had high cheekbones, cherubic and baby-faced, and the light turned his cheeks a Bonnard pink. He listened intently to one of the men in the group, while the others looked at him, but his full attention was on the speaker. A man who listened was an anomaly in my life.

He glanced up at me and hesitated. At first, I did not make much of it. In that room, I looked different from all the other women. I was also standing next to Joe, the guest of honor. David kept looking back at me, though. At the first break in conversation, he excused himself and walked over to Joe and Charlene. They exchanged pleasantries, and he was intro-duced to me as David Troubridge, senior vice-president in charge of the Western region. He was formal until he found out I was Joe's ex.

"It's wonderful you two are still friends," he said. "I wish I could say the same about my ex." That should have been my first warning, but I never listen to warnings, mine or any-body else's.

"Actually Sarah is close to both her exes," Joe said. "She's good that way. No acrimony."

"You have an accent." David had his full attention on me. "Are you Israeli?"

Joe chuckled.

"He wishes I were," I laughed, pointing at Joe. "Nour el-Din is a Lebanese name. I am originally from Lebanon."

Joe had to chime in. "Technically, the name is Druze, so it could be an Israeli one . . ."

"An Arab woman marrying a Jewish man," David interrupted, ignoring Joe. "What did your family think?"

"They didn't approve."

"I can imagine. Do you work for the company?"

"No," Joe said, trying to include himself one more time, "but she could. She's a good engineer." He stepped closer to me.

"Was," I said. "Was an engineer, but not a good one." I took a sip from my drink, but kept my eyes locked on David's.

"Why did you give it up?"

"I found out I hated it. I would call myself an academic engineer. I was good at solving problems on paper, but hadn't a clue when it came to the real world. Anyway, I could not function at all in such a structured environment."

"And what do you do now?"

"Professional divorcée," I said, thinking it a clever reply. His face registered confusion, followed by disappointment, which he tried quickly to mask. I lost him. He looked at Joe, wished him well in his new job, said his very-nice-to-meet-yous to Charlene and me, and withdrew.

I was sitting in the airport lounge waiting to board when I felt someone behind me. David smiled as he came around and sat next to me.

"Fancy meeting you here," he said. "Where are you going?"

Home, I told him, to San Francisco. That was where he lived as well. We were both surprised, each assuming the other was a Dallas resident. He suggested we sit together on the plane and said he would take care of it. He returned from the counter with a new boarding pass. It was next to him, in first class.

We talked the whole flight. I did more of the talking than he did, a pattern that would prove typical. I told him about my first marriage, my second, the relationships in my life. I brought up my brother, I told him about my son. In that confined space, with an avid listener, I poured out my feelings, my fears, my hopes. I felt heard. He asked all the right questions, wanting details of the story. He told me about his marriage, his life in New England before he moved west. He spoke about his divorce. He was caught cheating. No, it was not the first time. He had no children. How did I feel about abandoning my son?

I told him about Kamal, about the crushing choices I had to make, how much pain being without my son caused. I told him about my inadequacies as a mother, as a wife. He attempted to stem my tears with platitudes and admissions that he had not been the greatest husband either. By the time we left the plane we were holding hands. We kissed in the cab. We made love on the stairs in my flat, surrounded by luggage, with my cats watching.

In bed, where we were to spend the next three years, we talked and explored each other. His caresses were gentle, intimate. He asked me the most interesting questions. He was all ears and hands. We talked as he caressed my breasts. I found out more about him, about his work, how he became the youngest vice-president, his style of management. I was captured by everything about him.

He did not spend the night, saying he was unable to sleep well anywhere but in his own bed. He also left a little frustrated because he could not bring me to orgasm. He felt inadequate, even though I told him it was the best sex I had ever had.

David was more mature than any of the other men I had loved. Whereas Fadi, my first lover, Omar, ex number one, and Joe, ex number two, were emotional, David was reserved. Physically, they all had Semitic features, while David was as waspish as you could get. But more important, while all my previous lovers could make me laugh, David could make me cry as well.

For our second date, he showed up at my door carrying a smile and two bags of groceries. He was going to cook since I had told him I was not very good at it. His unkempt hair fell on his forehead. He wore khakis, a yellow merino sweater, his brown shirt had the top button undone, the left collar tucked beneath the sweater, light brown tufts of hair sprouting from the hollow beneath his Adam's apple.

He placed the groceries on the kitchen counter, took me in his arms and kissed me. "Won't it go bad?" I asked. He led me to bed.

He washed the vegetables in the kitchen, standing barefoot, in his khakis, shirtless, beltless, and underwearless. "You should stock your kitchen better," he said. He went through my cabinets. "Oh, my God. You don't even have a lettuce spinner."

I gave him my best helpless smile, shrugged my shoulders.

"You don't know what a spinner is, do you?" When he admonished, his voice rose a little higher. He shook his head in consternation. "It's a good thing I came prepared."

I studied an arabesque of sun-induced freckles on his back, walked up behind him, kissed them, tried to connect the dots. He reached behind and spanked my butt. "Not while I'm cooking."

"What are you making?"

"Can't you tell?" He handed me a computer printout with recipes for tabbouleh, fried potato and coriander salad, and fatteh, a dish of minced lamb, baked pita, garlicked yogurt, and sautéed pine nuts. "A full-fledged Lebanese dinner."

"Have you done anything like this before?"

"Nope. I just checked the recipes on the computer." He turned on a burner under the deep fryer. "I had trouble figuring out what to choose, what goes best with what. I wanted to ask you but I thought that would spoil the surprise. I ended up choosing this. I know it's two salads, but I thought the fried potato salad sounded more like a vegetable dish."

"Jesus. When you said you'll deal with dinner, I thought we were going to order a pizza."

"Order a pizza?" He pretended to be offended. "I make my pizzas from scratch using my very own pizza oven."

"Well, can I help with anything?"

"Why don't you chop the tomatoes?"

I did as I was told only to be rebuked again. "No, no, no. You're squeezing them. Leave it be. Why don't you open the wine?" I took out the wine bottle. "You're domestically disabled," he joked.

"This is Lebanese. Chateau Musar. I love this wine. Where did you find it?"

"At my favorite wine shop. I already tried a bottle just to make sure. It's quite good. Have to say I was surprised."

He chopped the tomatoes with the speed of an accomplished chef. His fingers, though long and thick, seemed delicate, feminine even, like a doctor's, or a surgeon's to be more precise. I began to entertain erotic thoughts again. The knife traveled deftly over vegetables.

"You went to so much trouble," I said.

"Say thank you."

"Thank you."

"You can thank me better by getting a knife sharpener. You don't have one."

"And a spinner."

"And a lettuce spinner. Come to think of it, I'll get them. I'm not sure I trust you in a kitchenware store."

As the scent of sautéed minced lamb wafted in the air, my cats, Descartes and Pascal, began to meow. David bent down and stroked them. Descartes licked his hand. David scooped some lamb into a saucer and set it on the floor. "I got more than enough lamb," he said.

I sipped my wine. I noticed the delicate hair on his arms. "One could fall for a man who cooks," I said.

"One could." He smiled.

In those early days, I was oblivious. I wanted nothing but to be in his arms. I wanted

Half and Half

A MEMOIR

Sarah Nour el-Din

For Dina

A MEMOIR'S CAST:

Mustapha Nour el-Din:	My father
Janet Foster:	My mother
Saniya Nour el-Din:	My stepmother
Hammoud Nour el-Din:	My grandfather
Amal Arouti:	My sister
Ashraf Arouti:	Amal's husband
Lamia Shaddad:	My sister
Samir Shaddad:	Lamia's husband
Rana Nour el-Din:	My half-sister, unmarried
Majida Salameh:	My half-sister
Alaa' Salameh:	Majida's husband
Ramzi Nour el-Din:	My half-brother
Peter Westchester:	Ramzi's lover
Kamal Farouk:	My son
Omar Farouk:	My ex-husband
Joseph Adams:	My ex-husband
Charlene Adams:	Joe's wife
Dina Ballout:	My best friend
Margot James:	Dina's lover
Fadi Arna'out:	My first lover
David Troubridge:	My lover

Chapter One–
The Beginning

I had a fairy-tale childhood complete with the evil step-mother. She arrived at our house a young girl. Only fifteen years separated us (twelve between her and Amal, the eldest). She decided early on she did not like me and set a course of discipline that would last until my teenage years. She was strict with my two sisters as well, but she was a Nazi with me.

I did not do well in a disciplined environment, not in my stepmother's house nor later with the nuns at school. I had an independent streak not easily vanquished, though my stepmother tried. My father and uncles used to teach us girls all kinds of pornographic swear words and laugh hysterically when we repeated them. When my stepmother arrived, she found them offensive and demanded a stop to all foul language. My father's compromise was to have us use swear words only when my stepmother was not around. My sisters never slipped. I did. I liked the shocked look on faces when I came out with a delicious curse. When she was not around, I received a hilarious response. When she was there, I got hot peppers. But still I slipped.

She was always upset that I never did what she asked. I was a precocious child, and all I ever wanted was for people to explain why they wanted me to do something. She never would. She always demanded and I wondered why. For every why, I received a smack. I never stopped asking.

Since I was the youngest until my half-sisters were born, I was the house slave. My stepmother was constantly demanding things. "Get me a bottle of water, Sarah." "My slippers from under the bed." "Get me the blue jar of face cream, Sarah. The one on the nightstand. Make sure it's the blue one and not the green one, Sarah. Not the green one." I brought the green one back and got smacked.

Every night, I walked on her back because I was the perfect weight. She had walked on her mother's back when she was my age, so I had to do it. She moaned with each step I took, and I imagined breaking vertebrae, my small feet making tiny indentations on her back. Skin turning pink.

I got revenge. Taking her shoes was my favorite. Once I figured which pair was her preferred, I would throw one of them down the garbage chute and listen as it clanked down the six floors and landed in the garbage containers with a tiny thud. No one ever looked in there. I always threw out one of the shoes, not the pair. That way she believed she had lost a shoe as opposed to someone having stolen them. I also liked to empty half of her perfume bottle down the toilet. When Violet, our nanny from the Seychelles, passed by her, my stepmother would smell the air. She was never able to pin anything on Violet, of course, and I don't think she believed Violet was capable of doing the things I was doing. Nonetheless, she sent Violet packing within a couple of years of her taking over our house. When she did that, I declared war.

I put Bic pens in her coat pockets to bleed. I placed a live mouse in her apron. I dethreaded the hems of her skirts. But my favorite act of mischief, for which unfortunately I was caught, involved the sachets. My stepmother made sachets by cutting old mosquito nettings into small strips, stuffing them with lavender, and tying them up in a bag. These she would place between the freshly laundered sheets in the linen closets; the sheets, when taken out and placed on the beds, carried the aroma of lavender. My father loved that. One night, I went into the linen closet, took out the bags, and placed them in the cats' litter box. The next night, I put them back between the sheets in the closet. My stepmother was furious. My father was the one who beat me for that, with the belt of course, in the bathroom.

I was a natural tomboy, and, knowing it annoyed my stepmother, I refused to wear dresses. I was frequently filthy, and I was better at games than any of the boys in the neighborhood. I did not wear makeup at all until I was fifteen, when I met my best friend, Dina. My stepmother taught my sisters, Amal and Lamia, household duties, such as cooking and sewing. I could not stand it. When she tried teaching me to embroider, I pricked my fingers until they bled. She never tried again.

She turned my father against me. I was his favorite daughter, his Cordelia. He always considered my uniqueness enchanting. After years of her nagging, he began to see me as a lost cause, an embarrassment to the family. The final disappointment for him was my skill at soccer. I had played the game as a child, on the streets with the boys. My father never considered this the problem my stepmother did.

However, during the years after the 1970 World Cup Finals, my stepmother was able to convince my father I was wicked. I watched the championship game with my family and saw the Brazilians tear the Italians apart. I did not know who the players were and actually thought Instant Replay was the best player because his name kept appearing at the bottom of the screen every time something really great happened. All I really knew was the Brazilians made coffee and Italians pasta.

But then I saw Pele pass the ball to Jairzhinho for one of the goals and experienced a soccer epiphany. From that moment on, I knew how the game was supposed to be played, and that knowledge marked the beginning of my spiraling descent into disgrace.

I was a scrawny child, neither fast nor strong. But I developed impeccable control with a soccer ball and was blessed with something intangible, soccer vision. I could see plays developing long before they happened. I always knew where to be, where to send the ball. Even in the small, disorganized street games, without a pair of tennis shoes to call my own, it was apparent to any bystander that I was special. And that I was a girl.

One day, my stepmother looked out from the balcony, saw me down on the street playing, and had a nervous breakdown. She refused to speak to anyone, took tranquilizers, and locked herself in her room. My father slept on the couch. The next day, when she allowed my father into the room, they had a long conversation. All three of us, her stepdaughters, not her daughters, ended up in a half-boarding school, *Carmel St. Joseph.* The school was only four streets away from our house, but we slept there five nights a week. We left for school on Monday mornings and came back on Saturday afternoons. We had to wear uniforms. The nuns had been warned about me and behaved accordingly. I was treated as a troublemaker and I did not disappoint. I was not allowed to play soccer or any other sport in school. I had to watch while the other girls played volleyball or basketball, considered acceptable sports for girls, but not for me.

Luckily, my stepmother's meddling in my life ceased, or more accurately decreased, with the birth of Ramzi, my father's first son and the reason for his marriage to my stepmother. I was eleven. Both she and my father stopped caring

about the girls and showered all their attention on the new-
born son, the boy who was the sole reason for my father's, and
all his forefathers', existence. Apocryphal stories abound about
that "blessed" event. It is said that my mother, Janet, whom
my father had divorced and sent back to New York because she
could not deliver him a boy to carry on his name, wailed for
one whole month beginning the instant the infant Ramzi
himself wailed for the first time. It is said my father cried. All
I know is that I was relieved.

Chapter 1

What I recall from all the craziness of that day is the sound of
the opening stanza of Deep Purple's "Smoke on the Water"
being massacred by Mazen, the boy living on the second
floor. Funny what we remember. Setting my memory in time
is easy. The first day of the war in Beirut, April 1975. I was
fifteen. Shells and bombs fell all around us, but we must have
had electricity since Mazen was playing his new electric guitar, had been for the last ten days since he had gotten it for
his birthday, and no "political skirmish" was going to get
him to stop. I distinctly remember wondering how he could
play so badly. Every boy in Beirut played "Smoke on the
Water" on his electric guitar, yet we had the misfortune to
live above the one boy who was tone-deaf. He took his guitar
out to the stairwell, while his parents desperately tried to
shut him up. The giddy days.

My whole family was out of our apartment. The stairwell
seemed the safest place, surrounded as it was on every side.
My father sat sideways, with his back facing the wall, one
knee close to his chest, crumpling his best brown suit. He
looked so handsome in those days. His hair was still dark
brown, his fierce eyes still indomitable. He smoked his cigarette, blowing smoke toward the upper floors. He spoke softly
to us throughout, to keep us calm. "They can't keep going on

like this," he said. "They'll stop soon." I noticed skin between
his socks and the hem of his pants. His sock garters must
have been loose. It was the first time I saw a flaw in his attire.
My father's name is Mustapha Hammoud Nour el-Din, M.D.
Everyone called him Doctor, even his children sometimes. I
called him *Docteur Baba*.

I smelled something peculiar in the air, what I discovered
later to be cordite. The things we learn. In time, the smell of
cordite, of garbage, urine, and decaying flesh, would become
familiar to us, banal and clichéd.

Three loud explosions in a row rocked the building. Too
close. Pallid-faced Ramzi, the youngest, screamed and bur-
rowed deeper into his mother's dress. My father winced. I
assumed he was wondering if Ramzi was too young to be
chided. Boys should never scream.

"They don't seem to be letting up," my stepmother,
Saniya, said. She held her son close, caressing his hair.
"Maybe we should move down and be with the neighbors."
She was rounded and soft, bearing an uncanny resemblance
to Anna Magnani. She sat between her two daughters,
Majida on her right, and Rana on her left, comforting them.
She would look at us, her three stepdaughters, intermittently,
wondering how she should comfort us. All three of us
remained separate from her and the young ones.

Amal, my eldest sister, then nineteen, was about to get
married. Gunfire could not dampen her mood. She leaned
against the wall, resolute, wearing Jordache jeans and a
lavender angora V-neck sweater, her face serene.

My other sister, Lamia, seemed unperturbed as well, but in
a different mood. No amount of gunfire could transform the
air of gloom around her. She sat, head bowed, not participat-
ing. She was almost eighteen. The dim light created shadowy
havoc on her acne-scarred face. Her morose expression was

only habit, through continual recurrence of an emotional display, the face reverted to it, habituated itself to it, even in repose. She did not seem to belong to our family, yet was an essential part of it.

I stared up at the water stains on the ceiling, at the peeling paint. I wondered whether the concierge would paint the stairwell if the building was damaged enough. Another shell fell close by.

"I'm sure it'll be over soon," I said. "They'll get tired." I smoothed my red dress. My hand curled a lock of my reddish brown hair.

My half-sister Rana wrote furiously in her diary. She wrote incessantly, considering the world nothing but material for her writing. My favorite sister was growing up to be a stunner, a heartbreaker in training.

"What are you writing?" I asked.

"I'm writing about this. Everything that's happening. All the noise. Where it comes from, how unexpected. Why the stop, start, stop and start again. All the different sounds. Always coming from different places. I can't tell where it's coming from next."

"No one can tell, my dear," said Saniya. "No one's sure who's fighting whom. We just have to wait it out."

"If I knew what to expect, it would be better," Rana said. "I just don't know what's coming next."

Something exploded not too far from us, making everyone jump. Ramzi screamed again. Rana reached out and patted his head. She seemed so adult. He began whimpering. I knelt down on the stairs below him and rubbed his tiny back. "It's okay, *hayatee*. Everything will be okay. I promise."

As if at my signal, the gunfire stopped. We heard men shouting, but we could not discern what was being said. "They seem to be on the roof of the building next door," my father said. "That's probably why the shells are dropping close."

"Do you think they'll go away?" Saniya asked.

"I hope so. Maybe I should go up and talk to them."

"No. We don't even know who they are. You can't talk to them."

"Maybe one of them is hurt," Rana said. "Would they need our help?"

We sat silent, wondering if they would fight again. Whenever someone tried to say something, my father shushed them. After ten minutes of silence, the electric guitar was back at it again. Lamia stood up, leaned across the railing, and screamed down, "Stop making all that noise. We're trying to think here." She sat back down.

PREMIER CHAPITRE:

Le commencement

Il est des histoires qui ressemblent à un conte de fées. L'histoire de mon enfance, par exemple, semblait être tirée d'un conte de Grimm. Et pourtant, mon enfance racontée ne fut jamais une histoire à faire rêver.

L'on dit souvent que les contes de fées laissent libre cours à l'imagination de l'enfant. La mienne (mon imagination), stagnait à chaque fois qu'on me parlait de sorcières. Je ne me prenais jamais à imaginer diverses figures féminines au physique hideux et aux cheveux hirsutes. Les sorcières des histoires qui m'étaient narrées avaient un visage qui m'était douloureusement familier, des cheveux longs et lisses comme de la soie, une élegance recherchée, et surtout une jeunesse hantée et menacée par la mienne. Invariablement, dans mon esprit, toutes les sorcières se retrouvaient en une seule: ma belle-mère.

Elle débarqua un jour dans nos vies, belle, jeune et impitoyable. Elle me prit en grippe dès le début. Et je le lui rendais bien. Elle m'était détestable. A son arrivée, elle imposa un système de lois et d'interdits qui transforma notre maison en une institution hautement disciplinée. Mes deux soeurs se plièrent sagement à ses règles. Mais mon esprit rebelle se refusait de se soumettre à ce régime qui semblait doubler de sévérité à mon égard. Si elle était intransigeante avec mes soeurs, avec moi elle se transformait en un despote Nazi.

Mon père et mes oncles prenaient un malin plaisir à nous apprendre des gros mots. Et encore, au fur et à mesure que nous nous perfectionnions dans cet art, ils enrichissaient notre vocabulaire d'insultes à caractère pornographiques. Avant l'arrivée de ma belle-mère, nous passions nos soirées à nous lancer des insultes. Bien sûr les oreilles délicates de celle-ci furent choquées par notre vocabulaire qu'elle trouvait aberrant. C'est pourquoi mon père avait trouvé un compromis. Il nous permettait de laisser libre cours à nos injures durant les absences de ma belle-mère. Mes soeurs avait tout de suite appris à éviter les dérapages compromettants en la présence de celle-ci. Quant à moi, je ne l'appris jamais. Et je dérapais souvent. Je me délectais dans mes dérapages qui faisaient surgir des expressions effarées autour de moi. En l'absence de ma marâtre, mes injures déclenchaient des fous rires. Quand elle était dans les parages, je recevais les piments. Mais je continuais à avoir ces lapsus quand même. J'en savourais la sonorité exquise.

CHAPTER ONE

My Mother and I

I wanted my mother to see her grandson, but she refused. My son, Kamal, was born in New York. When he was a baby, I took him everyday across the park, from the Upper West Side to the Upper East Side, to visit Janet. Once he left New York, she did not want to see him again. Kamal lived in Beirut with his father, but he came every summer to visit me.

One day, in July of 1993, I forced the issue. I walked Kamal over to her building. I told Jonathan, the doorman, to tell my mother Kamal and I were coming up. I did not have to do that since Jonathan knew me well, but I thought it would be better if she was prepared for us. Janet told him she could not receive us because she was leaving. I said I would wait for her downstairs and see her on her way out. Janet entered the lobby twenty minutes later, still beautiful as ever. Like a well-behaved boy, Kamal stood up to greet his grandmother. She shook his hand.

"You're a big boy now," she said.

"He's twelve, Mother."

"Well, I can't stay here and chat. I'm late for an appointment. We can do this some other time. Okay? Have fun you two."

She turned around and walked out, not allowing us to say anything more.

"Your mother is crazy," Kamal said.

"She's your grandmother."

"Sitto Saniya is my grandmother, not Janet."

"Saniya is your step-grandmother. Janet is your grand-mother. She's your blood and you can't forget that."

"I'm hungry."

I took him to a Greek restaurant across the street. We sat outdoors because I wanted to watch. He ordered pizza, the only thing he ate those days. Within five minutes of sitting down, we saw Janet walk back into the apartment building.

Chapter one

This, I learned from my father: "I don't think any man ever loved a woman as much as I loved your mother. But it faded, eroded slowly. One day I woke up and I was not in love. There was nothing I could do. We did not have enough in common to have a comfortable life together, not like Saniya and I. Once the love was gone, your mother got on my nerves. With Saniya, I don't love her as much as I loved your mother, but she makes me happy. Your mother made me crazy." There you go. My father divorced my mother and sent her packing, not because she could not give him a son, not because she was a terrible mother to his girls, but because he fell out of love.

In my family, love, like religion and politics, was to be avoided, a passion that vanquished reason and caused endless pain and heartache. I grew up angry with my father because he destroyed the fairy tale. My parents, Mustapha and Janet, their glorious love had not ended up happily ever after; it withered and faded. Unlike Amal and Lamia, my older sisters, I never heard them tell their story lovingly, since I was two when my parents split up, never as the grand affair. I was told the story, but only as a didactic fable of the folly of youth, the craziness of passionate love.

Janet arrived in Beirut in 1955, an independent woman of twenty, wanting to explore the world, picking the American

University of Beirut to finish her bachelor's, which she never did. Fate intervened in the form of a medical student at the university, my father. My mother was a beauty and, according to her, had had a number of beaus after her in New York, but my father had an irresistible charm.

The story goes like this: On arriving in Beirut, Janet went to a Lebanese fortune-teller who read her coffee cup. The fortune-teller saw the man who was to be the love of Janet's life. She told her the man was Lebanese, a healer who would save her from certain death, falling in love with her after curing her illness and then marrying her. They would live happily ever after.

Janet met Mustapha at the beach of the American University of Beirut (technically not a beach since there is no sand, only large rocks and cement walkways, making it a poor beach by Beirut standards). At the time, my father had a habit of walking around with a stethoscope, which identified him as a medical student and helped him talk to girls. Years later, he would apply the same principle when he put the stethoscope on his car's sun visor, thereby avoiding serious trouble or minor inconveniences when stopped at the checkpoints during the war. Whether Syrian soldiers, Christian soldiers of the Lebanese Forces, or the Druze militiamen, when they saw the stethoscope they did not ask for his ID, opting instead for a diagnosis of their ailments.

My mother was swimming that day. She was trying to climb on one of the rocks to rest when a sea urchin's spine inadvertently pricked her ankle. She screamed, but apparently had enough composure to swim back to the cement platform. People called to the man with the stethoscope to come look at the ankle. The stories differ here. My grandmother says the bleeding was so profuse, it took a heroic effort on my father's part to halt it. My father says there was no blood at all, and the prick was barely noticeable. My father examined the ankle and told my mother the only way to *save* her foot was for him to suck the poison out of the most beautiful ankle in the world. He then lifted her ankle and kissed it.

Their love affair was torrid and scandalous. They embarrassed the university by kissing publicly. The Druze community felt it was losing one of its brightest men and my grandparents were horrified. They objected to everything about Janet. They did everything they could to break up the couple, threatening and cajoling, to no avail. From the beginning, Janet tried to appease her future in-laws. She dressed more conservatively, held her tongue, and made Mustapha the most important thing in her life. When she appeared at Mustapha's uncle's funeral, following the precise rituals of the Druze, wearing the traditional black, everyone understood it was a lost cause. Mustapha and Janet were to marry.

Janet became more Druze than any Druze woman, even though she could not actually become one. One could not convert to the religion, but had to be born into it. Since there were no civil marriages in Lebanon, Mustapha and Janet had to travel to Limassol, Cyprus—technically, that meant that all their children were bastards. They came back to an apartment in Beirut bought for them by my grandparents. While Mustapha completed his studies, Janet became a Druze housewife. She learned to cook; her dishes became the talk of the town. To this day, it is said that her kibbeh, a dish of raw meat and cracked wheat, is unequaled in all of Lebanon. She became an impeccable hostess, generous to a fault, her house the cleanest it could possibly be. She never missed a funeral or a wedding, was the first on congratulatory visits when a birth was announced and the first at hospitals when an acquaintance was ill. She began to speak Arabic, with a mountain Druze accent even, which made her Druze contemporaries giggle but pleased the elders. She tried hard to be perfect and most likely would have succeeded had it not been for the daughters.

Amal was first, exactly nine months to the day from their wedding night. Everybody would have preferred a boy, but they were happy with Amal. She was healthy, a pretty baby, and there was time for boys later. Even her name meant *hope* in Arabic. They were disappointed with Lamia, but the marriage survived. When I arrived on the scene, it was too much. My grandparents convinced my father he needed a Druze wife who would provide him with a bushel of boys. Mustapha sent Janet back to New York.

Before she was married, Janet had been a lively girl, gregarious even. She had always been strong. After the marriage she became quiet in deference to her new position in the community. She became a steady and reliable woman who never said much, a woman who stood bravely and lovingly by her husband for six years as he finished medical school. She withstood most things thrown at her, but she finally succumbed to her husband's fizzled love.

After the divorce, she was never strong again. The first time I saw her after she left, I was eighteen. She did not resemble the woman described in any of the stories I had heard about her. When I moved to New York with my first husband, Omar, we grew closer, but it was a constant strain to be in her presence for she never forgave. She had been wronged, and lived that wrong for the rest of her life.

I did not forgive my father his treatment of my mother until I repeated the same story, taking on the roles of Mustapha and Janet simultaneously. Like Mustapha, I fell out of love with my husband, and like Janet, I am no longer with my child. I made mistakes.

Like Janet and Mustapha, Omar and I met at the American University beach in 1980, while we were both engineering students. I saw him with a group of friends, diving from a rock into the sea. I had noticed him before. He was two years ahead of me and would be graduating in a couple of months. He dove, holding a knife in his hand, coming back up a few seconds later with a sea urchin. He got out of the water, cut the sea urchin in half, and fed it to a dog. It was not the same story I grew up with, but close enough. He noticed me watching him and sauntered over. We chatted about school and the engineering program. I remember his smile, sly, demure. He was somewhat shy, yet playful. Everything about him intrigued me, how his bushy eyebrows almost met, how they lined up from side to side since his face was so narrow. I loved his nasal voice, how he took a quick, short breath before every sentence, the seconds it took him to think before every response. Like my mother, I was smitten on that beach.

We went out twice before we made love. I assume I shocked him. We had gone back to his house, his parents were out. We kissed and I did not stop him. Step by step, he thought he was seducing me, while I was fully ready. The lovemaking was a little dull, but I did not have much to compare it to. Although I was not a virgin, I was not experienced. I was frightened at times, mostly in the beginning, simply the fear of being touched by a man again, but I was determined, or, more accurately, committed. I went through with it and he fell in love. In the time we were together, our lovemaking never improved. Omar loved it, whereas I found it merely amusing. I never achieved an orgasm with him.

We became an item. I knew better than to tell my parents, my father and his wife. Omar was Greek Orthodox, more acceptable than Maronite, but still Christian. Though interfaith marriages were fairly common, they simply were not acceptable in my family. My father did not want me to repeat his mistakes. I guess I would have hidden the relationship anyway, even if Omar were Druze. I don't think my father could handle the fact that I was not a virgin. I confided in my eldest sister, Amal, who was married already. She thought Omar was a good match for me. He was intelligent, from a well-respected family, and was extremely rich. His parents, on the other hand, did not think I was a good match for their son. Yes, I was pretty. Yes, I came from a good family. They thought, however, I was after their money.

His parents did not do much to oppose our courtship. They thought since Omar was going to New York in the summer to get his graduate degree from Columbia, he would forget about me. Little did they know. I packed two suitcases and left with him. We eloped, were married within a month. I found out I was pregnant.

I loved Omar. There was never any doubt in my mind. Maybe not as much as he loved me, but I loved him. He treated me like a queen. The first year I was a housewife and took care of him as best I could. I was never a good housekeeper or cook, so he hired someone to do the menial jobs. While pregnant, I applied to Barnard and was accepted for the following year.

I delivered a beautiful baby boy, Kamal, on May 19, 1981. The pregnancy was surprisingly easy, but the delivery was nothing short of hell. I was in labor for twenty-seven hours. How anyone could accuse me of not loving my boy is beyond me.

I may not have been a good housekeeper, but I was a great mother. We lived on the Upper West Side, Eighty-third and Amsterdam. Most days during that summer before I enrolled at Barnard, when Omar went to the university, I would prepare Kamal and take him for a stroll all the way to Columbia's library. I walked as exercise to lose all the weight I had gained during the pregnancy. I studied. Even though I was sure I would make it at Barnard, missing a year might have been a problem if I did not spend the time in the library. On the days I did not go to the library, I walked across the park, taking Kamal to Janet. Those days were hard. Even Kamal could not lift Janet's moods. I believe I reminded my mother of her failures.

I am unsure of exactly what happened in September. I started school and hired a nanny for Kamal. Omar objected to my going to school, suggesting I wait another year for Kamal's sake. I did not think it wise, did not want to end up like Janet. My going to school was not the cause of our problems. Omar may have begun to nag at times, but his behavior changed little. My behavior did not change either, but my feelings did. He would still try to involve me in mischievous things, like the pillow fights we had had since we met, but I started seeing them as puerile. I began to hate the way he ate. I noticed in his interactions with other people that he was not just shy, he was a wimp. I do not know whether the change was sudden or gradual, but it was palpable. I hid it well, but I could not stand him anymore. My own fairy tale had ended.

We never fought. Only on one occasion was I curt to him. He loved tickling me. No matter what I was doing, he would tickle me and I would drop everything and we would end up laughing. The last time he tried, I was studying for a final. I screamed at him to stop acting so childish. He was terribly hurt, like a little boy, and I had to apologize.

He was the perfect father. He helped with Kamal whenever he was not in school, doting on him continuously. He thought we had a wonderful marriage, was still in love with me. His peace and happiness lasted till February, when he began talking about going back to Beirut in June as soon as he graduated. It took me completely by surprise. I needed another year to finish. He thought I could finish in Beirut, *if* I really wanted to. Beirut was a living hell in those days. The fighting was some of the worst of the war. The elections were coming up and no one knew what was going to happen. Most of the Lebanese were leaving Lebanon, not moving back. He was surprised at my stubbornness, as he called it. We were Lebanese, our place was in Lebanon. Kamal's place was with his grandparents, both sets, and his family. I tried to bargain. We could wait another year until I finished, until we figured out what was going to happen in Beirut. Omar would not budge. He missed his family, his friends. He wanted his parents to help with raising Kamal.

I made a mistake in underestimating Omar's desire to move back to Lebanon. I did not understand his alienation in New York. I loved the city, he hated it. I felt at home while he felt like a foreigner. It was only later that I realized he never made any friends in the city. All of our friends were mine. He tagged along simply because I asked him. I was having a ball, while he was counting the days until we could go back.

I also underestimated his sense of property. I belonged to him. I was his wife. Kamal belonged to him. If the man wanted to go back to Beirut, then we were all going. The more I objected, the more adamant he became. I do not think either of us realized the corners we were painting ourselves into. We never raised our voices, but we dug our trenches. War or no war, he was moving back. I was not. Did I want a divorce? It would be for the best. He was taking Kamal back to Lebanon. I could not do anything about it. How was I going to live in New York without any money? I could keep the apartment till I graduated, and I would get fifteen hundred dollars a month for as long as I lived. How could I live without Kamal? I could come see him in Beirut anytime. I was Kamal's mother. Omar would not stand in the way of my being with his son. That was it. In June, my husband and son left me.

That year, until I graduated, was one of the lowest times in my life. I missed Kamal tremendously. My parents in Lebanon were upset with me when I got married, and were more upset when Omar left me. For them, I was always to blame. The war in Beirut intensified, with the Israeli invasion, the blowing up of the U.S. marines, and the massacres at Sabra and Chatila. I was worried about my family, my son, and everyone. I concentrated on my studies.

I worried about the fact that when I graduated, I would not be able to stay in the United States legally. My student visa, an F1, would expire. I thought I could try getting an American passport since my mother was American.

Luckily for me, another graduate engineering student became infatuated with me. We were going to graduate at the same time, he with a master's degree and I with a bachelor's. Joe was the spitting image of Omar, but without the shyness or funny speech patterns. He was from a rich family. This time his parents did not approve of me both because I was not Jewish and because they thought I was after his money. I had practice with minor obstacles by then.

One

The last time I saw my mother was the day of my first and only New York opening, January 19, 1995. I went to visit her in her Upper East Side apartment. I had been dropping in on her the previous couple of days, trying to talk to her, not about my painting or the impending show and my nervousness about it, but about the problems I was having with David. I thought she would be able to help. All she could talk about were her memoirs. She saw herself as an artist, a painter, although she never really painted, having all the neuroses of an artist, but none of the talent. She had given up painting for the past year to concentrate on writing. "Write, write, write," she said. "All I do is write. It's so liberating." I asked to see, but as usual, nothing was ready to be shown. "I've hired a professional editing firm to clean things up before I'm ready to publish," she told me.

That day she was radiant, wearing a green dress, long, to the ankles. She was in a good mood, almost manic, moving constantly, nervously flipping her red hair back every few seconds. "I'm so excited for you," she said, "and I'm at a great place in my writing. It's going well right now, so we have more than one thing to celebrate." She would not elaborate. "You want to see something funny. I bought this voice recognition thing for my computer a couple of months ago. You speak into it and it types the silliest things. You know how awfully I type. I thought this would help, but it doesn't work, and I still have to type. Anyway, it's great fun. Come."

She led me to her office. The desk was impeccably clean, like the rest of her sparsely furnished apartment. I sat down at the computer and spoke into the attached microphone. "My name is Sarah Nour el-Din and I want to type something." The sentence appeared on the screen as "A cane barter poor meeting no finance upward to bin." It was hilarious. I spoke again and again. The words typed on the page had nothing at all to do with what I said. She laughed, called it contemporary poetry. I tried to type something, hit the keys repeatedly, but nothing showed up on the screen. I asked my mother if she knew why her keyboard was not working. She did not. It was obvious to me, a non-computer-geek, that the voice recognition software was interfering with the keyboard. For her to type on her computer, a technician would need to solve the compatibility problem. I did not mention it. We parted, kissing at the door, her hand surprisingly lingering on my face. I knew she would not show up at the reception, but I thought she would come up with some excuse the next day when I called her. I was wrong. That night she cut herself with a razor in the bathtub, not just her wrists, but all over, and bled to death.

CHAPTER ONE
On a Beach

It was endless, that afternoon. The ocean was calm, limpid, vast as the sky. But the color was wrong. It was gray, not the blue-green I was looking for. I had moved from New York to San Francisco to see the sun set in water. But it was wrong. The sun disappeared into oblivion at strange angles and with the wrong colors. I drove to the beach that afternoon to think. I sat on the sand, wondering what to do. I felt I needed some drastic changes. Should I move back to Beirut?

I wondered what percentage of the world's population had never seen the sun set in the Mediterranean. I remembered another afternoon, on a real beach, under a real sun.

We sneaked onto the beach, he and I. We were so young, both fourteen. It was our first summer together.

It was a public beach, not where either one of us would usually hang out. We were sure no one there would recognize us. It was less than half a mile away from the private beach club where our families swam and socialized, yet a world away. The masses on the golden sand were dressed in everything from swimsuits to full dress. The smell of lamb kebabs wafted through the still air.

The sand burned our feet through the sandals. "I know this place," he told me. He led me running to the waterline, where the sand was wet and cool. We walked hand in hand, the first time in a week. We walked until we reached a small hill jutting into the sea. As we climbed across he said, "In Norway, they have steep hills that fall straight into the sea. The bays these hills create are called fjords."

"Who do you think you're talking to, dummy? I know about fjords."

"We'll go there someday," he said, looking ahead, away from me. "I've seen pictures. It's beautiful and very, very romantic. You'll like it."

We jumped down on the other side, a secluded area. "Are you sure this will work?" I asked. "Some people might come and if someone walked on the top there, they'd see us. I'm not sure this is a good idea."

"We'll hear them coming. Anyway, we're not doing anything. We're just kissing."

We kissed and caressed until we heard people climbing the hill. It was another couple, older. They were shocked to find us there. She smiled. He glowered. They jumped down and sat facing the water with their back toward us. They whispered. They were obviously engaged to be married. Finally, she had the courage to reach over and hold his hand.

I reached over, slipped my hand under Fadi's swimming trunks and encircled his penis. His face registered shock. "I want to do it," he said.

"Not till we're married."

He kissed me and ejaculated silently.

CHAPTER ONE

ThE DIVINE SARAh

I grew up infatuated with Sarah Bernhardt, having been named after her by my grandfather. My stepmother considered this obsession, for that is what it was, to be dangerous. She objected to my grandfather filling my head with stories of the great actress, thinking they would lead me astray.

I did not realize when I was younger how much anguish my being a tomboy caused my family. The first day I returned from school wearing makeup—I was fifteen—I was greeted with mouths agape and eyes wide, followed by effusive compliments. I ran into the bathroom and cleaned myself.

My initiation into total femininity was conducted by Dina, my best friend. She took a wardrobe consisting of jeans and sweatshirts and converted it to fashionable dresses and eye-catching skirts. She took a face that had never had a dab of makeup and trained it to accept powdered and creamy intrusions. She took a girl who was notorious for being the best soccer player in school, better than the boys, and turned her into every schoolboy's fantasy. In my stepmother's eyes, Dina was a goddess.

Dina's arrival at school set a new standard of sexual tension among the boys. She was only the second girl in my class. I was one of the first five girls to enroll in the school when it was integrated. That first day, she was fully made up, wore a disturbingly short skirt and an even tighter shirt, which accentuated her cusped breasts. By the first day of school, she had earned a nickname that would stick: Crotale, after the French missiles.

It did not take long for us to become friends. She shattered my misconceptions about her within the first week. I had not known anyone who dressed like her. Because of the way she presented herself, I had mistakenly assumed she was dumb. Her grades displaced mine as the second highest. The highest belonged to my boyfriend at the time, Fadi, but his should not be considered because they were the product of a rare intelligence. I also thought she would be a tramp. She was not, of course, since she did not care for boys at all.

Dina and I grew ever closer. I was transformed, both by her example and by her free-flowing advice. I had always associated concerns about personal appearance with frivolity, and I had no role models to speak of. Who would want to look like Indira Gandhi or Golda Meir? In reality, the only true model of a successful woman was the Divine Sarah. Dina came into my life, intelligent, ambitious, and beautiful in a dress. While she taught me how to apply makeup, we shared our dreams of engineering school, of having our own company, of building a true skyscraper, not that ugly crap the Holiday Inn was forcing on Beirut.

The physical transformation was the easier part. Luckily, I am blessed with a good figure, and my soccer playing proved to be helpful in that department. My stepmother, thrilled by the metamorphosis, showered me with money to go shopping with Dina. The effect on the boys in school, and on Fadi in particular, was thrilling.

Unfortunately for Fadi, my transformation was not only a physical one. With the appearance of Dina, Fadi remained my boyfriend, but he was no longer my best friend. I found it easier to confide in Dina. That was not all, though. Dina and Fadi were opposites in many ways. Fadi was a leftist, a communist really. Dina, on the other hand, was a diehard rightist, a follower of Ayn Rand's objectivist philosophy. Fadi was a Sunni Muslim and Dina was Maronite Christian.

Whereas in America most fifteen-year-olds worry about who they are going to take to the prom, in Lebanon we worried about politics. The representatives we elected to our student board were all divided among party lines, right or left. Until Dina showed up, I had voted left. I was not as committed a communist as Fadi, but I had read Marx's *Communist Manifesto* and believed strongly in the Palestinian struggle against Israel. I marched in demonstrations, attended rallies, and during one demonstration picked up sharp stones for the boys to throw at the police. I must admit that I also derived pleasure from my stepmother's concern about my communism.

Our world was changing, even though at the time, we had no idea how destructive the change was to be. The civil war was starting, sides were being taken, and debates were heated. I began to wonder why the Palestinian struggle meant fighting the Lebanese. I did not particularly like the Maronites, but at least they were nationals. Dina gave me Ayn Rand's books and I was transformed into a budding capitalist, the poor be damned. I read *The Virtue of Selfishness.* Fadi did not take that transformation well. We stayed together for a couple of years after that, perhaps because we had nothing better to do and had no idea how to break up, but the relationship was not the same. It is ironic that our relationship lasted for two years, until my resolute Randian stance began to crumble. At seventeen I read Kant's *Critique of Pure Reason,* the book Ayn Rand blamed for the decline of Western civilization, and loved it. I dropped Ayn and Fadi at about the same time.

Dina taught me about myself. The daughter of an analyst, she posited many psychological theories about our lives. She thought my whole tomboy phase mirrored my father's wish for a boy.

Dina told me that a photograph of Sarah Bernhardt greeted every troubled and neurotic patient who entered Sigmund Freud's office. A photograph of the Divine Sarah greeted all my neurotic friends as they came up the stairs to my flat in San Francisco as well. I do not know why Freud had her in his office, whether he considered her a symbol of the eternal feminine or of the neurotic woman. If it were Carl Jung's office, I would suggest the former, but since it was Freud's, I lean toward the latter.

When my lover, David, saw her picture the first time he arrived at my house, he wondered aloud why I had it. He considered her a wayward slut and a megalomaniac. Having already fallen for him, I forgave his impertinence, giving him credit for being the first heterosexual man I knew, other than my grandfather (whom I had always wondered about in any case), who had even heard of her.

I was unable to find out which picture of Bernhardt Freud had hanging in his office. I had two, a photograph and a poster. The photograph was circa 1880 with Sarah as Dumas's *La Dame aux Camélias*, the role which made her famous, on a settee, looking despondent, away from the intrusive camera, wearing what appears to be a nightgown and a feather-trimmed *robe de chambre*. The poster was for the 1898 production of *Medea*, with Sarah holding a bloody knife, the supine body of a young boy at her feet.

Chapter One
Family Asunder

Count Leo Nikolayevitch Tolstoy lied. I do not know if all happy families resemble each other as I do not know any content families. In Lebanon during the war, however, all unhappy families were not unhappy in their own way. They suffered because at least one family member was killed. It did not matter why a family was unhappy before; death became the overpowering reason.

For our family, it was the death of Rana.

Rana was my half-sister, my stepmother's eldest. She was born in May 1964 and died on July 7, 1978.

I was her closest sister. Early on, she spied on me, mimicked my every gesture. I was four years older, which also meant she wore my hand-me-downs. When I walked with friends, she used to follow me, always pacing herself about ten steps behind us, not exactly a part of our group, but any passerby would recognize she was with us. She watched every soccer game I played in, always cheering on the sideline like an English supporter.

My eldest sister, Amal, and I called her *Beesy*, a diminutive of "pussycat" in Lebanese. When Rana was eight, a neighbor had a fight with my stepmother. Rana went to the neighbor's door two floors below us, pulled down her underwear, crouched, and peed on the neighbor's welcome mat, something that I would have been proud to have done at her age. She told only Amal and me about it. The neighbor complained about stray cats that came into the building.

Rana was beautiful, taking after our paternal grandmother. Our grandmother's sour disposition rendered her unattractive. Rana, on the other hand, was sunshine incarnate. She had shimmering black hair, light skin, large hazel eyes, and full lips, more a Botticelli than a da Vinci. By the time she reached fourteen, her beauty had become a general topic of conversation. My stepmother forced her to pin a small turquoise stone inside everything she wore to keep away the evil eye. It did not work.

The year 1978 was horrific. The civil war raged on. The Syrians wanted to become the major players in Lebanon, their army spread all over the country. Palestinians ran amok in Beirut. Eleven PLO fighters landed on Israeli shores and their carjacked vehicles ended up in Tel Aviv, killing Israeli civilians. In response, Israel invaded Lebanon, killing hundreds of Lebanese civilians. Instead of fighting the Israelis, the Syrians turned their guns on the Christians of East Beirut, killing hundreds of Lebanese civilians.

On July 1, 1978, the Syrians began an intensive bombing campaign against East Beirut, and a seventeen-year-old Syrian soldier, by the name of Izzat Ghalaini, laid his eyes on Rana. She was walking from our home to Amal's, what was once our grandfather's apartment, two buildings down. He cracked a joke as she passed by. She laughed, an innocuous laugh that would prove to be ominous. The pimply-faced sol-dier was besotted. He had misinterpreted. My sister's laugh never meant very much. She laughed easily, constantly, noth-ing could remove the joy in her eyes.

She arrived at Amal's house, told the story of the homely soldier to Amal and her husband, told it as something amus-ing that happened on her way over. On her return home, the soldier was waiting for her with a single daisy. She crossed the street to avoid him.

On July 2, the Syrians intensified their bombing of the Christians. In West Beirut, we had no water, electricity, or phones. It was worse in East Beirut. They could not even res-cue the wounded from damaged buildings. We stayed indoors the whole day.

On July 3, Rana and I walked over to Amal's, holding the hands of our youngest sister, Majida. The soldier ran over to us. "I've been hoping you'd show up," he said.

"What the hell for?" I asked.

He retreated a step, his face registered shock. "My inten-tions are completely honorable," he said softly, hesitantly.

"I don't give a damn," I replied. I pulled my sisters along and left him standing bewildered. "Don't you have work to do?" I yelled back. "Like manning some checkpoint or shooting at people instead of lurking about and harassing decent girls?"

On July 4, Kameel Chamoun, a Christian leader and for-mer Lebanese president, called for the withdrawal of Syrians from Lebanese soil. Prime Minister Hoss, a Muslim, rejected that demand. The Syrians kept shelling.

On July 5, the soldier showed up at our door in army fatigues, his rifle slung across his shoulder. He politely asked to speak to our father. When my stepmother, who had answered the door, asked him what for, he said that there had been some misunderstanding. He had come to ensure that our family understood that his intentions were honorable and that had his mother not been so far away, she would have arrived with him to our door. He intended to ask for my sister's hand in marriage. My stepmother inadvertently laughed. She then realized he was serious. She told him in no uncertain terms that Rana was much too young, that the family had many pressing things to worry about, not the least of which was an internecine war, and in any case, she was not sure he would be a very appropriate husband for her daughter.

On July 6, the Lebanese president, Elias Sarkis, threatened to resign, saying that the Syrians were carrying out operations without his consent or cooperation. Israeli planes began flying low over Beirut, their sonic booms rattling windows, their presence warning the Syrians off further bloodshed.

The Syrians heeded the warnings. They stopped shelling on July 7, after over four hundred Lebanese Christian civilians had been killed. Rana, celebrating the relative calm, walked out of the house to visit a school friend. The soldier did not approach. He shot her from across the street. She died instantly. He placed the butt of his rifle on the ground, put the other end in his mouth, and fired.

My stepmother cried on hearing the news. My father did not. My stepmother watched my father and dried her tears. She wanted to appear strong. At the burial the following day, even with the coffin in the room, she sat regally in her chair, her eyes moist but not flowing. The wailers, whose main purpose was to ensure that every female family member cried enough, failed.

The official condolences, on July 9, occurred at Dar el-

Taifeh, the main Druze building in the city. Our house could not hold the number of people that showed up. My stepmother, my father's daughters from his first marriage—Amal, Lamia, and I—and my half-sister Majida, sat in one of the large halls. Around us were our aunts, cousins, and other relatives. In the other room, which we could barely see because of the size of the halls, sat the men. My father insisted that my half-brother, Ramzi, all of eight-years-old, stay with him. Men and women entered both halls, offered their condolences and then split up. Every time someone came in, we stood up. We spent the entire morning on our feet.

My best friend, Dina, showed up, crossing from East Beirut. When she stood in front of me, I broke down. "May you be compensated with your health," she said formally, tears flowing down her face. She hesitated, slowing the line of people. "I'm so sorry," she added. She moved on to my sisters and stepmother on my right.

When she sat in the far corner of the hall, I left my seat and joined her. We held hands silently and watched as relatives and friends streamed in.

"I'm leaving," she said suddenly. "I'm going to Boston. I can't take this anymore. I don't think I'm ever coming back here."

"When are you guys leaving?"

"It's just me," she said. "They don't want to leave Lebanon yet. They think things will improve."

"They're going to let you leave by yourself?"

She looked at me sideways, scrunching her face. "After all this," she said, "you think they consider it better for me to stay in Lebanon?"

A couple of Druze men came in wearing army fatigues. Even though they were unarmed, the air tensed. They offered their condolences to the women and left for the men's hall.

"Are you doing all right?" Dina asked. Her face was lightly made-up, traces of wiped red lipstick clung to the left corner of her mouth.

"Not very well," I replied. "I just can't believe she's gone. I still think I'll wake up. How does one deal with something like this? You know, my family is very close in many ways but we do not talk about things. My father locks himself in a room. My stepmother shuts down. We try to pretend a crisis never happened. If we don't talk about it, it will disappear."

A short, dumpy woman walked in, wearing an old scarf and a tattered overcoat even though it was summer. Her face looked familiar, but I did not recognize her. She offered her condolences to the family, shook each hand quickly and moved to the next. She then sat alone on the side. My aunt began whispering to my stepmother. My relatives were abuzz.

Nervous chitchat moved around the room like a wave, up and down, side to side. Behind us, a voice said, "I can't believe the gall. Has she no shame? Someone should kick her out."

Dina looked at me uncomprehending. I scrutinized the woman and finally realized why her homely face was familiar. "It's his mother," I said.

Dina's face dropped. "Oh, my God. What is she doing here?"

"I don't know. She must have traveled all night."

The chair she sat in looked like it was a couple of sizes too big for her. She sat avoiding gazes, looking at the floor. The closest women to her were from our father's village and they stood up and left the room hurriedly, without shaking hands with anyone. The soldier's mother kept still, her head down, her hands on her lap, fingers entwined. Only her left thumb twitched sporadically. My aunt stood up, her eyes filled with menace. The chair she was sitting on fell backward, an earsplitting sound. She began moving toward the soldier's mother, but my stepmother stopped her. My stepmother strode over to the murderer's mother, sat down next to her. They did not exchange words. The room hushed completely. My step-mother reached over, covered the woman's hand with hers. The soldier's mother cried silently.

I, THE DIVINE

I, The Divine

A Memoir

by

SARAH NOUR EL-DIN

CHAPTER 1—

My grandfather, Hammoud, named me for the great Sarah Bernhardt. He was infatuated with her. Since he chose my name, stamped me, I immediately became his favorite granddaughter.

As a child, I spent as much time at my grandfather's house as I did at ours. My grandparents lived in a spacious apartment only two buildings away. Even though my father was educated, a physician, he viewed education only as a means of achieving a better professional position rather than as a process of satisfying intellectual curiosities. My grandfather, on the other hand, was a newspaperman. His mind was filled with information and trivia, which he shared with anyone who would listen, and I loved to listen.

I spent most of the time with my grandfather in the family room, a green-walled, well-lit room filled with books. I sat on his lap as he regaled me with stories. He told all kinds of tales, but his favorites were about the Divine Sarah, the goddess of the stage. These I came to know by heart.

"Her real name was Henriette-Rosine Bernard," he told me, "but she'll always be Sarah Bernhardt, the Divine Sarah, the greatest woman who ever lived. She broke every man's heart. When she was up on stage, the earth moved, the planets collided, and the audience fell in love. I was a little boy when I met her, not much older than you, but I knew I was in the presence of the greatest actress in the world."

"Her hair," went another story, "her hair was red like fire, bright red, and her voice, oh my, her voice was the most beautiful in the world. When she spoke it was like singing. I was a young boy when I met her, and she an old woman, but I would have married her, if I could. I would have married her right there. But everybody wanted to marry her. Her red hair was almost like yours was when you were a baby. If we colored your hair now, you would look just like her. And she was a firecracker, just like you."

I grew up believing I was the Divine Sarah. I could do anything I wanted. This gift from my grandfather was the greatest bestowed on me. Growing up female in Lebanon was not easy. No matter how much encouragement parents gave their daughters, pressures, subtle and not so subtle, led girls to hope for nothing more than a good marriage. Being the Divine Sarah, I was oblivious to such pressures, much to the consternation of many. As a child, I was a tomboy, unaware of how girls were supposed to behave. I became a good soccer player. I excelled at mathematics in school. I wore dungarees and tennis shoes.

His stories had little effect on anyone else. My sisters, Amal and Lamia, were unimpressed. My stepmother objected to my hearing stories of wayward women, but my grandfather persuaded her it was a harmless activity. Years later, she would blame my becoming a tramp, as she once called me, on those stories, which by the age of five I was able to repeat word for word. I wanted to be an actress. I would stand in front of the mirror in my room thanking my audience. I delivered incomprehensible monologues as Racine's Phèdre without having any idea what the play was. Lamia, who was two years older, got so fed up with the performances, she slapped me across the face. I cried, ran to my father, complained about her, and when she came after me to defend herself, I stood behind my father, orating a new monologue just to annoy her. To this day, with all her problems, what with being institutionalized and all, she is my least favorite sister.

As I grew older, I began to ask more questions of my grandfather. How did he come to meet the Divine Sarah? He was with his father, a highly ranked, poorly paid diplomat of the decaying Ottoman Empire who was visiting Paris on a diplomatic mission. They saw a play and my grandfather was taken backstage to meet her. How old was he? Eleven, the year was 1912. The play? Edmond Rostand's *L'Aiglon*. The hero of this play was Napoleon's son, who was kept in semi-captivity after the fall of the empire. The Divine Sarah was a middle-aged woman playing a boy's part. I was enthralled. Was she great as Napoleon's son? She was incredible. She ran across the stage, jumping from place to place, delivering her lines with such intensity, such integrity, the audience forgot they were watching the Divine Sarah. They were watching Napoleon's son walking the stage.

By the age of ten, I began to study the plays themselves. I loved *L'Aiglon*, but if the Divine Sarah was to do Rostand, why not be Cyrano de Bergerac with his panache? I asked my grandfather if he knew whether she had played Cyrano. No, he did not. She could have. The Divine Sarah could do anything. I wanted to know for certain, so I tried to find out. I went to the nuns at school. A kind nun, not typical of the Carmelites, took the time to show me how to use the *Encyclopédie Larousse*. I looked up the Divine Sarah.

I discovered the Divine Sarah performed *L'Aiglon* around 1900 or possibly even earlier, not 1912. The revelation shook me. As I was reading, I began to formulate excuses. My grandfather could have been four. No, no, he had not been born yet. She may have performed the play again in 1912. Just because it was performed twelve years earlier did not mean she could not have done it again. Then I read about the accident and tears ran down my face. In 1905, while performing in Rio de Janeiro, she suffered an injury to her right leg. By 1911, she was unable to walk unsupported, and in 1915, the leg was amputated. The Divine Sarah, my namesake, continued acting. When she could not walk, she used canes or was helped onstage by the other actors. After she was an amputee, she used an artificial leg. By 1912, she could not jump across the stage. She could not have done *L'Aiglon*.

I mentioned nothing to my grandfather, ever. He died unaware I knew. To this day, whenever I feel slightly depressed, I dye my hair red.

1———

The water stands ready. Bath foam, Caswell-Massey Bain Moussant, scent of gardenia. She prepares for the bath with her current book, Naipaul's *A House for Mr. Biswas*, a bottle of Crystal Geyser, her Sony cordless phone, and a Granny Smith apple—she loves to eat apples in the bath. Beethoven's string quartet in C sharp minor by the Tokyo String Quartet fills the room, not a great recording, but more than adequate.

White tiles rise only halfway up the walls of her small bathroom, followed by light blue enamel paint. Half of a wall is covered with postcards of paintings: the *Comtesse D'Haussonville* by Ingres from the Frick, the great *Portrait of Cosimo I de Medici* by Pontormo from the Getty Museum, *The Order of Release* by Millais from the Tate, and her favorite painting of all time, *The Toilet of Venus* by Velázquez from the National Gallery in London. Her faux marble sink, two faucets, one hot, one cold, like the English sinks. On the shelf below the mirror, Crest toothpaste, an Oral-B toothbrush, Listerine mouthwash, dental floss—have to keep up her almost perfect teeth. Mint soap from S. M. Novella di Firenze. Henna for her hair from Lebanon, two hairbrushes and a hair dryer.

She steps into the tub. It is smaller than the one in Beirut. Still, she remembers being lost in that tub, totally immersed, she remembers trying to get clean. She scrubbed herself with the loofah, over and over, as if there was some dark stain and she Lady Macbeth. Out, damn spot. She was dirty, all of her. She wanted to rub herself raw, remove any traces of herself. She wanted out of her skin. She wanted to be a different person, a better person, her tears adding salt to the bath. She scrubbed her arms, her legs.

The People in My Life

I had moved to New York with my first husband, Omar, when I was twenty. Two years later, he would take my son and return to Beirut, leaving me completely alone in an unforgiving city, without family or friends. I had no one in America except for my best friend, Dina, who lived in Boston. I visited her often out of loneliness, continuing even after I remarried. Like me, Dina lived apart from her family, but unlike me, she had adjusted better and much more quickly. It seemed she was adopted into a family in Boston the instant she deplaned. By the time she graduated from MIT, she had a coterie of friends so loyal, they functioned unlike any family I had ever seen. Dina is a lesbian.

Her lesbian family was a hodgepodge of strange characters. I was not sure at first how they could have accepted her so quickly, since her appearance was so different from theirs. Transcending the term *lipstick lesbian*, she dressed like a cheap whore who just came into a lot of money, whereas all her friends looked like regular dykes. Someone has to come up with a whole new definition for Dina.

I visited her and her partner, Margot, sometime in 1984. I watched her while she cooked dinner—both she and Margot were the worst cooks I knew—noticing how serene she looked, how content, how peaceful and composed, as if she had not a single sin on her conscience. I was so envious. I interrogated and pestered her endlessly, trying to discover her secret. In some ways, she had had a rougher life, yet she seemed at ease with every aspect of it, professionally, emotionally, and romantically, while I was floundering. We spent hours talking about the differences in our lives, our perspectives. By the time I finished my amateurish sleuthing, I came to the erroneous conclusion that the basis for her happiness was her care and support of those dying of AIDS. She was a volunteer with a number of organizations. I believed I should do the same once I settled down somewhere.

After my second divorce, I ended up living in San Francisco. I volunteered for an AIDS organization. I chose one that provided emotional or practical support to people with AIDS. Practical support was not an option for me. There was no way I was going to clean somebody's bathroom, no matter how sick he was. I never cleaned my own house. How could I conceive of cleaning someone else's? I also absolutely abhorred grocery shopping.

An emotional support volunteer provided peer counseling, which entailed listening to clients, agreeing with them, having them expound on their feelings, and then validating those same feelings with unconditional positive regard. This is not as easy as it sounds. In any case, in the first couple of years, I could not get any of my clients to express any feelings, let alone my validating them, because they all died on me. That was the thing with AIDS: it killed my clients, rather quickly, I might add. I could not figure out how Dina thought volunteering would help my state of mind. I became an emotional wreck, but all the staff at the organization thought I would be an incredible volunteer if I ever had the chance to work with a client, since I had no problems expressing *my* feelings.

My first client was Dominic, a Frenchman living in San Francisco. After my training, a weekend of intensive indoctrination, I was assigned to Dominic because of my fluent French. I was given all his particulars: age, relationships, medical symptoms, emotional symptoms, and so forth. He had been waiting for a volunteer for eight months. Unfortunately, my supervisor told me, he was at San Francisco General recovering from a bout of pneumocystic pneumonia. I began getting ready the instant I hung up the phone. I practiced what I would say to Dominic. I stood in front of the mirror making sure I had on my nonjudgmental face, my trust-me-and-tell-me-how-you-are-feeling face. I took my bulky training manual with me.

I arrived at the hospital and inquired about Dominic. I talked to his nurse, who told me he was alone in his room, not doing too well. I walked into his room and saw an emaciated person. He had breathing tubes in his nose as well as a couple of IVs in his arm. I was unsure what to do. Should I wake him to ask him how he was feeling? I sat down on the chair facing the bed to sort out my options. Dominic, lying inert on the bed, had a thin mustache and a wan smile on his face. He looked like a man who had experienced deep sorrow, sorrow without redress. His thin, knobby fingers clutched the blanket tightly. Suddenly he opened his eyes, looking slightly bewildered, as if he did not know where he was. That happened to me often, where I would wake up in my room uncertain where I was. He looked at me quizzically.

"Hello, Dominic," I said, using the correct pronunciation of his name. "My name is Sarah. I was sent here as your emotional support volunteer." I wanted to make certain he knew I was not a practical support volunteer.

He mumbled something. It took my brain a minute to register that the reason it was incomprehensible was because he was speaking French. I understood three languages, but it took me a minute to recognize anything outside the dominant language I was involved with at the time.

"*Salut, Alphonse,*" he said.

Oh, boy, I thought, he had the AIDS craziness. I had not prepared for that. Trust your instincts, the supervisor had told me, so I did. "*Pardon, Dominic,*" I said gently, "*mais je ne suis pas Alphonse. Je m'appelle Sarah.*"

"*Au revoir, Alphonse,*" he said and died, just like that. It was only the fact that my father was a physician that stopped me from screaming at the top of my lungs right then and there. I ran out of the room looking for a nurse and found one. Dominic was declared dead, and the nurse was nice enough to send me home with a tranquilizer.

My second client was Steve, with whom at least I was able to speak on the phone. He died between the phone call and the first visit to his home. His lover forgot to call and tell me, so I showed up at the scheduled time to meet Steve, who was already toast. Unfortunately, his memorial was that very afternoon; everyone was sympathetic, but it was embarrassing. I was not dressed for a memorial. I knew no one except Steve, and he was in an urn. I had no experience with American funerals or cremations. What could I say? Nice urn, is it Chinese? I had spent the day dreading our encounter, figuring out all different methods of trying to have Steve let out his feelings. Instead, I ended up dressed in a conservative, canary yellow Armani at a memorial.

To alleviate the stress of being an emotional support volunteer, we had weekly support group meetings where the volunteers *shared* their intimate moments with the clients.

"We spent the afternoon talking about his mother . . ."

"We lay in bed crying all day . . ."

"He is having so much trouble with his new medication . . ."

"I told him if you're ready to go, I'll support that decision . . ."

"He died. Just like that. He died right after our first meeting."

While the others talked about many different things, all I ever got to talk about was the swift and premature demise of my clients. After Dominic and Steve, I was assigned John A(dams), John B(elcher), Paul, Randy, John C(alipari), Juan, John D(eGroos), and Lance, in that order. Amazingly, the Johns died alphabetically. Ten men, clients, who died when they were assigned to me. Granted, the disease was unforgiving, but the rapid, headlong descent into death caused me endless anguish. All died within at most two weeks of becoming my clients. I moved to New York in the middle of that necrology (John C. and Juan), came back, but the cycle was unbroken. I was devastated. By the time I was assigned Jay, my eleventh client, I was barely sane.

I was so desperate to have a *working* relationship with a client, I was terror-stricken the first week, constantly expecting the dreaded phone call. Jay broke the death cycle, for a while at least. In the beginning, I treasured him for that, I loved him. He gave me something to talk about with my support group.

His name was Jay De Ramon, born and raised in San Francisco, in his forties, Catalan, his parents from Barcelona. He loved flamenco, his parents having been famous dancers. He could play the castanets, his fingers seemed disconnected from their joints. He was a biologist. Before going on disability, he worked for the government testing milk. His passion was his deceased mother, who had left everything to him and nothing to his brother. He was also the homeliest man I had ever seen by a wide margin.

Cows. Everywhere I looked I saw cows. Paintings of cows, drawings of cows, cow plates, cow vases, cow mugs, cow silverware, cow-patterned upholstery, sunglasses with cows, and even a cow snow globe. When it came to bovine paraphernalia, Jay was a major collector, a dairy-cattle maven. Everything in the apartment was black and white, which were the only colors he wore as well. He regularly joked about wanting to be buried in a cow-patterned coffin. He was easy to Christmas-shop for.

Our relationship was straightforward. He was lonely and wanted a companion, someone to spend time with. I arrived one day at Heifer House, hearing strident shouts from behind the door as I rang the bell. Jay looked agitated. "Come in," he said and then in a louder voice, "my brother was just leaving."

His brother stormed into the foyer, ignoring me. "This is not the end of it," he screamed. "Things can't go on this way."

"Don't worry," Jay said. "You'll have the house when I die."

"Well, you're not dying soon enough," his brother screamed as he slammed the door. The color drained from Joe's face. He stared blankly at the door. I moved closer, but he regained his fury before I could show my concern.

"He's going to be the death of me. Not AIDS. He's going to kill me. It's the Catalan blood. Angry and unforgiving."

Jay and I disagreed on practically everything when it came to politics. The tension grew between us when he became involved in anti-immigrant policies. This was long before Governor Wilson adopted his anti-Mexican stance to further his career. In his own way, Jay was a visionary. He wrote letters to newspapers that would be used by the proponents of California proposition 187 after he died. He wrote about the illegal immigrant population draining the resources of the state. He was the first to actually use the argument that the increase in population due to illegal immigration was destroying our environment, which was later appropriated by the Sierra Club.

As time went on, I began to argue vociferously with him. Instead of maintaining a nonjudgmental tone, I became polemical. I pointed out that were it not for immigration, he would not be in this country. Legal immigrants were not the problem, he would say, though he felt legal immigration should be reduced. It was illegal immigrants. It was those damn Mexicans who crossed the border, the parasites who sucked California dry and never bothered to learn the language. He wanted those damn Mexicans, those intruders, those uninvited guests, out.

He had been vilified all his life, had whined incessantly about being discriminated against. Yet he turned against a group even less fortunate. He was unyielding in his criticisms.

It was at his funeral that I finally understood. He had been my client for over two years and I thought I knew him. I did not. He lay in his coffin, surrounded by friends, but not family. A priest began to read to the mourners asking them to pray for Jésus's soul. It confused me at first until I realized he meant we should pray for Jay's soul. I looked down at the memorial announcement and saw that Jay's real name was Jésus. I questioned the woman next to me, a coworker from his days at the FDA.

"Oh yes, he always went by Jay. He didn't like the ribbing he got when people found out his name was Jésus."

"I can understand that," I said. "In the Middle East, the Arabic name for Jesus is not uncommon either."

"Well, with Jay, his father was José, his mother was Maria. So of course, they named the eldest Jésus. A fairly common Mexican name."

"But they were Catalan."

"By way of Mexico. His mother was born in Mexico City, but her parents had emigrated there from Spain. That's why she learned flamenco. I believe his father is Sonoran, but I can't be sure anymore."

Chapter 1

Sarah wakes up, but does not wish to get out of bed. She turns over on her side, closes her eyes, in hopes of catching a little more sleep. It is too early in the morning. The sun is still not up. It is July 4. Doesn't the sun come out at some ungodly hour in July? She turns over again, lies on her right side. Where does she put her right arm? Is it too squished? With her left arm, she reaches behind her for her Piggy, her stuffed toy. She hugs it with both arms. Closes her eyes again. She feels herself slipping, the pig pressing against her stomach, her left shoulder attempting to join her right on the mattress. This position hurts her back. She leans over with her left arm again and brings a pillow, places it between her legs. The chiropractor had said a pillow between her legs will prevent her sleeping on her stomach. The pillow feels too sexual. She takes it and puts it behind her. She lifts her head slightly, noting the time on the digital clock. Four twenty-three. Damn. It is much too early. She closes her eyes again. She must sleep, especially today.

Sarah looks at the clock again. Four forty-one. She must have dozed a bit. Try again. Closes her eyes. She curses. She should have taken Restoril. Too late now. She should have taken melatonin even though it makes her feel bad. Should she take a Xanax? This is not an anxiety attack. It may relax her though.

No. She should be able to relax herself. She has survived the Fourth of July before. She goes under the covers, just like she used to do in Beirut when it got too noisy, too violent.

Sarah turns over once more. She accidentally kicks her cat, Pascal, sleeping at the bottom left corner of the bed. He jumps, lands back on the bed, and then leaps off. She sits up quickly. Sorry, she blurts; Pascal trots away from her down the corridor. She lies back down, her head on the pillow. Closes her eyes again. No use.

Sarah uncovers herself, sits up, dangles her feet off the side of the bed. Should she get up? If she does, it means she is giving up. She lies back down, fetal position, closes her eyes. One sheep, two sheep, three sheep, lamb chops. She's hungry. Maybe that's why she's not sleeping. She pulls the comforter up around her. She realizes she needs new sheets.

Sarah switches on her bedside lamp. She fluffs three pillows behind her and lies down, rests her head on the headboard. Maybe she can read, but she doesn't feel like it. She looks at the books stacked on the nightstand. Too many. She picks up the top book, *The Age of Innocence*, and throws it in the wastebasket. She always hated that book. She feels guilty. Only last week she had wanted to reread it. She leans over and takes it out of the wastebasket, puts it back on top of the stack. No. She is not going to read it next. She puts it in the middle of the stack. The top book is now *Bridget Jones's Diary*. Why did she bother picking up that one? She got it for free. She had started it and could not get past page 20. She found Bridget to be stupid, dumbed-down, neurotic, and with an uninteresting career. Worst of all, Bridget is incompetent at being an adult. Every secretary can identify. No wonder the book is a bestseller. She takes it and throws it in the wastebasket. She slides completely under the covers again.

Sarah pulls the bedclothes down. Is it five yet? Looks at the clock. It's five past five. Five past eight in Boston. She picks up her phone and dials. A groggy voice answers.

Are you up? Sarah asks sheepishly.

I am now, Dina replies.

How come you're still sleeping? You're supposed to be going to work.

It's the Fourth of July.

Oooops.

You forgot, I'm sure.

Yes. But that's why I'm calling. It's the Fourth of July.

What are you doing up so early?

I can't sleep. Woke up and couldn't go back to sleep.

Sarah turns on her side once more. She reaches out to the clock and moves it closer so she doesn't have to crane her neck to see it.

So you thought you should wake me up? Dina asks.

I thought you'd be up.

Can this wait?

Yes. Sure. Call me when you're ready.

Pause. Sarah does not hang up.

Are you all right? Dina asks.

Depressed.

Drive out of town, Dina says. Go somewhere far from the city where you can't hear the fireworks. That's what I'm doing. We're driving to New Hampshire. It's quiet up there.

I will. I'll go up to Sonoma.

Why are you anxious?

I'm depressed a little. That's all.

Are the drugs not working?

I changed. Paxil was knocking me out. My doctor pre-scribed Zoloft. It'll take some time before it kicks in, but I'm not sleeping well.

You don't sound that depressed to me.

I am too.

How come you don't get depressed like normal people? You know, turn the lights off, draw the curtains, get under the covers and not talk to anyone.

I'm not normal. We figured that one out a long time ago. In any case, I *am* under the covers.

That's progress.

Oh, shut up. Do you want to call me when you're really up? Will do.

Five-twenty. The clock has not moved much. Maybe she'll run a bath.

Sarah gets out of bed, walks over to the bathroom. She looks at herself in the mirror, freaks. Dark circles under her eyes. She looks ghastly. Begins to rub a Lancôme *fond de teint* on her face. She is startled by Pascal rubbing against her naked legs.

Hi, sweetie.

He meows in reply.

No, no. You can't be hungry at this hour. I'm never up at this hour.

She ignores the cat and begins to fill the tub. A hot bath will do her good. She looks at her bath paraphernalia. Should she use oils or bubbles? Oils or bubbles, oils or bubbles? Why not both? She dumps in two balls of jasmine oil, followed by some gardenia bubblebath. She sits on the toilet and waits for the tub to fill. Pascal rubs himself on her shins. She picks him up and scratches behind his ears. He gets comfortable, digs his claws gently into her skin.

Let's hope this is not a bad day, she tells the cat. She looks at what she has on, a haggard T-shirt and satin Victoria's Secret pajama shorts. She shakes her head in consternation.

She waits. The tub fills slowly. Pascal purrs. She wishes she had a bigger tub. It would make taking a bath more pleasurable. She'll make do. The cat meows.

No, no. No food yet. I can't have you getting used to eating at this hour.

Sarah puts Pascal down. The tub is almost full. She undresses, steps into the bath. Her foot almost slips from under her. Too much oil. She settles in. The water is a bit hot. Using her left foot, she turns the cold faucet a touch. When the tub is full, she turns the faucets off with both feet simultaneously. Ambidextrous feet, years of soccer. She keeps her feet up and dunks her head in the water. She rubs her face underwater and realizes she has forgotten that she had begun putting makeup on. Fuck. She lifts her head, opens her eyes, is shocked to find Pascal staring at her, his black-and-white face close to hers. His paws are on the edge of the tub and he is looking in. The minute he realizes her eyes are open, he lets loose a loud meow.

No, no. No food.

He meows louder.

No food. I will not have it.

He meows louder still. She turns her back to him, pretends to ignore him. He meows again and again. She sighs, begins to stand up.

I can't believe I'm doing this. You run my life, you know that. I have to interrupt my bath just to feed your majesty.

She puts on her bathrobe. Pascal begins to lick her calf, always had a taste for fancy soaps. She walks to the kitchen, leaving water puddles along the hardwood floors of the corridor. Pascal follows, scampering between her feet. She decides to go down the stairs to make sure the front door is locked. Pascal whines as she comes back up. She turns on the kitchen light. Turns the small television on. CNN, maybe she can catch up on some news. Sarah stares at the screen. Pascal bites her calf.

Oh, sorry, she tells him.

She opens a can of turkey and giblets, pours it into his bowl, puts it on the mat. His head goes into the bowl. It will not reemerge until the dish is wiped clean. She changes the water, cleans the litter box.

I do all this for you, but are you grateful? Fuck, no.

She pets him, but he doesn't stop eating. She decides she needs a cup of coffee, decaf, doesn't want caffeine, which might bring out her anxiety. Turns on Mr. Coffee and waits.

It's almost six, four in the afternoon in Beirut. She can call her son. She'll worry him if she calls. She'll send him an email telling him she'll call and then call. She goes into the room to get her laptop. Comes back into the kitchen, sits at the breakfast table, and turns on the machine. Mr. Coffee announces he's ready. She pours herself a cup. Pascal, just finished eating, jumps on the counter to be petted.

No, no, no, she says. I told you not on the counter. Get off. Get off. How come you don't listen to me? I should trade you in for a dog.

She takes her cup back to the table and writes.

> Dear Kamal,
>   It's early in the morning here and it's the Fourth of July. I wanted to call, but I thought you might worry that something is wrong if I called now. So I am writing to tell you I am about to call. And I hope you get this before I call. Well, maybe I will wait a little before calling. How are you doing?
> Look forward to your coming here. Is Saniya doi

Pascal walks across the keyboard.

No, no. Get off. Why are you being a bad boy today?

He doesn't budge. She lifts him onto her lap and begins to pet him. She sips her coffee.

You're such a spoiled boy, you know that.

She looks at the television. More commercials. She gets up, still carrying her cat.

Let's go into the room. Dina will call soon.

She walks down the corridor and, as she passes the bathroom, drops Pascal.

My bath, she exclaims.

She walks in and tests the water. It's barely tepid. She shakes her hand dry and walks into the bedroom. Gets under the covers. Pascal follows, jumping on her stomach. She should leave town, rent a room in Sonoma or Napa, some out-of-the-way place. She doesn't want to hear any explosions. She wants this day over with already.

Chapter One

Here and There

This city is cold, slushy, and gray. It is only November, but the people have already journeyed inward. The never-quite-familiar labyrinths of city streets overflow with people going somewhere else, a sea of moving humanity. The trees are bare, forcibly divested of honor. Autumn carpets the ground in colors of decay. Ominous clouds dress the solemn pedestrians in gray-colored spectacles. With lonely eyes, she notes the subtle images of death and destruction. Here, she may be the only one with eyes to see.

In Beirut, death's unremitting light shines bright for all to see, brighter than the Mediterranean sun, brighter than the night's Russian missiles, brighter than a baby's smile. An interminable war rages. The city is warm, fall still hesitating at the gates. The brutal winter winds are still dormant, but drafts of deadly violence permeate the air. The city braces for the upcoming winter without its heart and blood, no electricity, no water. She wonders how her child will endure.

She feels alone, experiences the solitude of a strange city where no one looks you straight in the eye. She does not feel part of this cool world, free for the first time. But at what price? How can she tell the difference between freedom and unburdening? Is freedom anything more than ignoring responsibilities, than denying duty? She walks the morose streets, circular peregrinations that leave her soul troubled. Lost afternoons. Yet she cannot go back there. She does not feel part of that world either. She never did. The family she abandoned is there. Her husband. Her child. She will put it behind her. There will always be *there*.

In New York, she can disappear. What is the purpose of a city if not to grant the greatest of gifts, anonymity? Beirut offered no refuge from unwavering gazes, no respite from pernicious tongues. But her heart remains there. To survive here, she must hack off a part of herself, chop, chop, chop.

In America, a colorful national newspaper is born in time to report President Reagan's declaration of the war on drugs, while the war in Lebanon is shown in prettily colored pie charts. Snipers shoot innocents with cyanide-laced bullets, while here they lace Tylenol capsules with cyanide. She walks to class confused, tugged on by both worlds.

Can there be any *here*? No. She understands *there*. Whenever she is in Beirut, home is New York. Whenever she is in New York, home is Beirut. Home is never where she is, but where she is not.

Chapter One

These [Asian] paintings I could get into and they made me wonder who I was. By contrast, Western painters tried to tell me who they were.

—JOHN MCLAUGHLIN

DAVID AND I

I can almost see David, calm and inscrutable, disconnected, getting into his car, a gray older-model Nissan, and driving away. He arrives at his home somewhere in the city, some place I do not know, is greeted by someone I do not know, a woman most probably. His car may be modest, but not his home. It is where he entertains. The house has beautiful views of the Bay and the Bridge, floor-to-ceiling windows through which he and his woman can watch the sailboats.

I can almost see David at the Museum of Modern Art looking at the newly acquired Mondrian, thinking the master must have copied McLaughlin, the California painter whose work I taught him to recognize.

"Look," he will say to the woman. "This painting is by someone trying to imitate John McLaughlin. Why, look here. He left the masking tape on the painting."

"Who's this McLaughlin guy?" she will most probably ask, unconcerned with the answer, but, having been indoctrinated with inane politeness since her youth, she feels obliged to ask.

"A California painter who was the obsession of a woman I went out with once."

David left me before I could teach him Mondrian.

I can almost see David having a picnic in his backyard when his sisters come to visit. He may have a barbecue going. The woman entertains the sisters with stories of how she and David met, how she knew they were just perfect for each other. A laugh here, a giggle there.

The brother-in-law whispers in David's ear, "She's quite a catch."

"She sure is."

"Are you going to reel her in?"

"I'm seriously thinking about it." David smiles with his brother-in-law, two conspirators in the game of life.

I can almost see David everywhere I go. He has been an indecent obsession. I was always told time is the great healer, obliterates memory, sublimates passion. Not true. I was never a plaything of time. David left me over two years ago and I have not seen him since, yet I still feel for him as if it were yesterday. There are certain things that transcend time. Nothing seems to have changed with regard to my feelings for him. I am stuck in quicksand.

DAVID AND MCLAUGHLIN

I met David at a low point in my life and he gave me direction, became both my compass and my anchor. I was flailing and he gave me focus. For the first few times we were together, we did nothing but spend time in bed, exploring each other, literally and figuratively. I did not see him enough, since he was constantly busy, which meant that the minute he showed up at my doorstep, I dragged him into bed. I did not realize at first that he felt most comfortable in my bed, when we were alone, no one to see us together. It was in my bed, with me naked, irrespective of whether he was nude or not, that he felt the least threatened.

Our first outing was to the Museum of Modern Art. The curator had set up the corridor with paintings by California artists, Northern California artists on one side and those from Southern California on the other. David and I looked mostly at the Northern California painters because of their use of colors. As we were walking, a painting on the opposite wall stopped me in my tracks. It called to me. "Sarah," it said, "look at me." It was a simple painting, of a style that had never appealed to me and which I had considered pointless. Yet I was rooted to my spot, spellbound. It was a medium-sized painting, thirty-two inches wide and thirty-eight inches tall. The main surface was smooth, no signs of brush strokes, the color a yellowish white—it was actually a mixture of zinc white, cadmium yellow, and a touch of raw umber—with a yellow rectangle, slightly off-center. Eight horizontal and four vertical black lines of varying lengths and thicknesses intersected at various points in the painting. I was not seeing a painting at all, but a three-dimensional mobile object, a live sculpture. The black lines moved back and forth across the space. The yellow square pushed farther back into the painting, creating a depth difficult to comprehend. Colors burst through in unexpected places. It was my introduction to John McLaughlin, the painter who opened my eyes.

David could not understand why I refused to move from my spot. "You like this painting?" he asked me.

"Yes. It's beautiful." I looked at him, hoping he would not think me a complete lunatic. I could not understand my awe.

"What do you like about it?" He looked at me, intrigued more by me and my reaction than by the painting itself. I tried to explain, surprising myself by doing an adequate job. I could not elucidate the spiritual and emotional aspects of the painting I saw, but I showed him how the lines moved, how the intersections of lines changed colors as you looked at them, even though they were painted black. By the time I was done, he agreed it was a good painting, saying he would consider putting it up in his house.

"I wish I could take it home," I said. "I'd love to have it."

"Even if you could," he told me, "it would probably cost you a fortune."

"It would be worth it. I'd pay anything for this painting. If the museum would sell it to me, I'd buy it in a second. It's so grand."

"You're being silly," he said. "This is a nice painting and it would look nice in your house, but why would you want to pay so much for it? It's only paint on canvas. No, it says here it's on Masonite. That's probably cheaper. This isn't something unique."

"What do you mean it's not unique? I've never seen anything like it."

"No," he said in all seriousness. "I don't mean anybody can do the original, but anybody can copy it. You can do this. You're an engineer. If you like this painting so much, why don't you make one exactly like it? It shouldn't be too hard. Don't you think?"

I had never thought of that. I looked at the painting and began to wonder if I could copy it. I did not see why not. That was how it started.

It took me seventeen paintings to achieve an adequate copy of the McLaughlin. I tried painting it on canvas, on

linen, on Masonite, and learned about texture. I tried different kinds of paints. I painted the square by covering areas
with masking tape, by using a ruler, as well as freehand. By
the tenth painting, I got the colors right, but it was only on
the seventeenth, once I figured out the correct measurement
and placement of the lines, that the painting worked. David
was encouraging during the whole process. He could not tell
the difference between each painting, but he was patient as I
tried ineffectual explanations. He liked my first attempt as
much as he did my seventeenth, so as a present, I gave him
the first painting. I considered it the perfect gift. It meant the
world to me at the time. From the moment I put paint on
canvas, I realized a pleasure so primitive, so intrinsic to my
nature, it is hard to fathom how I could have gone so long
without it. I wanted David to share in my pleasure. I wanted
him to have something of me in his house. Little did I know
I would never see the painting again. Once the painting left
my house, I lost it. David never trusted me enough to tell me
where he lived.

David was instrumental in furthering my artistic career.
He had been to a small gallery's opening and told me about
it. He suggested I give them a call since they seemed to
exhibit abstract paintings. I spoke to the director, a wonderful
woman, younger than I, who supported herself as a waitress
and had converted a small garage into a gallery to show her
friends' artwork. I told her I was a beginning painter and
would like to have her opinion on my work. She showed up
within thirty minutes, saying she had nothing to do that
afternoon. She loved all sixteen of the paintings. She wanted
to exhibit all sixteen paintings, in chronological order, to
show the progression, even though the final painting was an
exact replica. The exhibit was not a resounding success, but it

was not an embarrassment either. We placed the sixteen paintings in order, with an elaborate explanation of the methodology used. It may have not changed the art world, but it was instructional. Having my work exhibited changed my whole view of myself. I was no longer as lost. I had a purpose for waking up in the morning. And for that, if nothing else, I will always be grateful to David.

David suggested I take classes, that I might learn more about painting. I took an extension class at the San Francisco Art Institute. On the first evening, the teacher told us there were two ways we could *not* paint in his class: we were not allowed to paint diagonally and we were not allowed to paint black. For the life of me, I could not figure out why a painter—of middling success, I might add, but still a painter—would come up with such arbitrary rules. What was wrong with the color black? My first instinct was to leave the class and never come back. I stayed, though, and for the entire tedious semester I painted nothing but black diagonals. I had black diagonal lines crossing solid-colored canvases, black diagonal lines crisscrossing each other, black diagonals all over the place. The teacher never said anything to me the whole semester. At the end of term, I was the only student to receive an A for the class. No other student received a grade higher than a C. I did not take any other art class after that.

By the time I had my second exhibit, I had developed a distinctive painting style, consisting of large, square canvases with colored bars on a solid color background, always two colors, thinly painted. The owner of a New York gallery wrote saying he would show my work in his gallery for three weeks if I was able to pay the expenses. The deal was fairly straightforward; I would get a New York show, in a SoHo gallery no less, if I paid two thousand dollars plus the cost of shipping my paintings. I was hesitant at first, unsure if it was simply a vanity exhibit. I agreed on the deal because of two things: the owner said all proceeds from the sale of the paintings would go directly to me until I recovered my expenses after which he would take his commission, and David thought it was a great deal because of the publicity I would receive. We scheduled the show for January of 1995, just over two years after I began painting. Luckily, I ended up recouping a lot more than my expenses from the New York show. I had shipped my paintings by UPS and they destroyed two of them, one on the way to New York and the other on the way back. I had insured them, thereby receiving four thousand dollars from UPS. So, of course, on my resumé, I include UPS as a major collector of my paintings.

David always came up with excuses for not attending any of the openings. He did show up for a reception in San Francisco, after I had nagged him for weeks about it. It was on a Thursday night, and that was not *our* night. He begged off, hinting over and over about other plans. I was surprised when he showed up. He stayed for about twenty minutes. We barely talked as I was busy with other people. He waved at me when he came in, walked around the gallery, and left without saying good-bye. For a long time after that I had to hear about how I had ignored him.

David's disillusion with my art matured slowly, reaching its apex with the emergence of Baba Blakshi. Baba was my response to the hypocrisy of the art world. She was never meant to grow, burgeon, and mature. A local gallery put out a call for entries in an exhibit called "Apparitions." The curator wanted artwork dealing with the concept of visions, apparitions, and materialization of icons. I am not sure why the idea intrigued me, not being anything I would usually have considered, but from the moment I read the advertisement in the art magazine, my mind was overwhelmed with possibilities. I proposed two pieces; both were accepted. The first was the now-infamous Jesus-on-a-Tortilla. I had a local printer make a metal plate with an embossed line drawing of Jesus, taken from *Head of Christ Crowned with Thorns,* a painting after Guido Reni at the National Gallery in England. I had wanted a Michelangelo Christ, but the Reni had the exact insufferable suffering look I loved so much. I heated the plate and threw flour tortillas on it. The result was a stack of Jesus-on-Tortillas. This, of course, was a reference to a true story from 1978, about a woman in New Mexico who was frying her tortilla and saw the picture of Jesus on it. She had it framed. Believers arrived by the bushel from around the world to glimpse the epiphany. I gave the world a whole stack. The second piece, Jesse-in-My-Toilet was a little more intricate. I had to have a plumber build it for me. I used an actual toilet bowl, with an internal pump to recycle the water. I had black light installed under the toilet's rim, which turned on when the toilet was flushed. Inside I had someone paint a portrait of Jesse Helms that could only be seen when the black light was on. Hence, whenever the toilet was flushed, a barely visible picture of Jesse appeared.

David did not appreciate my pieces. He suggested this could be the end of my serious artistic career; no respectable curator would take my paintings seriously if I presented a toilet as art. I explained Duchamp and the urinal, *Fountain.* I was not doing anything particularly new or shocking. I simply thought it was amusing. I told David I would not enter the pieces with my name, since I had no interest in them being associated with me. I would come up with a silly name, like Duchamp did, a joke name. I came up with Baba Blakshi. My serious painting would not be affected (I was wrong, of course, but for reasons different from the ones David mentioned).

The pieces were not only the hit of the exhibit—the other works in the show were childish—they were talked about for months afterward. There was more interest in the works of Baba Blakshi than there ever was in those of Sarah Nour el-Din. What I thought was a joke took on a seriousness all its own. Baba ridiculed the hypocrisy of the art world and the perfidious art world swallowed Baba up.

If I were to do it again, I would not have given birth to Baba. I allowed myself to be carried away by the attention directed toward Baba, thinking it innocuous. Slowly, but surely, I began to bestow upon Baba's work a respect it did not deserve. Baba pervaded my life, every aspect of it. Cynicism is a cruel, parasitic mistress. It seduces; like a succubus, it drains its flunky of any creative energy, redirecting all toward its own survival. Baba was nothing if not cynicism incarnate. No wonder she flourished.

I never had control of Baba, nor did she ever remunerate my efforts. Most of her work was difficult to sell (with the exception of Jesse-in-My-Toilet, which sold in an instant for more money than any other "piece" of art I had produced). Since Baba was ephemeral, she received more attention than her creator. I finally lost Baba a year and a half ago, at my last exhibit. To further a joke that was no longer amusing, I asked a few artists to come up with Baba works. They produced a number of pieces which the gallery liked more than my originals. My Baba exhibit included nothing of mine. She is going strong somewhere now, but has nothing to do with me. The art world still loves Baba, although she does not ridicule hypocrisy much anymore. Baba's work has become less funny and more cruel, a natural progression.

I lost David during the transition from Sarah to Baba. He did not leave me because of it, but there was never any doubt that he disapproved vehemently of Baba. He considered her tacky, classless, and contemptible. I cannot blame him for that.

PROLOGUE

As a young girl, I always felt my life was being filmed for posterity. I thought of myself as an actress in a documentary or a piece of cinéma verité. I imagined myself being the subject of a future episode of *This Is Your Life*. I even practiced it. I sat in front of the mirror, trying on different facial expressions. Shock at being considered *worthy* of a retrospective of my fabulous life, surprise for when they called my elementary school teacher, tears for when they called my mother, Janet, and glee for when they called my father.

The practice sessions stopped as I grew older, of course, but my self-focus never allowed me to diverge from the belief that my life must be recorded.

Goethe said:

Whatever you can do or dream you can, begin it;
Boldness has genius, power and magic in it.

I begin.

Marsyas Flayed

If I were to write our love story, no one would believe it. My real-life story is unbelievable. I tell my friends, but they dismiss my love for you as puerile, inconsequential. I tell them what happened and they consider me foolish. Perhaps I never manage to convey how much I loved you. I say it: I love you. I love you so much, my heart aches, a physical hurt. But what does it mean really? Words, nothing but words. If I could show them how much I loved you, how much I love you still, they might see why I stayed, how I let the story unfold. If I could show them, I would be able to explain how I let the cruelest man in the world destroy any remaining dignity I might have had.

So how? How can I describe to a passerby the way I felt about you? I can't tell stories of what we did together. We did nothing. We never went anywhere, an entire relationship spent in my bed not having sex. Do I describe in loving prose how you look? Do I tell how you held me, how I felt in your arms? I don't know how. It would have to be something different. I can talk about how it felt when I knew it was over.

In front of a painting. That's how I knew. Titian. *The Flaying of Marsyas*. Apollo killed the satyr Marsyas by skinning him alive. His muscles exposed, every vein and sinew seen. Repulsive. Left with nothing to hang on to, no honor, no decency, shamed. I opened myself to you only to be skinned alive. The more vulnerable I became, the faster and more deft your knife. Knowing what was happening, still I stayed and let you carve more. That's how much I loved you. That's how much.

Chapter one

On an exceptionally hot evening early in August, I stood on the sidewalk in Beirut waiting for a taxi to take me home.

The Mediterranean sun was still blazing and I was about to faint.

I had recently recovered from a nasty bout of bronchitis and was just beginning to realize I should not have gone out.

Beirut is detestable in August.

Even the air is filthy.

I wanted to be home, in my bed.

It was 1976. The city was beginning to look damaged.

I could feel the ripening sun burn my skin, pale from having spent most of the summer indoors.

I was too skinny, my stepmother said.

Too sickly.

I wore a black linen dress.

The linen was perfect for the weather, but the color was not.

The dress was covered with tiny colorful flowers, a happy motif.

The black was a stark contrast to my skin.

The dress exposed my shoulders, which the sun attacked mercilessly.

Merciless. That evening was merciless.

I watched the cars drive by. No taxis in sight.

I felt a little dizzy, cursing my luck for having to be in Beirut instead of the mountains.

I was sixteen. I should have been invincible.

A taxi approached. It was full. Five passengers already in it. I felt crushed.

The dress was French, bought from a catalogue. I loved it.

I looked at the sea behind me, oblivious to the play of colors.

that we had three months of talking on the phone and his telling me how happy he is that we're talking again. His saying we can be friends. You still think I killed Descartes, I said. He started accusing me again of every bad thing I ever did, of how unstable I am, how unfeeling. I told him the vet was the one who suggested I put Descartes to sleep. I told him there was no hope. He thinks he loved Descartes more than I did. He says I have no heart, underneath this soft exterior, I'm hard as granite. I'm someone who abandons her son. He delivers this with an emotionless voice, controlled, venomous. What's ironic is he's the one who's unfeeling, not me. I have problems playing Hearts with my computer because I worry how the other three people feel when I beat them. I know there aren't three people there, just the computer, but I can't help it. I'm very sensitive, I love most people, and I love my cats. Descartes was adorable, a tiny, tabby-colored Persian. I got him when he was no bigger than the palm of my hand, the runt of the litter who barely survived. One day he got sick and it turned out he had a congenital kidney problem. The vet suggested a kidney transplant for my cat. How could I put him through that? I changed vets. Descartes lasted for about six months. Then he started getting worse, until one day at five in the morning, I woke up wet. Descartes, who slept every night on top of my right shoulder, had peed on me. He peed without moving. I got up, changed the sheets and lay back in bed wondering what to do. I dozed off only to be woken up an hour later wet again. Since his kidneys were not functioning, his urine was only water, no smell. I called David and told him what had happened. He thought it was amusing that Descartes peed on me. My heart ached and he was laughing. I took Descartes to the vet, who told me it was time. He first gave Descartes a strong sedative. I asked him to leave me alone with Descartes before he gave him the second shot.

respect each other? I shouldn't wax philosophical when I'm drunk. I shouldn't write when I'm drunk, but what the hell, I'm not writing when I'm not drunk. It gnaws at me that he hates my guts. Okay, I grant you, I was not the easiest person in the world to be in a relationship with. I am by nature very negative. Not all the time, but I do criticize a lot. I'm not a victim. I admit to my faults. He doesn't admit to his. Maybe the reason I was so negative is because of the circumstances he put me in. What would you do if your lover was embarrassed by you? I want to make sure you don't think I'm an embarrassment. I was an embarrassment to him only, for a number of reasons. I'm twice divorced and living off two alimonies. Supposedly, I also had mood swings, but I don't see it as such a big deal. I can be happy one minute and angry the next. So what? I know a lot of people like that. My whole family is like that. Hell, we're Lebanese. I think that was also a problem. I wasn't just a foreigner, but an Arab. He says I attack him viciously, which is not true. Okay, so I did say he was emotionally constipated, but that wasn't an attack, that was stating a fact. I simply point things out to him because he refuses to see what he's doing. He gets me frustrated and I start saying things to help him see how he's so annoying. If he got into therapy like I keep telling him to, I wouldn't have to point all these things out. I have to take responsibility for what happened and not make the same mistakes again. It's hard to conceive of loving another man again, and even harder to think of another man loving me the way he did. I do have to try, though. What's frightening is that after all this, if he asked me to try again, I would in a second. This is difficult for me to admit, and worse, I admitted it to him. I told him I still loved him and he rejected me again. I don't want to sound like the women who love too much or any of that crap. He had his good points. If he wasn't upset, he treated me wonderfully. He was thoughtful, considerate, never forgot a birthday or an important occasion. Unfortunately, I always forgot his. He could have helped me by reminding me his birthday was coming up, but he loved it when I wronged him so he could become the martyr. He wasn't a great lover. I was never fulfilled with him, which made me frigid in his eyes. Other women always had stupendous orgasms with him. In any case, I didn't mind the sex. I loved lying in his arms in bed. Cuddling. He didn't say let's make love, let's have sex. He'd say, let's cuddle. We'd zip to my room, undress, our clothes flying apart, jump in bed, and cuddle. It was so romantic and I miss that terribly. He's a good cuddler. He always said I was the most beautiful woman he'd ever been with. I don't think that was true. I think I was the most exotic woman he'd ever been with. Compared to Buffy and Mandy, how could I not be? Hell, after the women he'd been with, Mrs. Butterworth would be a step up. After he described his fiancée on the phone, all I could think was yuck. I think if I were with her for five minutes, I'd buy a gun. Graduated from Vassar with a "speech communication" degree. What does that mean, I ask you? Did it take her four years to figure out how to speak? Speech communication as opposed to what? Speech non-communication? As opposed to sign language? Boy, would I love to give her a sign. I bet you she flips her hair incessantly. I shouldn't have asked him if he bought her clothes from FAO Schwarz. But it wasn't an attack. I said it because it was funny. I can't help it if he loses his sense of humor when he's upset. We used to laugh at things like that. I mean, come on, her name is Dotty. From Dotty to Barbie is not that big of a jump. Everyone tells me I should think before I speak, but at least I'm unpretentious. What you see is what you get. Unfortunately, David doesn't like what he sees. He has distorted vision, that's all I can say. I'm not saying this because I'm drunk. I'm rarely, if ever, drunk. I don't han-

Chapter One

When my father divorced my mother and sent her back to America, she put a curse on our house from which none of us escaped. Everyone misunderstood, thinking it was a curse ending my father's line. The end of my father's name could have been a result, but it was primarily a side effect. The curse was a life of loneliness. If you took all eight of us, the parents and the six siblings, scrutinized our hearts, you would come across a loneliness so enveloping, so overwhelming, it frightens the uninitiated.

My family's leitmotif is loneliness. We exhibit characteristics of the curse differently, deal with it differently. We have different forms of loneliness. However, whether we are in a relationship, whether we are surrounded by close friends, we are never separated from it.

On September 13, 1997, I received a call from my stepmother, Saniya, at two in the morning. Groggily, I tried to make sense of what she was saying. I should fly to Beirut as soon as possible and bring my half-brother, Ramzi, with me. We were needed. I asked if my father was all right. My father was doing well under the circumstances. My sister Lamia was in trouble. What kind of trouble? I asked. She would not elaborate. Emotional problems of some sort. Her husband was fine, her children were fine. But we should fly to Beirut the next day. It was important. I asked to speak to my father. He was with Lamia.

Sleep was impossible. I called the airlines and made reservations for Ramzi and me, without consulting him. I did not wish to wake him, but then I had to because the flight was at eight in the morning. He needed time to pack. I called his house and Peter, his lover, answered.

"Do you know what time it is?" he hissed into the phone. "It's three-thirty in the morning. You shouldn't be calling at this hour."

"I have to speak to Ramzi, Peter. Please put him on."

I heard Peter say, "It's your crazy sister."

In the background, "Sarah?"

Ramzi came on the phone, alert, "What's the matter?"

"Lamia."

Lamia is the sister closest to me in age, two years older, yet the farthest in temperament. She was awfully shy, neurotically so, and so homely—elephantine nose, wide brows, bulging eyes, and pitted skin that looked like it needed a good scouring—that even at an early age my stepmother worried Lamia would grow up to be a spinster. She did not. Lamia married a low-level insurance salesman with the personality of a sheet of plywood. Surprisingly, she made something out of her life. When the war got heavier, she and her family moved to Cairo, where she studied nursing. When she moved back to Beirut, she lived with her in-laws, worked at a hospital, and continued her bland existence.

We did not get along. She was not close to me in any way,

but I did not hate or despise her. I believe she hated me and always felt inferior, or at least, I can say, she was filled with envy. I usually spent the entire month of May in Beirut. She was always the last to come visit, after a whole week had passed, enough time for it to be an insult, but not enough to be considered an egregious one.

Peter and Ramzi picked me up. Even though Peter did not apologize for his behavior earlier, he seemed contrite. I had gotten used to him and his bitchiness, so it was not that big of a deal. He is a good person who is easily lost when people do not follow his rules. "Do you have any idea what this is about?" he asked me as he started the car.

"No," I replied, "I wish I knew more. All I was told was that Lamia is having some kind of emotional problem."

"Probably having a nervous breakdown," added Ramzi. "Not rare in our family." The last comment was for Peter's benefit. I did not need a reminder, of course. "If I were living with her husband and in-laws," Ramzi went on, "I'd have a nervous breakdown for sure."

"Did you pack everything?" I asked Ramzi. A stupid question; not only would he have packed everything, Peter would have checked up on him. They would have gone over their list of things at least twenty times, shirts, sweaters, pants, socks, brown and black tassled moccasins, immersion heaters, inflatable hangers, and herbal teabags. Ever since he was a boy, Ramzi had been meticulous. Whenever we went to the beach, he wore a tight Speedo and his penis always pointed upward. To this day, whenever I see him in a bathing suit, his penis is never pointing left or right, always up. Peter was just as anal. They actually glued the strands of tinsel on the Christmas tree so they would not move or fall down. They feared ever finding themselves at the mercy of the random, dreaded the disturbing effect of arbitrariness. No one would be able to guess Ramzi and I are related. My apartment looks like a hurricane went through it, his is ready for a photo spread in *House and Garden*. They cooked salmon soufflés that never, ever, collapsed for Princess, their white Persian cat. They made a perfect couple—too perfect, for they were carbon copies, exact replicas, never challenging, never arguing, never having to allow the other within the boundaries of their erected walls, a relationship based on mutual convenience, complementary neuroses, and loneliness.

"Do you have any idea how long you'll be?" Peter was probably considering what to say when he called UCSF, where Ramzi was interning, how he would explain: Dr. Ramzi Nour el-Din had to fly back to Lebanon because his half-sister flipped.

Lamia is the middle sister, and I doubt she ever forgave God for that misplacement. She was envious both of Amal for simply being the eldest and getting all the attention and of me for being special. She was a taciturn child, though not exactly peaceful. She always got me in trouble. The only severe beating I ever received from my father was because of her. My stepmother, always trying to impress my father, made sachets of dried lavender flowers stuffed into old mosquito nettings, which she placed between clean sheets in the closet. One day, I took out all the bags and placed them in the litter box. I replaced them the next day among the sheets.

"Who did this?" my stepmother screamed over and over.

By that time, I had perfected a look of utter innocence. No

one suspected such an angelic face. My stepmother called us all into the room, even my father. "Who did this?"

Lamia, as calm as can be, pointed at me. "Sarah did. I saw her do it."

I wanted to kill her. She lied. She did not see. She was not in the house when I did my deed. "She's lying," I said. "She didn't see me. I didn't do it."

"She did it. I saw her do it with my own two eyes. I swear on my mother she did it."

Before I could jump her and commit fratricide, my father lifted me by the collar and dragged me to the bathroom. He took off his belt and whipped me so hard the welts lasted for two weeks. After the beating, she still would not recant, insisting she saw me do it. No matter how much I argued, she did not budge from her invented story.

We had a six-hour layover at Charles DeGaulle Airport. We tried calling Beirut, our parents' house, Amal's house, everyone, but no one answered. I left Ramzi, who was using his laptop, and went to look at the duty-free stores, window-shopping diversion. While looking at the window display of the Hermès store, I heard my name being paged. I picked up the courtesy phone only to hear Ramzi yelling, "Come back, come back." I ran back to him. He was fluttering nervously, his face red as a beet, palm hitting forehead every ten seconds. "Not possible. Not possible." I panicked even more. He was prattling in Arabic, not his preferred language. I took the laptop, the object of his mortification, stared at the screen, and my mouth dropped. He had used his wireless modem to connect to the AP wire. One of ours had made the news.

Nurse Killed Patients to Have Quiet Shifts

BEIRUT, LEBANON—A nurse confessed to local police to killing 7 patients so they would not disturb her while she worked at night.

Lamia Shaddad routinely killed patients by injecting them with lethal drugs stolen from the hospital. "I did not want to be disturbed," the 40-year-old nurse said. "The patients were demanding and made too much noise."

The nurse attempted suicide Friday after her confession. She is recovering at the same hospital where she worked.

I am ashamed to admit my first reaction was not concern for Lamia, but for my father. Ramzi echoed my sentiment. "Poor dad," he said. "He must be going through hell. As if he doesn't have enough to deal with." Our father was a respected physician at the same hospital. How he was going to survive this scandal, I had no idea. The black sheep of the family were supposed to be us, Ramzi and me—he, the out homosexual, and me, the twice-divorced adulteress who abandoned her son.

When I was growing up, my father was the center of my universe. I considered him the handsomest man in the world, tall, dark hair and eyes, with the ubiquitous Lebanese mustache. He was a ladies' man. In a culture that idolized virile, bed-hopping males, he flourished. He charmed the pants off everybody. We, his children and his wife, forgave him all his sins, all his indiscretions.

He was anachronistic, a traditional man in a rapidly changing culture. Yet he valiantly attempted to hold off the inevitable moral and cultural collapse, as he called it. While the country's mores adjusted and mutated, he still held the belief that a man's reputation is all he has. He still believed in honor in a society which now honored criminals and marauders. Having an offspring's name in police files would surely shame him.

At first glance it might appear that my father's traditionalism and his lascivious womanizing were contradictory. Not so. The behavior was typical in the culture. When I was fourteen, my father was the one who explained the birds and the bees. My stepmother had already prepared me, but it was my father, the physician, who provided the medical details. The talk was in our main living room, to give it a more formal air. It was early afternoon, after he had arrived from the hospital. He was still wearing his suit, adding to the seriousness of the occasion. Usually, he left a trail of clothes behind him the instant he came through the door going straight to his bedroom, my stepmother picking up after him, after which my father emerged seconds later wearing a T-shirt and pajama bottoms. Around his neck that afternoon was his stethoscope, which he carried at times to give weight to his medical authority. The talk was serious, but not dreary. He made easy jokes, smoked his cigarettes leisurely. One statement stuck in my mind. "A boy's sexuality is like a plastic tablecloth," he said. "If a carafe of wine is spilled on it, you can easily wipe it off. A girl's sexuality, on the other hand, is like fine linen, much more valuable. If a carafe of wine is spilled on it, it will never come off. You can wash it and wash it, but it will never be the same."

I never compared notes with my sisters to find out whether they received the fine linen speech. I always felt he told it specifically to me because I was fooling around with my boyfriend at the time. Of the five, I was his only daughter who was deflowered before marriage. Amal, Lamia, and Majida all earned their wedding dresses, whereas I had eloped with my first husband. Rana, my stepmother's eldest, was killed before she tasted love.

We were picked up at the airport by my son, Kamal, who had grown even more since I had seen him four months earlier. He had turned sixteen. On my arrival in Beirut, my ex-husband, Omar, used his political clout as a minister in the government to go through all the restricted areas and whisk me out of the airport. Ever since I married him, I had never had to stop at passport control or customs in Beirut. Kamal was waiting for us as we disembarked, the chauffeured car on the tarmac.

"How did you know we were on this flight? We tried calling, but no one was answering. We tried everybody."

"This was the first flight in."

"What happened? Tell me."

"Lamia killed patients at the hospital. At least seven. That's how many she remembered, but it could have been more. They're checking. Everybody's going crazy. The hospital was about to start an investigation. Another nurse was telling Lamia about the possible investigation and Lamia must have just told her she killed the patients. Just like that. The police were brought in. They asked Lamia if she killed the patients and your sister said yes."

"Just like that?"

"Yes, just like that. She thought it was no big deal. The patients annoyed her so she killed them. Your sister's definitely wacko." He began chewing on his thumbnail. I slapped his hand away.

"How's your grandfather dealing with this?"

"Seems okay so far. He's been talking to everybody. He doesn't want a trial. I think she's going to be committed."

"How's Lamia doing? How's her husband?"

Kamal shrugged, and the corners of his lips curved down. "I can't tell. He seems fine, as unperturbed as ever. So does she. She tried to kill herself, but failed. Ironic, huh?"

"That's not funny, Kamal."

I ran my hand through his soft hair.

The family gathered at the hospital. In crisis, our family pulls together like no other. My sisters, their husbands, and older children were there. So was Lamia's husband, but not her children. There were no outsiders. In normal circumstances, when one of ours is hospitalized, the hospital waiting room would have been filled with people out of deference to my father and his position in the community. In this case, the community stayed away. The air was funereal. Saniya was wearing black, but that was expected. Amal was wearing black as well, which is what gave the gathering its solemn appearance. My ex-husband Omar was there. He always stood by me in times of crisis.

Our entrance was greeted with tears all around. When my father saw Ramzi, he cried like a baby, hugging his son, shaking uncontrollably, which only increased the flow of tears from the family. In all my years, I had never seen my father cry. He had aged, white hair and wrinkles, stooped posture. I joined in the crying. It was the closest I had felt toward him in a long time.

It took a couple of minutes for my father to compose himself. Until he did, Omar was in charge, which was disconcerting at first, since he was not exactly part of the family, but became understandable as he spoke, explaining what happened. He had arranged everything. Lamia was to be institutionalized. There was no doubt she was mentally unbalanced. There would be no trial, no more publicity. In time Lamia would be forgotten by the community.

"What about the children?" I asked.

"They seemed okay," Amal answered. "You have to transfer them to a different school, don't you think?" The question was directed at Lamia's husband, who was not paying attention. He was sitting in his chair, seemingly nonplussed by the events surrounding him, in his own world as usual. Two folds of fat hung over his starched back collar. "Samir, do you think you should transfer the kids to another school?" Amal asked again.

He looked up, awakened from his reverie. "Maybe I should. I guess so. Put them in a new school where no one knows them."

"Yes," Amal said. "It's for the best and school hasn't started yet so there should be no problem."

"I'll tell my mother," he said.

"I'll talk to her," Amal said. "Don't worry about it." She looked at me, shaking her head, and whispered, "It's a good thing he still lives with his mother. She's the only competent one in the whole family. The kids will be fine. I'll make sure of it."

I trusted her. My sister Amal had devoted her life to one single thing, being a good mother. If she said she would make sure Lamia's children were taken care of, the job was as good as done.

The scene was unlike a funeral in one respect: the men and women were not separated. My half-sister Majida, whose seri-

ous burgundy suit and pulled-back hair made her look older
than her thirty-one years, sat between my father and Ramzi,
all three involved in a heavy conversation. My father nodded
his head, agreeing with what Majida was saying, took off his
glasses and wiped them with a tissue. Saniya was lecturing
Lamia's husband, and Omar and Kamal were involved in a
discussion.

"Can I go in to see her?" I asked Amal.

"She's heavily sedated," Amal replied.

"I'd like to see her anyway."

In a darkened room, the heavy curtains drawn, Lamia lay
on her bed, looking almost dead. A fairy tale came to mind,
Sleeping Beauty, except Lamia was no beauty. She looked
peaceful, a hint of a smile creased her lips. Someone had
brushed her black hair, which surrounded her head on the
pillow like a halo. The presentation was discomforting.

When we were little girls, Lamia's favorite game was playing dead. She played it in secret, only Amal and I were privy to
it. One of our aunts died as a young spinster, and Lamia had
sneaked a peak at the funeral, intent on finding out what happened. She wanted us to play the mourners while she died. She
darkened the room, just like it was now, lay in bed, and waited
for us to cry. We did not. We could not play her game. Watching her on the hospital bed, I finally cried for her.

Amal held my hand. "Strange, isn't it?"

"Yes," I said. "It's too weird."

She waited a couple of seconds before saying, "I'm having
an affair."

"What?"

"I'm having an affair," she repeated. She was still holding
my hand, looking intently at me.

"Why are you telling me now?"

"I have to tell someone. There's no one else I can talk to."

"But now?" I asked, gesturing to include the dormant Lamia. "Here? Can't you wait till later?"

"No, I can't wait," she snapped. "When is the right time to talk about this? When we're all at dinner or what? I want to talk to you. Do you realize how hard this is for me? I thought you'd want me to talk to you for a change."

For a change. Amal was one of my confidantes. Since my first boyfriend at thirteen, I had always shared my men problems with her. When I fell in love in college and wanted to elope with Omar, she was the only one I could talk to. My best friend Dina, with whom I had shared everything, had already immigrated to the United States. Without Amal's steady support, I would not have been able to leave with Omar.

"You're right," I said. "Maybe we should go to the cafeteria."

"No. We can talk here. It's not like she's listening."

I sat down on a chair facing the bed and Amal sat next to me. "Is he married?"

"Yes, of course." She raised an eyebrow and smiled with only the left side of her mouth.

"Is he in love with you? Are you in love with him?"

"No, no, it's not like that."

"You're doing it for the sex?" I asked incredulously. After my parents, Amal would be the most difficult to imagine having sex.

"No. Stop that. It's not about sex. I wish it was as easy as it is for you."

"You *are* having sex though? I mean you did say you're having an affair. Usually, that involves more than afternoon coffee."

"Yes, yes," she said, slightly irritated. She leaned back in her chair and adjusted her dress. "We are having sex, but that's not why I'm having an affair. I want to be with someone. I'm lonely, really lonely. Twenty years I've been married to that idiot and I began to realize I don't like him. I know you never liked him, but I thought I did. One day I woke up and realized I don't like him. He's not the best kind of man, he's not the worst kind of man and I didn't care. After everything he's done to me, I don't hate him. I just don't care. Twenty years of my life spent with someone I don't like. It's a terrible blow. I woke up one day and the first man who flirted with me got me. A prize, huh? Are you upset?" She looked away from me, down at her hand as if examining her fingernails.

"Upset?"

"Are you upset with me? I thought you'd be the only one who would not be embarrassed by what I'm saying."

"Embarrassed? I'm proud of you. If there's anything that's upsetting, it's that you're still with the asshole. Divorce that son of a bitch and send him to his mama. I told you that a long time ago. Dump his haggard ass. I'm surprised it took you this long."

We sat in the dark, no longer looking at each other, but staring at poor cataleptic Lamia. I wished there was something more I could say. Amal suddenly whispered, "Well, if not a divorce, then a frying pan again." She began giggling uncontrollably. It took me a few seconds to join in, enough time to recover from the shock of her bringing up the frying pan incident at such a stressful time. We giggled like schoolgirls again. "Boing," she would say and try to keep her laughter low enough not to be heard. "Boing," I would reply.

The frying pan incident. Another family scandal. Amal's husband slapped her once, ten years earlier. She was furious, but had to live with it, or so she thought. She com-

plained to Saniya, who told her she was lucky her husband
was a nice man. Amal should look at the marriages around
her and consider herself fortunate. My father agreed it was
a terrible thing for her husband to do, but he was her husband after all. She called me. I told her if any man ever hit
me, I would deck him and damn the consequences. Apparently her husband got upset with her one day a couple of
years later while she was cooking. He slapped her. She
turned around and banged him over the head with her frying pan (full of butter). His first reaction was, "What did
you have to do that for?" Like a little boy. Our father had to
stitch his bleeding forehead. Her husband was the butt of
jokes for a while, but he never laid a hand on her again.
Whenever Amal and I got together, all one of us had to say
was, "Boing," and we would crack up. People were unable
to stop talking about the crazy Nour el-Din women for a
while.

Lamia remained unconscious throughout our hysterical
giggling. I sat looking at her, wondering what part she played
in our family's problems. A friend once drove me from Brook-
lyn to John F. Kennedy Airport. Along the way, while stuck in
traffic on the expressway, I noticed a black family in a small,
brownish, older-model Toyota. Dad driving, Mom in the passenger seat, four kids in the back, the eldest no more than
ten, the youngest no less than four, all singing at the top of
their lungs, in discordant harmony, with the radio blaring, a
song called "I Believe I Can Fly." As I watched them I was
uplifted at first, but a feeling of envy overcame me. Our family never sang, never came together in joy, not as long as
Lamia refused participation. If my father wanted to tell a

story, she made sure to mention she hated fairy tales. If my mother suggested a game of trumps, Lamia commented on the silliness of card games. We had no family outings. Our family did not believe it could fly.

1-

I have a great story to tell you. I was there. This is what I saw:

I saw a principled man regretting his past actions and attempting to correct the course his young life had taken. I saw him cruelly divorce his blameless wife. For a few moments, he had taken a risk, stepping beyond the imaginary circle Lebanese men drew around themselves in colored chalk. He had married nontraditionally, an American woman, for love, the riskiest of all. He divorced for comfort, for tradition, for safety.

I saw a young woman, still a teenager, marry a man many years her senior, for duty, to fulfill her destiny. I saw a woman who looked at the principled man finding him a worthy husband, a doctor, a provider, a father for her future family. She saw a good name, and an upward move in the community. She saw the pride in her mother's eyes.

I saw a debonair city man choose a mountain girl for a wife. I saw him pick an uneducated girl he could train, mold in time, sculpt as his Eliza. I saw a man from a titled family decide on a peasant for a wife, someone who would always look up to him, never challenge him, never threaten. I saw a man choose a girl for a wife.

I saw a silly young woman, the butt of her in-laws' cruel jokes. I saw an incompetent homemaker trying hard to learn on the job. I saw a horrendous cook ruin every meal, the aroma of burned food stultifying. I saw a naive girl stand for hours in front of modern appliances unable to figure out how to work them. I saw a crying girl murmuring heart-wrenching apologies for placing an electric kettle on a stovetop burner. I saw an unforgiving family snicker.

I saw an inexperienced girl look at the man's daughters and recoil in terror at the prospect of responsibility. I saw her unsure what to do, make many mistakes. I saw a little girl take full advantage of these mistakes.

Chapter One

Mirror, Mirror, on the Wall,
I Am My Mother After All

And boy, was my father surprised.

My father divorced my mother in 1962, when I was two. She died in 1995. In all those thirty-three years, he never saw her, wrote, or called her. She no longer existed. I, through no fault of my own, reminded him of her. I was my mother's daughter.

As I grow older, I notice how much I look like my mother. The eyes are the same, the hair is almost the same, mine is more brown than red, but I do dye it red every now and then. The nose, the forehead, the same. My sisters take after my father's side of the family. I inherited the exotic looks.

When we were children, my father would regale us with stories, some fairy tales, some real stories from his days as a child, and some that were entirely made up. He used to love telling us "Sleeping Beauty." He would show us each a mirror and in a solemn voice, tell us in English, "Mirror, mirror, on the wall, who's the fairest of them all?" My sister, Amal, would shout, "Sleeping Beauty." Lamia stayed silent, as if she were being asked a trick question. I would shout, "Me!" My father loved that.

These days, the rhyme is different. I look at myself in the mirror and can't help myself. I begin to chant:

Mirror, mirror, on the wall,
I am my mother after all.

And I start crying.

It isn't just the looks. I notice how my life ended up and realize I am my mother, even though I hardly knew her

Chapter one

Had I known the opening of my New York exhibit would turn out to be a complete fiasco, I would have stayed home. My friend Dina and I reached the gallery at ten minutes to six, breathless. The gallery was empty. One of the assistants was still sweeping the concrete floors. The reception was from six till eight.

I was lucky to have Dina with me. I was a nervous wreck, floating in a rough sea of anxiety. For nineteen years, she had been my anchor. She had taken a week off from her job in Boston to be by my side, flying out to San Francisco to accompany me across a continent to New York.

"Do you need me there?" she had asked over the phone.

"No, I'm fine. It'll be nice to see you in New York, but you don't have to come here. I think I can manage. Look, it's no big deal. We just had another fight. That's all. He didn't want to come to the opening. He was surprised I asked. That's all the fight was about. No biggie. It's not like he usually shows up at any events."

"Lovers are supposed to support each other."

"Well, maybe he's not my lover."

"I know that, but do you know that? I'll be there. I'll fly to San Francisco and we can come to New York together. I'll feel better that way."

And that was that. She arrived in San Francisco to escort me.

I thought the exhibit looked wonderful. My paintings had never looked better, they had breathing space. Even though my best painting was not hung since UPS had damaged it during shipping, the rest of the work was good enough. I was elated.

The gallery had three rooms with three different exhibits. Mine was in the main room. In the smaller gallery there was a group exhibit of New York artists, both paintings and sculptures. In the smallest room was a conceptual exhibit by a Russian émigré.

It was January 19, 1995, and I felt my life might be going somewhere. It did, just not where I expected.

I had not been painting for a long time, but I had reached a style all my own. Having been influenced by what some people called hard-edged abstraction, from Mondrian to McLaughlin, I began painting symmetrical rectangular bars on a plain colored background. The canvases were always large.

INTRODUCTION

I drove my black Honda Accord on the freeway for the simple reason that I needed to get out of the house. It was Sunday morning and I wanted time to think. I crossed the bridge, unconcerned where I might end up. In time, I would turn around, returning along the same route, without even thinking about it. I wondered what to do, as the rolling hills of the East Bay flew past me. My ex-lover, David, had not called in over six months, but I still wished fervently he would. I was stuck in a relationship that had been over for years.

For someone who had believed the main point of life was relationships, I had done a poor job of living. If relationships were the crucible of transformation, I had shattered those fragile containers. I had failed every romantic relationship I had plunged into. The reasons for these failures continued to elude me, but the resulting feelings did not. I sometimes felt like I had been dropped into a sea of overwhelming sadness. I was unsure whether the feelings were the direct result of my incompetence at relationships or the effect of a biochemical imbalance. For sometimes, like this moment, as I drove on the freeway, I cried for no reason.

The enveloping sadness began in my belly, moved up to my heart, and inundated me. Tears flowed down my cheeks as I drove. I was in the midst of a feeling explosion. I zipped past a highway patrol car on my left. I panicked. The patrol car was behind me, the disco lights went on, and I slowed down. I breathed deeply, slowly, trying to control myself as I parked along the side. I could not let a policeman, a stranger, see me in that state. I tried to stop crying, but was unable to. What the hell, I thought, go for it. I allowed myself to sob and heave loudly. The policeman came to my window, Mars, the god of war, personified, all pomp and circumstance capped off by reflective sunglasses. "Can I have your registration and driver's license, ma'am?"

"Yes, of course, officer," I replied between sobs. I began looking through my purse.

"Are you all right, ma'am?" he asked, beginning to visibly deflate.

"Yes, yes, I'll be okay. I'm just having emotional problems." It was a miracle I could even be understood. I was practically in hysterics as I handed him my driver's license. "It's an old picture. I looked better then." The last sentence was followed by a loud heave and a renewed bout of crying.

"Are you sure you're all right, ma'am?" he muttered, no longer sure of himself. His hand trembled.

"Yes, I'll be okay in a few minutes. I'll just stay here for a bit until this passes."

"Where are you going, ma'am?"

Go for it, I thought to myself. It was Sunday. "To church."

"Will you be able to drive?" he asked me, his voice hesitant.

"Yes, just let me catch my breath. I'll be able to drive as soon as this passes. It always does." Another loud sob.

"Well, ma'am," he said, giving me back my license without having looked at it, "please take your time before getting back on the highway."

"I will, officer," I said compliantly. "I'll just wait here for a while." No ticket, not even a warning, nothing.

Chapter One

A Serial Killer in Our Midst

Unlike me, my sister Lamia was not the sort of person who would attract attention, preferring to blend into the background. She was such an anonymous presence in our family we sometimes forgot she was even there. Though she was the sister closest to me in age, we were not close in any other way. She was a reticent child. She spoke so little many assumed she was a deaf-mute or incapable of understanding our language. Adults spoke to her slowly, loudly, as they would to a foreigner, and she rarely replied unless it was absolutely essential. When she did reply it was aggressively, snapping back at whoever had the audacity to engage her. Every now and then, she surprised us by interrupting, using a polemical tone, disagreeing with what was being said. Her utterances were not usually a statement requiring an argument or further elaboration, simply an assertion of her disagreement like, "You're wrong," or "That's absolutely untrue." She uttered such remarks whenever my grandmother or my father made a disparaging comment about our missing mother.

My eldest sister, Amal, says Lamia was not always a troubled child. I would not know since she was older than me. I only remember her after her troubles began. Amal remembers her as playful, if not too rowdy, before our parents' divorce and our father's remarriage. Our mother's sudden disappearance was the final in a series of blows that forced her inward. Around herself she wove an impenetrable cocoon from which she never emerged. My father remarried when Lamia was five. By that time, her personality was struck.

Our mother simply vanished. One day, she was not there. Without any explanation or elaboration. "Your mother went back to America," our father said. That was all. We were supposed to live with that.

I always thought that being the youngest, I suffered the most from my parents' divorce, but I was wrong. By the time Lamia had succeeded in pulling herself out of our world and was institutionalized, I had come to the realization that I knew little if anything about her. Apparently no one else did either.

Our mother rarely wrote to us. At first we assumed our father had intercepted most of her correspondence. Later on, when I got to know my mother, she explained away her lack of letters as distaste for epistolary communications (her exact words). She did, however, send us cards on our birthdays. Whenever Lamia received hers, she burned the card after reading it. She placed the card in a crystal ashtray, poured rubbing alcohol over it, and lit it with a match, never a lighter. Her eyes bore into the beautiful blue flame. She did not remove her gaze until the flame died out, until the card evaporated.

I had stupidly assumed Lamia hated our mother and blamed her for leaving without an explanation. Lamia had never attempted to contact her or try to visit as I did. Lamia never mentioned her to either Amal or me. After she was institutionalized, Lamia's husband asked my sister Amal if she would help pack some of Lamia's things. While doing so, Amal discovered a well-hidden cache of letters. They were folded sheets of papers, no envelopes, no addresses, undated, frayed, having obviously been read many times. All of them were addressed to our mother. All of them in English so our mother would understand them better since her written Arabic was not advanced enough. None of them sent.

The letters spanned thirty-five years beginning the day our mother disappeared and lasting long past the day our mother committed suicide. The first one, written in crayon on a sheet of paper torn from her school notebook, simply stated in a childish handwriting, "Come back, Mommy." The last, written with her Dupont fountain pen on light blue stationary, was a six-page letter detailing in jumbled, nonlinear prose all that had transpired since the previous letter, all the pain, all the loneliness, all the insanity. In between those two, there were over four hundred and fifty letters, written about once a month, in which Lamia chronicled her life and feelings in a mundane, running conversation.

My sister Lamia was a murderess, a serial killer. She hated her job as a nurse. She thought the patients too demanding so she systematically killed those who most annoyed her while under her care. Her methods were not ingenious, mostly overdosing them. By the time the dust settled, it turned out she had killed seven patients and was suspected of one more death, though the authorities could not prove the last. The first time she was asked about the deaths during the investigation, she confessed to everything. The patients irritated her; she killed them. She gave the authorities as many details as she could remember. Luckily there was no trial. She was declared insane and institutionalized to avoid any further scandal. In actuality, she had killed seven patients and failed in killing two more. She stated so in the letters. She had told our mother about each killing, the reasons, the methods, everything.

Most of the letters are simply ramblings. It would have been clear to anyone who read them that they were the product of a disturbed mind. Unfortunately, no one read them until it was too late, and then we did not dare show them to anyone else. Only my sister Amal, my stepmother, and I read them. Their presence was kept a secret among the three of us. We never told my father.

My sister was what we Druze call a "talker." It is a difficult word to translate. A talker is one able to say things as a child that related to her past life. Those who follow the Druze faith believe in reincarnation. "Talkers" were not rare among us. She began getting into trouble at the age of three. When she was given a sandwich for dinner, she refused it, saying she would only eat if the dinner table was set, she was too good to be given sandwiches. She told everybody that when she lived in Jabal al-Druze, in Syria, she always had lavish feasts for dinner. She stomped her feet when she was asked to bathe. She wanted her old bathtub, the one with intricate turquoise-colored designs on the side. She asked to be taken back to her husband and children. Usually such behavior is taken with a degree of acceptance among Druze families, allowing the child some leeway until she adjusts to her new life. It is considered normal. Unfortunately, Lamia was insulting the family so she was made to shut up. She was forced to eat sandwiches, use cutlery not made of silver, and bathe in a regular porcelain bathtub. It was at that time that she began to withdraw.

When my grandfather began investigating her previous life—one goes to the area where the "talker" was supposed to have come from and asks around to see who died at the time of the "talker's" birth—he discovered that what Lamia was saying was true. She had come from a rich, landowning family and had three kids of her own. Apparently she had lived a normal life, married to an ostentatious man who constantly berated her for not being perfect. On the day she died, she took a saber to her husband's throat, slashed it, and killed herself, leaving her children orphaned. Those in the village from which she came warned my grandfather that if her soul was back, our family should be wary. We were not. My grandfather told my father who told my stepmother who told me. It became a tale, an interesting family story. No one mentioned anything to Lamia. In her letters, though, it was obvious that she knew the exact details of her life in Jabal al-Druze.

I had always thought I was the one who took after my mother. After all, I inherited her exotic looks, her artistic tendencies, her mood swings, her Americanness. I was the one who was perpetually lost, always trying to find myself in the rubble. But in the end, I realized it was my sister Lamia who took after my mother. She inherited her insanity.

It is quite possible that I am not the best person to describe my sister or to speak for her. I am biased and cannot write objectively about her. I will let her speak for herself:

*   *   *

Dear Mother,

My husband is very strange again because about five weeks ago, he bringed a mannequin home for what reason he will not say but I don't know how to say mannequin in english but you know what I mean like the big doll. The children have liked it in the beginning and they called it Madonna but not too long and they don't like it anymore, why I don't know, and I

wanted to throw her out but my husband he said we
might use her some day but I did not like her naked all
the time so I dressed her and put a wig on her hair and
The children liked her now so I put her in the salon
room in one of the couches. Well I liked the way she is
looking now and I start to dressing her in different
every two or three or four days and I put makeup on
her face and I gave her some new looks wonderful and
it was fun and so the children talk to her as if she was
someone human being. But my motherinlaw thinks its
realy crazy but I said to her maybe she better talk her
son because he says he want her in the house at the
beginning so she said I should not be dressed her but I
told her Madonna only wear things I dont'd wear
because I don't have a body like her and she is very
thin, don't you think and I can't get far away with what
she puts on. Why is she blaming me all the time?

I argued another time with my father because he
still has the same temper. He got upset with me
because I gave Ashraf some Cypro and hee said only
doctors are suppose to proscribe strong antibiotics and
he was so holyer than thee but He agreed with me that
all the symptoms of Ashraf's were a bacterial infection,
but he thinks I should have talked to a doctor but I
think he just hates me. Amal selfproscribes valuums
and Majida takes Prozac whenever she has depressions
like candy and bonbon but if I give my son antibiotic, I
did the wrong thing, don't you know? You know of
course that Ashraf was better and it was the right thing
to do of course but my father didn't said to me that I
gave him the wrong medicine but only that I need to
talk to a doctor. He went on and on and on like running

water all the time about the danger of all medicines are over the counter in this country and as if that had anything to do with me so I said to him what can I do about that but he didn't tell me so he treats me like a little girl who doesn't know right from wrong. And my husband doesn't do anything because the fat thing only sit there and let my father shout at me and I keep thinking that one day, he shall'll stand up for me and tell my father stop but he doesn't know whats going on so I told him a couple of time that if my dad shouts at me it means he's insulting him since he was the man of the house and not my father who isnt the man of the house at all, don't you think? He doesn't understand it and I dont depend on him for anything because its all up to me and I am the rock of Gibraltar and My husband is a weakthing and he can't even answer up to his own mother, so how can he answer up any one personne like my father. People will always run all over him and ride him and wipe there feet on him like a outdoor carpet and he lets them because he's been passed over for better job at work over many hundred times. I swear on you, if he didn't married me, he would'n't have gotten anywhere in this life but being with his mother at home all day crying over spoiled milk. Do you watch ER? I watch every show even though the children try to harass me during the show but I like it because it shows how much better American hospitals are than Lebanese hospitals and much better hospitals and all the nurses and doctors are pretty and they have all the best machines and none of the patients are as demanding as the patients are demanding in Beirut. My father still doesn't give me

enough appreciate me and I have to say to him all the
time that I am a nurse and I am a good nurse too But
he doesn't see that, does he, but I'am just happy that we
don't work on the same department because I swear on
you, he treat the philipino nurses better he treat me.
Because at one time when we were over at his home to
have dinner, he start talking about a procedure he did
on that day and then he looked at me with a bad smile
and asked me what *uterus* was in Arabic because he was
just making a joke of me because I study nursing in
Cairo and start to learn anatomy in Arabic as if that
make my nursing degree bad, Can you believe that? If
I had graduated from the American University of
Beirut, then I was a real nurse and as if it was my fault
that we had a war and I go to Cairo to make sure my
family is safety and you know, at the least I have a
degree, don't you think? I'am the first woman in the
family to come out a degree. Sarah says she graduates
from Barnard, but I know she is lying, she is, and she
does'nt have a single picture in a hat and graduation
dress and she says she didn't go to the graduation celebration because she thinks graduation celebrations are
for children and the only reason she thinks its for children is because she couldn't go and I'am sure she did'nt
have a graduate. I told her one every time to show me
her degree and she asked me in a realy angry way,
Why? You want to hire me? Because If she realy come
out a degree, wouldn't she show a degree papers to me,
don't you think? but my father loves her and always
Sarah this and Sarah that thing and she is graduate
from Barnard and shes the smart one and she is the joy
of his heart and she is the apple of his eye and she is

the flower of every four seasons. They can all go to hell on a quick basket.

I shouldn't talk about my father because I know it makes you upset and I promise not to do it again ever but you realy should stop upsetting over it and I say this with the kind heart, the whitest heart like yassmine flower because it pain my nerves when you are upset. Don't let him make you angry like that because he's not worth much and hes an unhappy man and he will always be an unhappy and he is sad and he does nothing with his life because he hass very little work no more and all the new doctors are much better than he and he should retire a long time ago but he goes to the hospital every morning and does nothing al the time. Then he comes home and all he does is make his wife sad and angry and she deserves it, but realy, what kind of life is that, don't you think? You shouldn't get upsetting when I talk about him because he's a nobody and he's a loser and he is a painful neck but I hope you can see that.

I made another doily for you, better than last two because the last two have faded and gone bad and faded and you will see because I sawed flowers on it with gold thread because you'll realy like it for sure. And as I'am writing this, one Israelien plane just shaken my windows and I can tell you how much I hate that. Your so lucky you left before the Israelien planes start to fly over Beirut all the time and you never know when they are going to bomb but realy worse, because they fly always near the ground and break the sound boom and the boom shatter many windows all over and its very bad all the time and they do it on purpose just because it pains my nerves.

I better leave now because I have shaked too much to write and I have a pain corn on my left foot and I dont understand why because I had been wearing the same shoe pair as if my left foot is growing because I am growing up. Okay, I willl stop writing now.

       Love,
       Your lovely daughter Lamia

       *   *   *

I only wanted to tell you that Sarah is in Beirut and I went to see her yesterday but Shes still the same and still arrogant and all about her and nose in the air like someone who smell kaka all the time and she believes the world should pay her a living and I don't know what makes her think she is someone. Only to make her nose break a little I said to her in front of her old husband that I saw her first boyfriend, Fadi but realy I said I saw *one* of her boyfriends and Omar wanted to know who he was this Fadi so you see, good Sarah, smart Sarah, wonderful Sarah, never said to her husband about her boyfriend so okay, they are no married more but she never said to him about her affairs about her love about her sex before she met him her husband. The stupid fool thinks she was a maybe virgin when he first went to bed on her but she's a sexmachine and that how she fished her men in the sea. But I told her Fadi he looked terribile because he had one eye and walked with a cover eye like Moshe Dayan, don't you think? But she knew anything about that, Can you believe that? Because She loves this man at one time but then when she fished a

more important fish like Omar she no longer cared with
Fadi and she never cared to know out what happened to
him her boyfriend because she doesn't care and she all
the time is insensitive. Only to make her feel bad I told
her that at the beginning the early days of the war, he
didn't fight but he was a member of the communist
party but he never fights so he was took by the Syrians
and beat so hard he lost one eye and he can no more
think right because he has no more shorterm memories
and he forgets what he only said to you right away but
he remembers what happened to him twenty years ago
as if it was now happening and of course, he wasn't to
get married after that and he can't have a job and he
lived with his parents. He cannot understand a lot but
he's still in love with Sarah and he remembers her like
she was all the time back then so I did say to him to forget her and I said to him she married twice and has
many boyfriends but you see, he can't remember no
more now and all he knows is what happened then and
his what happened that was my cruel sister.

She changes men like magic and I don't know how
she did it but I think I know how because she opens
her legs to any man who will make her rich and better.
I'am sorry to mean this about your daughter, but its the
truth I swear on you and I know you saw her now and
you know her and you know she is that way, don't you
think? Everybody here know about her sexmachine and
thats how she fished herself with Omar but I don't
know why she let him leave and go without her and
leave but he maybe found her with another man but if
she worked hard she could have made him to forgive
her because He was so in love with her. But he is better

off now with better wife who take care of him all the time not like Sarah she swallows life out of her men. look at poor Fadi.

This is very depressive but I'am happy I can talk to you about this things because I dont talk to anybody and when I try to talk to Amal she attacks me because she thinks everybody is a good personne, and you know it is not true all the time at all but she likes Omar and I can know why because he is inviting her and her children all the time up to his chalet to ski and last year it was four times with him but he never invited me or my children, don't you think my kids good enough?

I opened another bottle of wine and it was rance like sour vinaigre also like yesterday and why this is happening to me. Can I ask you a question which is do you still have the green woolend dress I always like and I know there is about thirty years but it was a nice dress and I thought you maybe still had it maybe I doubt you still wear it but maybe you saved it because a penny saved is a penny saved. If you did, can you save it for me? Don't leave it to any of the other girls because I don't think they loved it as much as I did and they don't appreciate beautiful things, dont like pretty things, don't know nice things, they don't do they?

Love,
Your good daughter Lamia

*   *   *

Dear Mommy,
I'de been thinking a lot about you this days and Sorry because I did not write to you but busy all the

time because Ashraf my oldest boy been sick and got the grippe last month but he is over her now. You will be very proud of him if you saw him because he looks like you and your eyes but his father says his eyes not your eyes but are like him but you know my husband he is not intelligent and very fat also and he never met a food he does not say hello to all the time.

I took a long car to Suida because I was wanting to go there for a long long time like from here to eternity and I drive there at last and all by myself and it was so good and you will be proud of me. I woken up at four in the morning and took my car but I did not tell you I had a new car because Saniya bought a car only for me for my birthday and she thinks she can buy my love don't you think. She thinks she is better than me because she has money and she buyed the car and gave it to me because she sknows I dont know how to say no because my old car was dying all the time slowly. But she picks the car and not me and she made the color choice and I hate that but it is a good car and I like it all the time and now I can go to Suida all the way.

I drive all the way to the Syrian border and the Syrians give to me a lot of trouble there and they ask me again and again why I was going to do in Suida. How can I tell them don't you know? I'am not stupid. I couldn't say to them I was going to find my children and say I'am sorry for killing there father because they would have put me in jail for sure right away don't you think? I say to them I want to meet family in Suida and They asked me what was there name was and I said to them and they asked me how they were family and that is maybe how I got in trouble at the first because nor the family of my husband nor my family are fam-

ily to my old family you see. So all the time at the end I
said to the guy who was asking the questions to me that
all Druze families are one family don't you know? He
at last believed me and let me go to Suida but I should
said to him I was only a tourist in Syria and that is no
problem but who goes tourist to Syria I don't realy
know and I know what you a're thinking because I
know you and I should had said to the man I was shopping but I thought about that only after they let me go
and don't you hate this when you think of something
that would only have been perfect to say but it was only
after it was time to say it like at the lip of your tongue
because I always do that. Dommage realy.

it drive me a long long time to reach Suida because
the roads are terribile and everything is so primitife and
the village was just like I remembered déjà vu and
nothing changes because it was old and dirty and very
old at the same time but not dirty like dirty but there
were cans of garbage all the time but no one had picked
them up in long long time. Suida has many *ajaweed* and
everyone wearing black and covered there heads with
white with a silly hat or a foulard and it was like the
fourteenth century but when I was there there was no
electricity in the village but now here it is. Everyone I
saw stared at me very much because I'am an outsider
but I wasn't of course but how do you tell that to stupid
people don't you know? I drove all the way up to my
home and nothing changes there only for the terràce in
the front and now it had pots of flowers, most of all
hydreyngeas and some pensees but it was still the stone
house and shutters of the wood was not changed also.
The paint had gone bad and the color of green of the
shutters was not there anymore at all almost because I

was the last one to paint green paint on them there is fifty years ago. It did no longer look special like fifty years ago and not the best house in the village any more and look very smaller. I want to see under the pot of flowers next to the door to see my key but I don't do that because it was long ago I left it there.

So an old woman come to the door and answer and she is also one of the *ajaweeds* and her mandeel cover her hair and she bites on one side to cover her mouth but she let go when she see its only me at the door and say hello to her so she smiled. She told me come in without realy asking who I am or what I want from her at all and she walk first to her salon room and I second and the salon was the same one because furnitire has no changes only they put better material on top of the chairs you see. I told her my name and said I had drive from Beirut a long way here and I ask her who she was and she was surprised because she was askin how I could come see her if I do not know who she was but I told her I lived here in the house a long long time there is many years back. Her eyes knew me and I should understand who she was but I did not think and it is not my fault all the time but only when I looked at her after she knew me I think I know who she is my own daughter you see. You see funny because I want to see my girl like when I left her not like she is now because when I left her she is only twelve but now she is older than me my own daughter but it is funny so I did not know in the beginning but now I knew that. You know she ask me for coffee and she is a good hostess because she ask me to take lunch with her because her husband is away for after lunch and she is not letting me go away with no lunch. She walk first in the kitchen and me second after but the kitchen was old but had new cooker and fridgerator but not very new but new more than other things in the kitchen. She cook lunch and say to me she knew I will come one day soon but this surprised me because I ask her why she thinks I will remember and she says when she is six- teen reddy for marriage my grandfather came to Suida and asked all for me all the time. The bastard never say anything to me. You know, he was an evil man, a horri- bile human being and very stupid and I said to my daughter that and she said the same back because she did not like him at all when he came up all important and asked things like everyone was his servant. The bastard known about me and did'n't say anything because he knew He knew I was always saying the truth yet always he said I was lyer. I hate this son of a bitch. So my daughter said she knew when he came up all the way to Suida I must remembered and she hope I come up to village also all the way and I told her I want to come there is many years but it was hard because we had war there for many years and she say she all the time prayed for me.

She told me the damn Israeliens killed all my two sons in 1967 and I feel so sad because of this and I cried for them many tears like river and she said my heart is kind because I cry for them now so long ago and I say I think of them all the time for so long now and maybe they have a better life now I hope and I pray. She told me about her family because she had three sons and a daughter and all are well and all married with there children to them and I said to her I am very young and not reddy for a great grandmother and we laughed hard as a rock and when she laughs all her whole body shakes and she have a good life and all her hopes have come true all the time you see.

I asked her about her husband and she said he was a good man and he loves her and he from a good family and was a stoneworker and worked hard and he with the family in good and bad time and I ask her if he makes a problem when before she married and she said no problem and asked me why I ask her about a problem and I said did he know she not pure when he marries her. She looks sad and cry a lot and said he did know nothing because he is simple man and did not know anything about women. She surprised I remember all that but I was upset because she thinks I forget something like this because all the time I rememeber what happenned that day all the time never forget you see and how can she think I forget what my husband he did and I killed him because he did when I see him over her on top. what can I do? so I killed him and cut the throat and then cut my throat because after I cannot explain why I killed him because she will never have a husband if I say why and she was not pure you see. She said she know all the time and is smart because she knows and she says thank you to me and then she make me eat a big lunch with her and we talk to each other all the afternoon all the time and she cooks good like me and we change cooking recettes to cook better. Then she walks me to see her children one by one all of them and was realy wonderful but I did not see her husband because I want to go and come home before midnight but I say to her I come back soon all the time you see and I now feel I have family.

This is secret between you and me don't tell any personne about my car to Suida because I don't know what
to say to people how I went because I don't want problems now. so you see you keep secret.

Lamia

*   *   *

Dear Janet,
   Very worse day today and you don't believe what
happen because Ramadan is over and everybody celebrate and have good time and celebrate and noisy and
everybody fire fireworks all the time and noise all over
and not sensitive for other people and no one thinks of
anyone but them self. You know all the month there is
one man that is a drummer and he wakes all the people
for two in the morning all night and every night and
he bangs his drum boom boom and shouts wake up
wake up for everybody to wake up and eat before fast-
ing in the morning but I do'n fast so why wake me? he
calls all muslim to wake up but muslims have there
party at cafes and dance and eat all night and not sleep
until next day but he wakes me you see. The drum boy
makes me crazy all the time so I throw potatos at him
but I am not a bad person because I cook the pototos in
microwave for one minute only so potato is not too hard
on his head and I hit him with only one and I did not
want to hurt him but want him stop banging the drum
all the time and it was not raw potato. The shit drum
boy come all the way to my home and complain to my
husband about me hitting him on the head with a
potato. He asked my husband why I do that and he is

little man because he is very short and why are most
bad people short don't you think? Good thing Ashraf is
not short at all. So my husband says a big sorry to the
short drum boy and he says to him I have much stress
in my life now but I don't have much stress if he did
not drum all the time every night now you see but my
husband does not take my side anytime. All the time I
am wrong to him and I hate him. Well Ramadan is
now finis and now all the time for two days muezzins
call there prayers on microphones for two mosks and
one on one side of my house and one on other side of
my house and they say sermons on microphones and
each one is more loud than other one and its not right
they do that but also the one church now microphone
the bells ringing because the mosks are loud so the
church has to be more loud. The two mosks hate them
self and my husband says there is blood between them
and we get noise in stereo now. Every one shut up now
please but there is more noise all the time and firework
and all wrong religion all the time and there is no
quiet for me you see.

And the shit drum boy comes to the house today and
says he want money so please pay because he helps up
for Ramadan and wakse people like the Koran says to
do all the time. I could not believe he come and wants
pay for waking me up don't you think. But he is serious
he wants pay because he thinks we are muslim and
that is his job so my husband say okay he pays but I
shout at my husband and then shout at him to get out
my house now but he did not know anything so he
stays in sofa all the time and is confuse him self and
why do I shout at him like this so I go to kitchen and
bring a knife and he scares and runs out the house but

my husband runs second and says he is so sorry and I
do not know why he does that all the time say sorry to
people. Why say sorry because this drum boy is annoying and he wants money so we must pay? why you see?
He is stupid not me.

> Only Love,
> Lamia

*   *   *

Dear Mother,
    I should tell you I saw a play there is a week ago and
it was realy strange and supposed to be alegorie of civil
war and imperialism and people say the play must be
banned but the goverment did not understand the play
so no ban was given tonight at all. The play attacks the
goverment like knife in butter but the goverment is
stupid ad doesn't understand. It is Very hard to say
what the play is because it opens with a woman chorus
screaming then men chorus screaming and all women
wear things like vegetables but men wear things like
animals and my husband says this if from a king of
lions in new york but I know nothing about that. Then
a chorus of people who all die during the war sing
together We die, We die, But why we die. I shout
because you sing realy bad so they say I need to leave
because no one shouts in a theater you see but I say I
didn't know this but I go home anyway and it was better anyway because I made better tea for myself. Do
you have theater like this in America?
    And I killed another patient today and I know you
dont like it when I do this but I did it because it was

okay and he is old now and a bad personne and he likes
very much drugs and wants more morphine and I gave
him more morphine but he wants more and more and
more and again and again. His wife calls me all the
time every half an hour to make sure he is okay all the
time and I say donot call me all the time and I say if
there is changes I call her but she calls me more and
more and he calls me and buzz me and says what time
is it and I tell him. Then there is five minutes and he
calls again and says what time is it and I say I'am not a
cleaning woman so stop calling now but he calls again
and he says he has much pain and wants morphine and
he says more morphine because he has more pain and I
say I gave you morphine and he wants more you see.
He says the morphine is bad and I say not my fault and
he says morphine is not good anymore and I say it is
good morphine and he say he going to die and I say
okay but he says he tells my boss that I am the very
worse nurse he ever sees. He is a baby and I say pain
don't kill anyone and stop calling please so he calls me
and says I'am ugly and he asks for a pretty nurse. I
want to give him so much morphine he flies to see god
but then he is happy so I gave him potassium IV and
thats better because who knows what happens with
morphine. So he start shaken and has heart attach and
bye bye blackbeard and he died. I feel good and I relax
my shoulder. I know what your thinking now because I
know you and you say I need more patience but realy
I'am very patient and I don't kill every first personne
and I care for people and I am a good nurse and everybody says I am a good nurse only not the other nurses
and doctors but I don't bother people but people are
rude because of the war and no one behaves much. All

the rude people come to me because the nurses hate me
and send me rude people and its not my fault. I know
you understand and one day you will sit me and we
will talk and I wil say why all this happens and you
will understand and I know you love me but I want you
to see everything and not sit in new york and worry
about wrong and right you see. I do the best thing for
people because I'am solve problem. Okay I have to go
make food for the children because if I donot make
food no one eats and they will go hungry all the time.

Love,
The Good daughter Lamia.

Chapter One

One of my earliest memories is of the day of my father's wedding. I remember crying, wanting to ride with him in the motorcade. I must have caused some confusion. After all, Druze tradition says nothing about a bridegroom's offspring. His three girls stayed behind, waving our brief good-byes to all the men in the cars. They were leaving and bringing back a bride. I was carried by our nanny, Violet, and cried onto her shoulder as the blaring car horns became unbearable.

Sometimes I wonder what it must have felt like for my stepmother. A girl is supposed to be ecstatic on her wedding day. According to tradition, getting married is what we live for. *Hope your wedding day is soon*, they say. To young girls even, barely ten years old. *May we all celebrate your wedding day*. What did it feel like for her, though? She waits at her father's house, all dressed up in white. The men in her family all proud, happy, one less mouth to feed, one less honor to defend. All parade in front of her, congratulating her, sauntering away, getting drunk. All the men happy she is marrying a man of a higher station. Good things to happen for the family. The women ululate, the groom is a doctor. She sits with her back to the window, hears the cars honking, looks back to see the caravan approaching. The ululating grows louder. The men go out to greet the arrivals. A hundred men come out of the cars, some with machine guns. Shots are fired in the air. They scream, they shout, they hail the hero. The groom will be getting some tonight. The men have come to collect their prize. More men shouting, some come into the house. She stands. The strange man, the groom she has met only twice, smiles at her. She walks out with him. Her whole family follows. She rides in the first car with her husband. Her husband's family follow, and her own family after them.

How did she feel? I cannot begin to imagine.

My father divorced my mother, an American, and repented. He decided to marry a woman according to the traditions of his forefathers. He found himself a much younger girl, not too pretty, not too ugly, never even looked at a man, who would look upon him as her god. A simple girl from a poor, uneducated, mountain family. A girl who had been to Beirut only once even though she lived less than half an hour away.

She arrived home an outsider. She desperately tried to please the family, to belong, but we were already entrenched. We three girls saw her as a usurper, taking our mother's place. My grandparents saw her as a usurper as well, from a lower-class family pretending to be part of ours. We criticized her cooking, we made fun of her dress. We laughed at her. Even my father did. I remember walking in on her crying in the kitchen. I have to admit I did not feel sorry for her. She was making burghul and had burnt the bottom. It was too late to make anything else because my father had to have his meal at one-thirty every day on the dot. She served the burghul, and for days my father and grandfather made jokes about her new method of cooking, smoking the meals.

Slowly, methodically, she took control of the household, and of the family. She began instilling a discipline unheard of in our home. I rebelled.

Before my stepmother arrived, my father used to teach us

girls all kinds of curses, mostly pornographic swear words that would make grown men blush. Whenever his card-playing friends visited, he would trot us out and we would recite our teachings. All would laugh hysterically. In Lebanese, cursing is an art form; I was its Rembrandt. My stepmother was horrified when she heard us. She instilled a no-cursing rule. She took away my main attention-grabbing activity, my star-making vehicle. I saved my best curses for her and was severely punished. In later years, she would adopt a stray African gray parrot who would make my cursing sound amateurish in comparison, a feathered demon who would become in some ways her best friend.

Around
an
Empty
Grave

A Novel

Sarah Nour el-Din

And Polo said: "The inferno of the living is not something that will be; if there is one, it is what is already here, the inferno where we live every day, that we form by being together. There are two ways to escape suffering it. The first is easy for many: accept the inferno and become such a part of it that you can no longer see it. The second is risky and demands constant vigilance and apprehension: seek and learn to recognize who and what, in the midst of the inferno, are not inferno, then make them endure, give them space."

—ITALO CALVINO, *Invisible Cities*

Chapter One

Mustapha usually woke Saniya up early every morning by repeatedly poking her side with his fingers. He no longer slept much, getting up much earlier, their age difference causing irreconcilable sleep patterns. His daily finger poking annoyed her, which was why he continued to do it. Annoying her, a pleasant diversion when they first married, had become his only entertainment in old age, teasing and ribbing his only merriment. In the beginning, the jokes at her expense were constant, but as the marriage matured, there emerged a zone of respect he rarely breached. However, in his old age, the marriage turned full circle. Her husband believed they had reached a time in their marriage where they were one, no respect needed when one is with oneself.

Mustapha did not poke her awake that morning because it was their anniversary. He lay close to her, face to face.

"Good morning, darling," he said in his most romantic voice.

Saniya opened her eyes gently, noticing a strand of his white hair approaching her face. He surprised her by kissing her, a simple peck. She tried not to show her revulsion. She still loved him, yet she could not overcome her distaste of his smells. She realized he could do nothing about it. He bathed three times a day, which did nothing for his early morning

aroma, musty, subtly tinged with putrefaction. A month earlier, she had opened the suitcase in which she had stored her
wedding dress. Mustapha was on the bed. "That stinks," he
had said. The suitcase smelled exactly like he did in the
morning, Saniya thought. She never mentioned anything,
not then, not now, knowing fully well how preoccupied he
was with age and the ensuing decay. They lay next to each
other. His face was slightly asymmetrical, still handsome, not
to him though. When he thought no one was looking, he
would pull at his slack cheek muscles, staring in the mirror,
trying to recapture a time when muscles behaved. His face
close to her on the pillow, gravity skewing his cheek in an
unnatural, slanting angle she found charming.

"Who would've believed?" he asked. The timbre of his voice
still deep, attractive, unchanged from the day she met him.

"Happy anniversary, darling."

He smiled. She smiled. He got close to her and burped,
taking her by surprise. She crinkled her nose. He laughed.

She looked away, wishing the newly installed mosquito net
was two singles as opposed to a double. He wanted a mosquito
net even though there were no mosquitoes. He kept scratching
imaginary bites until she relented. He had secretly hoped a
mosquito net (such nets have all but disappeared long ago,
even from mountain houses) would allow him to sleep like a
little boy again.

He rolled over, his pajama bottoms drooping, exposing
unnecessary flesh, and got out of bed, energized, headed
toward the bathroom. She stayed in bed, staring at the daisy-
patterned wallpaper, hazy at first, the net acting as a scrim,
clearing as her eyes adjusted. Three inches from the bottom,
a peel in the wallpaper was exacerbated by Kooky, who had
turned an unnoticeable tear into something that required
attention. I must call to have it fixed today, she thought, just

as she had every morning for the past three years. I have the extra rolls of wallpaper. I'll tell Tariq to take care of it this afternoon. She closed her eyes for a minute. I should tell Tariq to get someone to wash the windows as well. They need to be cleaned.

"I had another strange dream," he said over the sound of the filling bathtub. He always shared his dreams in interminable detail. The sound of running water caused the inevitable pecking on the bedroom door. The pets had been banished from the bedroom when the mosquito net was installed. Alfie, the dog, and Trumpet, the cat, waited patiently for the door to open, but Kooky began pecking as soon as he heard her husband running the bath. She pressed the maid's buzzer.

"You were in the dream," he said, "only younger."

Miki came in carrying a silver tray. One would think it was an extension of one of her limbs. The uniform looks good on her, Saniya thought. She should get two more in the same yellow color. Sri Lankan skin color is probably the only tone that could pull off that yellow. Kooky tried to trip Miki, biting at her big toe through the shoes. Alfie and Trumpet entered the room and waited patiently for Miki to lift the hateful mosquito net.

"Good morning, madam," she said, placing the coffee cup on the nightstand, trying to ignore Kooky.

"Good morning, Miki. Is my son up?"

"Yes, madam," as she put the other coffee cup on Mustapha's nightstand and began to lift the net.

"Did you make him tea?"

"Yes, madam, and orange juice."

Trumpet was on the bed the minute the net was off.

"You had green hair," her husband said, "and I mean bright green hair, which doesn't make sense because I think your hair is the best thing about you, if you know what I mean."

"Yes, darling, I know," usually enough of an answer to satisfy him.

Trumpet curled up next to her. Alfie waited until she had her first sip of coffee before placing his head on the bed to be petted. Kooky began climbing at the foot of the bed and made his ritualistic daily journey till he reached her chest and squawked.

"Tell your bird to keep it down," her husband said from the bathroom. "It's too early in the morning." His standard response, every day.

"Shh!" Kooky and Saniya nuzzled.

"So what did you think of the dream?"

"It's interesting."

"Yes, it is, isn't it?"

Ramzi appeared at the door. "Are you up?" he asked.

"Oh, yes, come in, come in."

"I want to get my email," he said.

"Sure. How did you sleep?"

"Got up at six, which is not as bad as usual. I should be over it by tomorrow if I take a nap this afternoon."

"Do you have diarrhea yet? You always have diarrhea when you first arrive here."

"I don't know, Mother. I haven't eaten anything yet. Don't worry about it, okay, Mother?" He was at her computer, the modem dialing. It was only eight in the morning and he was dressed in pleated, tan, casual slacks, a pressed burgundy shirt, and brown loafers with what had become his signature, gold tassels.

"Is my son up?" Mustapha walked out of the bathroom stark naked but dry. Even his pubic hair was now white. "On the computer already, definitely your mother's son."

Ramzi stood up and kissed his father. Clothed facing naked.

"You should have woken me up when you got here," Mustapha said as he began dressing.

"You looked too peaceful sleeping."

"You," Mustapha pointing at Saniya, who was still sipping her coffee, "you should have woken me up."

"I will next time, dear." Another sip.

He finished dressing in his customary ten minutes—as meticulous in his clothing selection as his dapper son. Still used garter belts to keep his socks up. Drank his coffee in two gulps. "Well, I'm off to work. I'll see you at lunch, son. We can catch up then."

Mustapha left the room. Ramzi waited till he heard the distant door to the apartment close before taking a compact disc from his pants pocket and turning on the stereo behind the computer.

"I just love the fact that you have everything you need in your bedroom, Mother."

"It'll be your bedroom when we're gone. Do you ever listen to anybody other than Joan Sutherland, dear?"

"Sometimes."

The first call of the morning was always at eight-thirty from Amal, her oldest stepdaughter. This morning was no different. The phone rang, in asynchronous stereo for Kooky always followed with an exact trill replica.

"Happy anniversary, Saniya." Amal, always cheerful in the morning, was probably in the office already. "Is Father out already?"

"Yes, of course. It's twelve minutes past eight-twenty. The schedule must be kept."

By the time she finished her coffee, every family member would have called to wish her a happy anniversary and con-

gratulate her on the safe arrival of her son. She was surprised
to receive a phone call from her other stepdaughter, Sarah,
from America. Sarah was not calling about Ramzi—it seemed
those living abroad did not view international travel as an
event worthy of a congratulatory call—she simply wanted to
wish her a happy anniversary. Somewhat perturbed, Saniya
asked if she needed money. Not at all, she was just calling
because of the occasion.

She found herself considering what she should wear, how
she should appear to her son on his first day back in over a
year. What impression should she impart? What attitude did
she want to reveal? In fall, on a rainy day like today, she
always wore trousers, shirt, and a sweater, comfort and
warmth over wide hips. She hesitated, contemplated a
designer suit.

When Ramzi left for the United States, leaving her alone
with her husband, a knell sounded. Her children had grown up,
her husband was acting childishly, and she felt discombobu-
lated and distraught. It was her expected retirement, but she
was not prepared for it. It felt like a combination of stud farm
and glue factory. She had to reinvent herself, change herself
but not appearances. She adjusted to a new life without allowing the family to perceive threat. She picked the trousers, shirt,
and a sweater. She would appear to be the kind of mother her
son expected.

By ten o'clock, she was at the office, the Lebanese International Cable Company, LICC, her bastard baby. Although she
was no longer needed for the day-to-day running of the company—Amal managed quite well on her own—she still

managed to show up every weekday morning. People assumed it was Amal's brainchild, and Saniya preferred it that way. She had thought of it when her husband bought a satellite dish.

When the war ended, everyone in Lebanon who could afford it installed a dish. The black and gray circles replaced the straight lines of antennas on Beirut's rooftops. She wanted to "share" her good fortune with those not lucky enough to afford the price. Think of all the children who do not have the choice of good television because their parents are not hard working enough to be able to afford the five or ten thousand—dollar price, she told her husband. Don't they deserve to see the same programs the rich children do? It won't take too much of my time, she said. No, no, she said, I won't be dealing with people. I'm not good with people. I'll let Amal do that. I know, I know, I don't have the technical understanding, but we have a satellite, and we have cables that run from it to our television, so it can't be much harder to have cables running to other televisions. I'll hire some engineer. Her husband finally relented, allowing her to dirty her hands, for the sake of the children. Although he did not know exactly how much she now made, since she was in charge of all finances, even his, her income the year before was ten times what he brought home.

When she looked back at how her business had started, Saniya was surprised by many things: the ease with which she made decisions, the decisiveness itself, the sheer audacity of her actions, her understanding of the logic of investment, and her lack of self-doubt. The company was set up easily. She opened an office, hired an engineer, and bought a huge dish from which they ran cables to any customer for only ten dollars a month. Her cables crisscrossed the city like dribbles in a Jackson Pollock painting. She had two hundred clients signed up within the first week. She recouped her investment in a little over six months. The problems arrived when men—it's always men, men with money—began to copycat her idea. The solution arrived when she hired Tariq, the driver.

Tariq was a young Shi'ite from the south, a cousin of her husband's driver. Her husband objected to him because of his connections to Hizballah, labeling him a fundamentalist because of his beard. Although Tariq was religious and had fought with Hizballah—could any teenager avoid the peer pressure of belonging to a murderous clan with a war raging on?—he was not the fanatic her husband assumed. If he looked with keener eyes, Mustapha would have noted the pitted skin. The short, unkempt beard was an attempt to cover up acne scars. Her husband saw a face that suggested the personality of a ruffian. Looking further, she saw the eyes of a boy desperate to please. She hired Tariq. He became her partner in crime.

When her competition began to take root—three different companies, owned by men with political connections—Saniya realized her only hope lay in dealing with them quickly and decisively utilizing the Lebanese Business Method. She asked Tariq and friends to hijack and destroy a truck carrying equipment belonging to one of her competitors. The owner of the company blamed the other two. The Lebanese cable war broke out. No one suspected her company or its principals—Amal, who was oblivious to what was going on, or her—for women knew nothing of "business" matters. Satellite dishes were riddled with bullets, generators blown to smithereens, cables cut. Her competitors left her alone for she had nothing to do with the battle. By the time the dust settled, the police got involved, and the newspapers ran their stories, her company was well entrenched. Other than the first blow, Saniya and Tariq remained uninvolved in the skirmishes with the exception of occasional tinkering with "independent" satellite dishes, impairing the reception, forcing their owners to subscribe to the only working cable company in Beirut, LICC.

She went into Amal's office. Her stepdaughter was on the phone. Saniya sat down and waited for her to finish. She noted for the umpteenth time how sparsely the office was furnished. Functional, nothing decorative, no paintings, no pictures of children, no knickknacks or trinkets. Amal moved her arms in circles, suggesting the conversation was endless. Her fingers then returned to drumming on the desk.

Saniya had never seen her so happy. She wondered whether Amal's flowering was due to finding out after all those years that she was a good businesswoman or that she was a desirable lover. It could have been a combination of both, but Saniya would have put money on the latter. After being in a dull marriage, Amal began to discover the pleasures of being desired. She assumed no one knew about the affairs. But she was not very discreet. So far, Saniya knew of at least three affairs, each with a successively more prominent man. Mustapha, Saniya's husband, had indoctrinated his children to believe that passion was the antithesis of morality. Only when she discarded stifling morality did Amal find passion of any kind.

Amal, unlike her sister Sarah, was a conglomeration of contemporary ordinariness. Her average face was congenial, making every child she came across wish it had her for a mother. She kept her dark hair in a bun. The very angle of her ears suggested ordinary. Her eyes were unastonishing. An appearance which belied the fact that she was sleeping with one of the most powerful men in Lebanon.

"Ramzi called while you were coming over," Amal said

when she finished on the phone. "It seems Kooky now sings opera, so he had to kick him out of the room." They both laughed. "Ramzi is so much like his father in many ways."

She had found Kooky a long time ago. The year was 1979. The war seemed endless. Saniya was utterly broken down. Her eldest daughter had been dead a year, killed at the hand of a lunatic, a stalker. Saniya felt she was no longer part of life, living in an anteroom of grief while the rest of the world reveled in the large living room. She walked home. This was long before she bought a car, long before a driver. For great distances, her husband or his driver would take her. Otherwise she walked.

She noticed the parrot on the way home. At first, she spotted leaves dropping. One leaf, two, three, two at a time, a small branch. She looked up and saw him, did not trust her eyes on first glance. Kooky was on a mission. He wanted to make sure not a single leaf was left on the tree. He had thousands left, but he was intent. She trusted he would do the job.

"Hey," she called up to him. "Hey, you." The parrot stopped his destruction. He bobbed up and down, reminding her of the silly dog dolls in the back windows of cars, popular before the war.

"What are you doing up there?"

He emitted a funny noise, bobbed up and down some more. She raised her hand, her finger pointing to form a perch. Kooky played coy for a bit, before beginning a climb down. He bit her finger to make sure it would not move and climbed on it.

She brought him closer. He surprised her with a kiss, beak to mouth. "You must be a boy," she said.

Saniya had never seen a live parrot before. She did not

expect to come across a dull-colored one. Kooky was predominantly gray, an African gray parrot.

She considered trying to locate Kooky's owners. Maybe he belonged to some child somewhere in Beirut. Before she went home, she stopped by the local veterinarian, who was infamous for killing more pets than treating them. She assumed he might know if this gray belonged to anyone. She was right.

The minute she rang the doorbell, Kooky started laughing. Short bursts of laughter. "Hehheh, hehheh, hehheh." Bobbing frantically up and down on her finger. Intriguing behavior, she thought. He squawked loudly. A woman's voice from behind the door screamed, "Take him away from here."

Kooky yelled back at her, "*Sharmoutah, intee sharmoutah.*"

"I'm not a whore," the woman replied to the parrot. "I'm not a whore, you son of a dog. Take that cursed parrot away from here. I'm not opening the door."

"I only want to know if he's owned by anybody," Saniya said, terrifically amused.

"Satan. The damned parrot is owned by Satan."

"You obviously know him," Saniya said. "Who owns him?"

"No one. No one owns him. Take him away and burn the devil's spawn. No one wants him. They left Kooky to die. He's nothing but trouble. Burn him."

"His name is Kooky?" Saniya asked her innocently.

"Kooky wants to fuck you," the parrot yelled. "Kooky wants to fuck you."

Saniya laughed. For the first time in over a year, she laughed.

"Farid," the voice screamed. "Farid. That damn Kooky is outside. If you don't do something, I'll kill myself."

Saniya walked home, Kooky nuzzling her cheek.

"You're a bad boy," she told him.

"Hehheh, hehheh, hehheh."

Kooky became the lord of the manor. Her husband felt the competition, did not want him in his house, but Saniya put her foot down. Mustapha noticed her spirits lifting and relented. The children loved him. Kooky became Ramzi's constant companion.

Kooky had a fascination with big toes. He attacked her big toe whenever she walked barefoot, which was all the time. When she wore shoes, he tried to bite through them to get to the toe.

The devil's spawn had a large vocabulary, mostly obscene words, which he had learned to place in different combinations. He rarely used them on her, but whenever guests arrived, he rattled them off one after another. It made her husband furious, but amused her to no end. He even had a basic understanding of feminine and masculine words to use on visitors. When he made grammatical mistakes, he sounded like an Armenian.

Kooky's relationship to Satan manifested itself clearly as the bombs fell. Ronnie, her husband's dog, was the only other pet in the house at the time. Mustapha had wanted a hunting dog. Ronnie's pedigree was impeccable, except he turned out to be more a *chien de salon*, terrified by the mere sound of gunfire. It was Ramzi who ruined him. When Ronnie arrived as a puppy, Ramzi began playing with him, dressing him in elaborate outfits, allowing the dog to sleep with him at night. Ronnie ended up not going on a single hunting trip.

Kooky and Ronnie were best friends. They slept together, ate out of the same bowl, and chased each other around the apartment. A slight difference in personality was the main problem. Kooky was afraid of nothing, and Ronnie was afraid of his own shadow. Whenever minor gunfire erupted, Ronnie cowered in a corner, and Kooky got excited. When the large guns erupted, and Saniya had to go down to the shelter, she spent at least fifteen minutes trying to convince Ronnie to come down with her, whereas Kooky would scream obscenities at the dog. He wanted action.

It was the missiles that turned Ronnie into a quivering mass of jelly. When the whistle began, he would quail, his four limbs a study in vibration. By the time the explosion happened, his bladder would be empty. Within a short period of time, Kooky had assessed the situation. In calm times, while the family was at the dining room table or watching television, and Ronnie was lying down nearby, Kooky would begin a missile whistle. The devil's spawn had it down to a science, except for the explosion at the end, which he could not imitate. Ronnie would stand up, quiver, and pee in place, without even lifting a leg. Kooky would laugh.

For the following ten days, the duration of her son's stay, the cook would make Ramzi's favorite meals for lunch. The cook, who was from the same village as Mustapha, did not particularly like Saniya. He was devoted to her husband and simply worshiped Ramzi. For the next ten days, the meals would be impeccable.

The meal was *gigot*, leg of lamb. Amal and her husband were already coming, but Saniya knew that would not be the entire lunch crowd. She returned home at noon to find out that her daughter Majida and her husband had called the maid and told her they were coming for lunch. While she was getting into her housedress, her husband's sister called. "What's for lunch?" she asked. Saniya told her.

"Count me in. I'm coming." Mustapha's sister was seventy-six years old, lassitude incarnate, but when it came to good meals, she moved heaven and earth to be there.

Some time to herself before the crowd started arriving. She looked at herself in the mirror. Getting older. Thunder thighs. I must lose a little weight, she thought. At least there was still someone who found her sexually attractive. That was a blessing.

"How many people for lunch, madam?" Miki asked. She came into the bedroom to turn down the beds for the afternoon.

"Eight so far, but I think it'll be ten."

The phone rang on cue. Kooky, sleeping on his perch, imitated the sound until she picked up the phone, and then went back to sleep. "What's for lunch?" No hello, no small talk. Her husband's nephew was a busy man. He was coming. She knew there would be one more, the other nephew. She knew it would not be long.

The phone rang.

"I hope you won't be late," Saniya said. "I can't believe you waited this long to call. Are they working you hard?"

"You know, business stuff. Have to keep up on all the news."

"*Gigot.*"

"That's all the news I need. I'll be there. Is he making it with pine nuts?"

"Yes, I'm sure he is."

"Chestnuts?"

"It's not the season, silly. It's only September."

"Well, tell your son to come back during chestnut season."

"I'll make sure to mention that."

Ramzi came home at one o'clock. Tariq had been driving him. At one-fifteen sharp, Mustapha walked through the door. She could set her watch by his schedule. As was his habit, he began undressing the minute he walked through the door, Saniya picking up after him. The jacket in the ante-room, the tie in the living room, the shoes in the corridor, the shirt on the floor in the bedroom, the pants on the bed, the underwear, the socks. Emerged seconds later in pajama bottoms and undershirt. Saniya followed him with warm socks. "Put these on. It's cold."

By one-twenty, everyone had arrived. By one-thirty, they were seated at the dining table, all ten of them. Timing was essential for Mustapha. By two they would be done.

The conversation at the table covered a lot of ground. Ramzi's health, his work. Mustapha asked his son about clients. Ramzi practiced medicine in a part of San Francisco where clients were not all genteel and white, but a procession of multicolored flesh, a new cause of consternation for his father. Even Saniya was surprised at her son's choices, not prejudice, but a seeming distortion of the immaculate image she had of him. Mustapha's pointed questioning had its usual effect on Ramzi. He raised and lowered his eyelids slowly while his father spoke, a sure sign of his waning interest.

"How's Sarah doing?" Saniya asked, coming to her son's rescue. "She called today to wish us a happy anniversary. I was surprised she remembered."

"Of course, she would remember," Majida said. This was a conversation the whole family could participate in. "Ramzi must have told her before he left."

"I did tell her. She's doing fine, still as lost as ever."

"I wish she'd move back here where she belongs," Mustapha said. Always the same refrain.

"She never will, Father. You know that."

"Is she still writing her book?" Amal asked.

"I'm not sure. She hasn't mentioned it in a while."

"That girl was just spit out by her mother. She behaves in exactly the same way." Mustapha's statement was the usual one, which ended any conversation about Sarah. Saniya could see the girls wanting to find out more, but they would wait until Mustapha had gone in for his afternoon nap. Amal would want to know whether her sister was still obsessed with the man who had dumped her. They could not talk about Sarah's relationships while her father was present. They could not talk about Ramzi's lover either. Relationships, the unmentionable topic.

"Can Tariq drive me this afternoon?" her son asked.

"No. I need him. Can you drive yourself?"

"Sure." He turned toward his father. "Are the players coming this afternoon?" Mustapha simply nodded.

The lunch was over. Two o'clock. Mustapha stood up. "I guess we'll see you all tomorrow." Laughter all around.

"Bring the kids tomorrow. It's Saturday."

"Ramzi should visit more often."

By two-fifteen, Mustapha and his wife were in bed for a brief siesta. At two forty-five, Miki came in with the coffee. By three the cardplayers began arriving. They had been playing *quatorze* every day since before Saniya was married. The same five people every single day, from three-thirty till eight. All of them worked half days, even though they were all professionals. Mustapha played *quatorze* on his wedding day—they did not have a honeymoon—on the day Rana was born, the day Majida was born, and even the day Ramzi was born.

She started dressing when they were four. She would greet the fifth and leave as was her habit. For the first ten years, she was there every day making sure all their needs were met. She finally began to train the maids to do her job. When the doorbell rang, she was the one to open the door.

"How's the little business lady?"

"Fine. How are you today?"

"Going off to work?"

"Someone has to." The last she said as the elevator door closed.

• • •

By four-thirty, Tariq was going down on her, his Hizballah beard proving to be functional after all.

Tariq lay with his arms around her, her back against his chest, their feet touching. He fell asleep nuzzling her neck, a hand holding her breast. She wept, silently, careful not to wake him. Tears dropping into her open mouth, she whimpered softly.

Premier Chapitre

Il faisait chaud ce jour-là. Elle avait porté sa longue robe noire et fleurie. Elle aimait cette robe. Sa belle-mère disait qu'elle la rendait trop maigre. Mais elle en aimait le fin tissu frais. La chaleur l'ètouffait. Elle était au bord de la route depuis bientôt dix minutes, et aucun taxi ne semblait vouloir s'arréter. Ses cheveux lui collaient au front. Elle détestait Beyrouth en été. La chaleur et l'humidité rendraint la ville sale.

Une voiture s'arréta. Elle regarda furtivement le conducteur, puis, lui fit signe de la tête qu'elle n'en avaint pas besoin. On lui avait toujours dit de se méfier des jeunes conducteurs. Elle regarda sa montre. Déjà six heures . . . Elle était lasse et fatiguée. Elle voulait rentrer à la maison. Les séquelles de sa récente maladie commencaient à se manifester. It faisait tellement chaud qu'elle se sentait au bord de l'évanouissement . . .

Chapter One

Spilt Wine

It was hot that day. Sarah wore her long black dress with a flower motif, tiny yellow-and-white daisies and red poppies. She loved the dress. Her stepmother had told her it made her appear too thin, the black making her skin look too pale. But she loved the fine cloth, billowing linen perfect for the weather. The heat was suffocating. She had been waiting at the side of the road for more than ten minutes and not a single taxi or jitney seemed to want to stop. A couple had passed filled with the maximum five passengers. Her hair stuck to her clammy forehead. She hated Beirut in the summer. The heat and humidity made the city filthy.

A car stopped. She glanced at the driver furtively, then signaled him with a slight movement of her head that she did not need a jitney. She was always told to be wary of young taxi drivers. She looked at her watch. Already six o'clock. She was tired and weary. She wanted to be home. The symptoms of her recent illness were beginning to reappear. If it were not for the bout of pneumonia, she would have been up in the mountains instead of in Beirut. When she got sick, the family packed their summer home, returning early to Beirut to make sure she could be hospitalized. She ended up spending a couple of days in the hospital when her fever ran too high.

It was so oppressively hot, she felt faint.

A white car stopped, grimy, needing a vigorous wash. She looked inside. The driver was a man about as old as her father. In the back sat a young man of about twenty. She was so tired, she decided to take the two seats next to the driver. After all, she knew she did not have to worry because the driver was a seat away and she was not alone.

She rode in the car distracted, thinking of other things: the strange behavior of her boyfriend, the engagement of her sister, the pleasures of air-conditioning.

She did not know exactly when she no longer recognized the route. She told the driver this was not the road to her house. The driver looked at her, smiling, showing teeth that turned her stomach. The passenger seemed imperturbable. What was going on? She told the driver to stop, but he addressed her with the same nauseating smile. This was strange. She realized she must escape, get out of the car. The man in the back seemed indifferent to her complaints. Why would he not help her? She should get out, but the car drove fast in a neighborhood she had never seen before. She was not afraid. Not yet. She felt overwhelmed, unsure what to do, but not afraid yet. She knew she must act, and quickly. She put her hand on the door handle, but she felt a coldness on her slick temple, a metal coldness. She did not dare look back. The driver landed his large brown hand on her arm. When she tried to free her arm, his grip tightened, like a vice. The contrast between the whiteness of her arms and the dark of his fingers frightened her. Her dry throat tightened when she heard a click. The click of a revolver. She felt the veins in her temple pulse with such force, she thought the hand holding the gun would certainly feel the palpitations. It was only at that moment that she realized the passenger held the gun. She also realized she was at their mercy. She tried to master her mounting terror. She anxiously calculated the value of everything she had on her. This process reassured her. She would give them the gold watch, a gift from her father. She would give them the gold chain she had received from her stepmother six months ago for her sixteenth birthday. And of course, all the money she had on her.

Lost in her thoughts, she did not notice the car had stopped at an indistinct plot of land. The driver got out of the car, made the round to her side and opened the door. Her first reflex when she got out was to give him a kick on his shin. The cry which escaped him launched a horrifying panic in her. She knew she was going to bitterly regret her action. The man with the gun was already behind her, holding her firmly by the shoulders, the revolver aimed at the nape of her neck. She received the first blow on her stomach. *Slut. Fucking bitch.* The second blow, a slap across her face, caused a rattle in her head. She did not pay attention to the pain in her jaw, or the blood running from her lips. She came to realize what these men wanted. They did not want her money, or her watch.

For the first time, she dared look the driver in the eyes. What she saw froze her. A scary mixture of lust and disdain. The desire was not of coveting, or lust, not even of possessing. It was a primitive desire, dominance, aggression. For the first time, she wanted to die. She did not wish to suffer what these men wanted to inflict.

The man who held her shoulders, raked his gun along the naked skin of her back. She did not know if the shiver that ran up her back was from fear or disgust. The driver dragged his palm along her chest. His hand glided the length of her throat and rested on her bloody lips. She did not know where she got the courage to bite. She bit, gripping his fingers with her teeth the way her dog held on to bones. She did not want to, could not release her prize. The taste of blood, was it her lips or his fingers? She never figured it out because the punch she received in her kidneys blinded her. The younger man threw her on the ground, while the other, holding his injured fingers, kept repeating, *Slut . . . Whore . . . You will pay me for this, bitch . . .*

The man with the gun was stretched out on top of her, holding her arms with one hand, pulling the thin straps of her dress with his revolver. Her bust was now naked. She looked with horror as his mouth engulfed one of her breasts. He bit savagely. He lifted his head, a smile plastered on his lips, a smile disfigured by ugly desire. *Are you feeling pain, whore?* He lowered his head to kiss her, but she tried to turn her head. *I don't want to kiss you, bitch! I want to shove the gun in . . . Slut!*

She tried to strike out, but the other, the older one, crouched down and held her arms. With his free hand the younger man rubbed her breasts, with the other, lifted her dress, then pulled her panties down with the tip of his gun. He ran the cold gun along the inside of her thigh.

She did not want to believe this was happening to her. She wanted to wake up and realize this was nothing more than a nightmare. She raised her eyes and saw the pale sky. Blue, no cloud in sight. The chill of the gun as it touched her vagina brought her back to the cold reality. She was going to suffer. Of that she was certain. She would not look at them.

The sky was hazy, or was it her vision? She felt the gun moving in and out of her vagina. The man placed his knees on her legs, forcing her to remain open. The gun was practically in her now.

The sky . . . Where was the sky? It had disappeared . . . She felt she was about to dissolve as well. She heard the older man heap insults. No, just one. *Whore.* The word rang in her ears. She continually searched for the sky, but she saw nothing but the man with the gun, standing, blocking her line of sight, unbuttoning his jeans, one button at a time. He pulled down his pants and threw himself on her. She felt the heat of his erect penis enter her. She only saw the sky for a second because the pain caused her to faint. When she regained consciousness, the pain seemed intensified by the frenetic movement of the man within her. She heard his breathing accelerate. She heard his groan. Or was it her that groaned? Suddenly, the body of the man stopped moving, and he fell heavily on top of her in a death rattle. She lifted her head to look at the sky. It was darker, but the sky was there, assuring her. She was still alive. She was not dead. When she saw the older man take the place of the younger man, she folded herself up, as if, with such a movement, she would be able to stop his penetration. He kicked her, forcing her to curl up more. It was not the sky she looked at now, but the muddy earth. He yanked her by the hair, forcing her to turn around, hitting her. She was suffocated by his weight. The other man took his turn holding her down. *You see these fingers you bit? I am going to shove them in like* . . . The rest of the phrase hung in the air, suspended, because the pain this time was so sudden, she could hear only her own cries. He penetrated her savagely. She thought he was going to pierce her.

The sky had disappeared. She closed her eyes, out of pain, out of bitterness, out of shame. She felt him going in and out of her like an animal in a rut. With every movement of his body, he emitted a cry, and she groaned in pain.

When at last, with a cry, he fell on her, she dared to open her eyes. She allowed her eyes to wander along. She felt dispossessed of her own body. She tried to recapture a visual support, something to get a hold of, but she could only discern a frail silhouette in the distance. The end of the nightmare? Salvation? Someone was there. She felt a strange relief. The person would call for help. She would not die.

The man holding her down noticed the spectator. But instead of panicking as she had hoped, he called out to him. The silhouette approached slowly, with a hesitant step. She realized he was only an adolescent, maybe a year or two younger than her. She read in his gaze a terror akin to hers. Run, she thought. Go call for help. He regarded the scene with a mixture of fascination and disgust. A child in an adult world. The man stood up, arrogant in spite of the fact that he was naked from the waist down, his penis covered with blood. *You want to remain a virgin all your life. Come. Come find out the pleasures of being a man.*

The adolescent hesitated. Looked at her. From pathetic and poignant, his look transformed to desire. It burned with the same fire which animated the driver after he hit her. The man snickered. *Come on. What are you waiting for? Inspiration?* Both men burst out laughing. The boy began slipping out of his pants. *You know what to do, right?* The older man had a conniving smile. The boy nodded. He jumped on her, penetrating her brutally and clumsily. She did not have time to close her eyes for already he emitted the strange cry. She felt him being picked up. *Why didn't you take your time? She is ours.* One of the others went back inside her. She did not know which one. She remembered that she sobbed, begged the man to stop. He slapped her. Her tears did not stop, but he did not hit her anymore. Then the man penetrated her again. But she felt nothing other than pain.

The sky was darker now.

She had not noticed the men dress and leave. She found herself suddenly alone, filthy, covered in dirt and blood. She put her dress back on. Though dirty, it remained intact.

She must return home. She was late. She looked at her

watch, which they had not taken, and saw that it was only seven o'clock.

One hour. In only one hour, her life had come to an end. In only one hour, her dreams were shattered. In only one hour, she thought bitterly, she had become a woman. She was no longer a virgin.

She did not know how she returned home. By taxi . . .

She had only one worry; her parents must never know what happened. No one could know. No one.

Her father was home playing cards when she arrived. He did not notice her come in. She went into her room and undressed. There, she saw the marks. She placed herself in front of a mirror reflecting back the image of a girl who had been raped. Here was the bruise. She was raped. She was not guilty, she kept reminding herself. She was a victim. She felt soiled. There, between her thighs, on her naked legs, the dark blood mocked the pallor of her skin.

She placed herself under the waters of the shower, vigorously rubbing her skin, to erase the marks, the bruises, any trace. She scrubbed.

She put a new dress on. She covered her face with makeup. She left her room to face the tribe. Everything must go on like before.

Hello everyone, she addressed the card table. A chorus of hellos. *That's a wonderful dress you're wearing.* The man overflowed his seat with his girth. *You like it?* She twirled coyly. *It's a beautiful dress*, her father said. Did he still love her? she wondered.

She sat in front of the television. Her stepmother watched her intently. *Are you all right? Yes, I'm fine. I'm fine.* For a minute, but only a minute, she considered how many girls must have gone through what she did and sat silent. *Are you sure you're all right?*

. . .

Her best friend was spending the night. They were in bed together. *What's going on? It's been a while since you've been yourself. Don't you think I'd know if you're not all right? I'm your best friend.* For the first time since the incident, tears ran down her cheeks. Her best friend gently touched her cheek. *I missed my period. Oh, my god. You didn't tell me you went all the way with him. I didn't. Oh, my god! I was raped.* There. She said it. *I was raped.*

A best friend is someone who cries when you do.

We'll go see Dr. Baddour. What if he tells someone? He won't. But everyone will know. No one will know. There's something inside of me. I know it. We'll just get rid of it. Who'll pay? I have some money, and anyway, I'm sure he'll give us a discount.

Dr. Baddour scheduled her in the morning. She did not dare look down while he worked. She looked up. At the white ceiling, which became hazy sometimes.

The pain in her stomach was unbearable. She stayed in bed, told her parents she had stomach flu. She tried to be quiet for fear her father would want to examine her. Her best friend held her hand for a whole week.

Six months later, a group of her friends were over for dinner. Bombs were exploding somewhere in the distance. The electricity went out. They played a French version of Pictionary by candlelight. They were divided into teams of two, one to draw and the other to guess what was being drawn. She was teamed up with her best friend. They had been playing for over an hour. The next word was in the category of action. The first artist looked up the word. *Oh, boy. This is going to be hard.* He passed the card to the next artist and then to her best friend. She saw her best friend's jaw drop. *Okay. Time.* The artists began drawing. Her friend put the pencil on paper, but was unable to make it move. Stick figures in various forms of coupling appeared on the other artists' papers. *Have sex.* She was looking at her best friend, who still could not draw anything. *Making love.* The other guessers yelled out possible answers. A lump stuck in her throat. *Fucking. It has to be fucking.*

Her best friend finally looked at her, her eyes moist. *Rape?* she asked quietly, incredulously. *I can't believe you figured it out. You should have drawn it differently. How can I tell this is rape and not just fucking? I put those lines around the figures. That means it's violent. Those lines mean violent? You're crazy. Well, sorry, I don't know how to draw rape. I can't believe you figured it out. You two must be psychic. You must have some kind of connection.*

For the rest of her life, she would try and figure out why a game of Pictionary would have the word *rape* in it.

How does one draw rape?

The Fall

<hr>

BY

Sarah Nour el-Din

I don't believe artists know half the time what they are creating. Oh yes, all the tralala, the technique—that's another matter. But like ordinary people who get out of bed, wash their faces, comb their hair, cut the tops of their boiled eggs, they don't act, they're instruments which are played on, or vessels which are filled—in many cases only with longing.

—PATRICK WHITE, *The Vivisector*

Chapter One

She wakes up from her afternoon nap feeling heavy. She is still trying to adjust to sleeping on her back. Her neck aches. So does her back. She hears steam building in the heaters. Soon the apartment will transform from a freezing cold to a stifling heat in time for those returning from work. She does not understand why the most advanced country on earth still has apartments where you cannot regulate the heat.

Sarah gets out of bed slowly, puts on her terrycloth robe, which she abhors but has to make do with because it is her only maternity robe. She will not buy one she likes. This will be her one and only pregnancy. She toddles over to the window. Looks out. She has to crane her neck at an unnatural angle to see the sky. Blue, not a cloud in sight. Must be cold outside. She looks below, confirms the snow still on the ground, probably ice as well. The usual hordes walk the streets of the Upper West Side. She sees the Haitian woman coming out of the building across the street with the white baby. The nanny pushes the stroller down the five steps, one step at a time, until it is on the street. She comes around, bends over to see if the baby is well wrapped. From her height, Sarah can see nothing of the baby but a large, multi-hued bundle. The nanny pushes the stroller past the side of Sarah's window. How lucky, Sarah thinks. How fortunate to have to take care of a baby during working hours only, to be able to trudge back home and leave everything when her time is up.

With each step, her feet sink slowly into her thick slippers as she walks to the bathroom. She did not realize one could gain so much weight. She sits on the toilet and empties herself. She keeps sitting even after she is done. She thinks she is getting a headache. Without getting up, she stretches, reaching her bottle of Tylenol, and swallows two pills without water.

———————

He walks home from the university after classes. It is still early, but light is fading quickly. He has yet to adjust to the disappearance of light this early in the day. He longs for the Mediterranean sun. The colder it gets in the city, the more vivid his azure dreams.

It is a decent walk from Columbia University to his apartment. Omar walks the thirty-three blocks briskly, never takes the subway. He can't stand the stench of the underground. He does not particularly like the aboveground smells much either. At least winter ameliorates the city's horrific odors. As he thinks of the smells, he instinctively breathes deeply and gauges. Musty ammonia with a subtle tinge of putrefaction. Disgusting. He feels weighted down in so much clothing, oppressed by the sweaters, the ski hat, the woolen scarf. It is difficult to move. He is wearing long johns, for crying out loud. He did not realize he would ever have to wear long johns.

———————

Sarah walks into the kitchen. She needs a cup of coffee. She turns on the magical Mr. Coffee, the greatest invention.

Omar hates American coffee. She likes it. Or has she gotten used to it? She never cared for Turkish coffee, too thick, too permanent. When in Beirut, she drank Nescafé, and anything Mr. Coffee makes is better than instant. She leans back on the counter and stares into space. Looks at the black-and-white clock on the wall, realizes it is time for Omar to come home. He did not notice the clock in the kitchen. She bought it two weeks ago thinking it was cute. Instead of going from one to twelve, it has one, two, three, and then etc. She loves that.

She should cook something for Omar, surprise him with a meal. She tries to think of a meal he likes, but cannot come up with anything. She thinks the pregnancy must be affecting her thinking. She cannot even think of what her husband likes. The kitchen is too small. She has to agree with Omar about that. Not cozy, like she said when they moved in. With her size, it is immensely difficult to maneuver in the kitchen. Anyway, she is weary. The pregnancy is taking a lot out of her. She will order pizza. She likes pizza. She has a craving for pizza. She is sure Omar will like it.

———————

Omar walks home trying not to notice his surroundings, taking small steps to avoid slipping. He thinks of his friends back home. He misses his parents. He misses his dog. But it is his friends he misses the most. He wants someone to whom he does not have to explain everything. You can't say anything to Americans. They don't understand. They did not grow up with you. Anyway, what Americans? They are such a hodgepodge of people, all so different. African, Puerto Rican, Chinese, Indian. They do not have the same history. How can they possibly have shared experiences? Do they know what friendship is? He does not think so. He stares at the ground as he walks.

A year and half. That's what is left. A year and a half and he will have accomplished what he came here for. He will be free.

Sarah plops herself onto the couch, the only one in the room. She must figure out a way of fitting another in the cramped space. She cannot keep her guests sitting on chairs. She considers turning on the television. Listen to the news. The remote control is on the table on her husband's side of the couch. She cannot stretch that far. She is too weary to move. She stares at the black screen. Gray, it is actually dark gray, not black.

Above the television hangs the painting. She wonders why she bought it. It is not particularly pretty. An imitation impressionist painting by some American. A nice pastoral sunset. It does match the colors of the couch. She had hoped it would give her home an aura of serenity. Actually, she had hoped it would give her home something, not necessarily something specific, anything that would alleviate the feel of a motel room or a furnished temporary rental. Her husband thought it was too expensive.

She picks up the princess phone and dials her mother. The phone rings three times before the machine picks up. "Janet, it's Sarah. I've been trying to reach you. Did you get my last message? Call me soon, please." Her mother lives across the park but it feels like continents away. Sarah is fascinated by her mother. Such beauty, such pathos; her life the stuff of novels. She had to leave Beirut and come to New York when Sarah was two. Now that they are living in the same town,

Sarah cannot get enough of her mother. The feeling is not mutual. Janet can only take so much of Sarah.

———————

As Omar walks home he thinks of himself as a lumbering giant. He is not tall, around five foot seven, but with every step he takes, he feels his feet sinking into the slush as if he weighed a ton. He notes his appearance in a store window as he passes by. Not a giant, a massive mobile bundle of clothes in Timberland boots. That's what he is. A bundle of clothes that do not match. His camel's hair coat is tan but his ski hat is light gray with a black vertical line. How can one wear matching clothes if one has to wear so much? Quantity supercedes style.

He is not feeling well. He thinks he might be having a relapse of the flu. He feels a headache coming on, possibly even a migraine. A glacial wind blows and he thinks his nose is going to freeze. He wipes away wind tears. It must be below zero. A shiver runs up his back. He thinks he may already have a slight fever.

———————

She stares at the cream-colored drapes. The previous tenants had installed them incorrectly, facing out. They were so drab, one would not notice that they were installed backward unless one looked at the hems, which were facing inward. She should reinstall them. Her husband will not do it. She has to wait till after her delivery to do it herself.

For the second time that day, she feels the stab in her stomach. A piercing pang followed by a dull twinge for a couple of minutes. Her doctor says this is normal. She feels as though she is being eaten alive from the inside, something is slowly devouring her. A vampire sucks her soul. She must not allow herself to think these thoughts. The bats must be fought back, turned back to the dank caves from which they come. She feels the baby is changing her, transmuting her, into something she no longer recognizes. The real her is being slowly consumed, ingested, day by day, hour by hour, minute by minute. It starts in her belly and emanates outward, spiraling insidiously, overpowering her mind, vanquishing all her defenses. She must stop thinking these thoughts. This is her baby and she loves it.

It's a boy. And she loves him.

He walks along Broadway, from One Hundred and Sixteenth to Eighty-third, thirty-three city blocks, every day. Thirty-three blocks of complete anonymity. The passing crowd is always the same, always different. In all the times he has walked, he has never encountered anyone he knows. He would recognize everyone if he took a walk in Beirut. You felt human in Beirut.

The sultry voice of Umm Kalthoum wafts seductively out of a cassette player perched atop a hotdog cart. A twinge of bittersweet nostalgia. The Egyptian hotdog vendor stands next to his cart, customerless, lonely.

Omar arrives at the intersection of Eighty-sixth and Broadway. He stops to light a cigarette, takes the right-hand mitten off and places it in his coat pocket. The red Don't Walk signal is lit. He notices no car coming. He steps off the curb. His left foot alights on a metal grate. It takes less than a microsecond for his foot to slip from under him. His right foot follows suit, imitating the left in flight. His arms flail helplessly. The cigarette falls from his lips onto his chest in midair. His right hand instinctively reaches out to break his fall, reaches the grate an instant before the heavy thud of his butt, followed by his right elbow. The pain is instantaneous. His right hand is chafed, his left elbow is bruised, and the small bone at the bottom of his spine hurts. He attempts to pull himself up quickly, wobbles unsteadily.

"Are you all right?" asks a black man in a business suit, half of a couple.

"I'm fine," Omar snaps.

He almost slips again standing up. A group of teenagers, a couple of Puerto Ricans and an Indian, snicker from across the street.

"It's the ice," the black woman, the other half of the couple, says. "It's slippery."

"Yeah, right."

"Are you sure you're all right?"

"I'm fine," he growls back. He walks away.

The cigarette has burned a tiny black hole in his coat. His hand is not bleeding. He feels he is about to start crying. Fear. He is terrified. Not a normal kind of fear, primal, nothing he has ever felt before. He feels goose bumps all over his skin. His testicles ache. There is a metallic taste in his tongue. His breath comes fast, shallow. Dark spots appear before his eyes circling clockwise. He stops for a second to regain his breath. His mittened hand instinctively reaches out to the building on his left. He needs to steady himself. He wants to be home. He resumes walking, this time at a brisker pace. This must be primordial, cellular. He is unable to control the feeling. His bones ache. He wishes to wail. He wants to be in his own bed, his mother taking care of him, making him hot tea with a little bit of cognac. His head pounds.

———————

Omar walks through the door, sees her sitting on the couch. His wife. He smiles at her, a forced smile. She worries. She can't discern his expression. She thinks he is either about to cry or crack a one-liner. She tries to stand up, but he comes over and kisses her. He begins unwrapping himself.

"You burned a hole in your coat," she says, not an expression of concern, but a conversation starter.

"I know. I dropped a cigarette."

"They don't warn you about the sartorial dangers of smoking."

He hangs his coat on the coathook, takes off one sweater, the scarf, the hat, gradually regains his natural form. He takes off his boots. He comes over and lies on the couch, his head on her lap, his legs draped over the armrest. She strokes his hair gently.

"Did you lose a mitten?" she asks.

"*Mitten*?" She had used the English word. "What is mitten?"

"It means a glove without fingers."

"I know what it means. I know exactly what it means. Why do they use a different word? Why did you use it?"

"Because a mitten is different from a glove and you lost a mitten. That's why."

"Couldn't you have used the Lebanese word? I mean when did *we* start differentiating between a mitten and a glove."

"It's just more precise."

"Precise. Yes."

He stares at the ceiling as she continues to stroke his hair.

CHAPTER ONE

That Which Is Written

Régine and Fatima giggled, huddling together on the couch, arms entwined. Janet stood in front of a floor-length mirror dubious of the reflection. She liked the kohl. Not the rest, though. The braided hair made her look prepubescent. The gold chain with dangling trinkets around her forehead, the yellow eye shadow and the blood-red lipstick had the opposite effect, made her look adult, in her thirties. The dichotomy was disconcerting. She did not look Lebanese, yet was no longer American. She knew no Lebanese woman who dressed like that. She stared at the girl in the mirror. She appeared so exotic, straight out of a Sinbad Hollywood movie. Yes. Sin and bad. That was the girl in the mirror. She shuddered. She thought she was losing her footing again, though her feet had not budged. She quickly grabbed the mirror to steady herself. She looked like something out of *A Thousand and One Nights*. She was Shahrazad, a drunk Shahrazad, spinning tales.

"Do you like it?" Régine asked her Galatea.

"It's strange," Janet responded, which induced another bout of tittering from her friends. "I look so different."

Fatima fixed herself another drink. Her parents were in the mountains for the weekend so she had no worries. She placed a single ice cube in the miniature glass, poured the glass jar of *arak* until the glass was half full. The clear liquid whitened as it hit the cube, turning milky when she topped the glass with water.

"To your health," she said to no one in particular as she lifted the glass in the air, then gulped down the whole drink.

"You didn't make me one," Régine pouted.

"Sorry. I'll do it. Do you want another, Janet?"

Janet was entranced. "Mirror, mirror, on the wall, who's the fairest of them all?" Janet heard, "I am," coming from behind her, but was unsure whether it was Régine or Fatima. She begged to differ. There was no doubt Janet was the most beautiful of the three. How many times had she seen her face in the mirror? She knew every minute detail of it. Yet what stared back at her was a face she did not recognize. She raised the corners of her mouth for a smile, attempting to recapture some glimmer of familiarity. The face staring back at her became more distorted. She shivered perceptibly.

"You don't like it?" Régine asked, supine on the couch. Fatima was making more drinks. "Isn't that what you wanted?"

"I don't know. I wanted to look Lebanese so that I don't look so different from everybody."

Why was she here if not to feel different from the way she did back there? She wanted to experience the world. She wanted to change how the world saw her. Then why was she so terrified of the transformation she saw? She stared at the reflection. She must force herself to like this amalgam of East and West, to embrace it. The reflection might not be the new her, but she should accept any discernible change, no matter how incongruous it appeared. Any change was good change.

"Pour me a drink, Fatima," she said.

"You're so remarkable," Fatima said. "I can't believe you like *arak*. I bet you no other American would drink this."

"I want to celebrate the new me."

Janet kept looking at the mirror. She saw looking back at her a middle-aged woman, sad, lonely, desperate. She saw someone bitter. The woman in the mirror shook her head and told her, "Don't." The phrase repeated in her head over and over, a ringing. She was terrified. She covered her ears with her hands, felt faint.

On the corner of Bliss and Abdel-Nour streets, Janet waited for Régine and Fatima, looking in a store's picture window. Nothing interesting so she regarded her insubstantial reflection. She looked good. Janet had an abundance of bright red hair and was well aware of it. She took out a cigarette as a group of young university men walked by.

"Hi, Janet," one of the boys said.

She glanced up at him, unsure whether she knew him. She smiled anyway. "Hi there." The young man puffed up, obviously proud he knew her. One of the boys hesitated, wondering whether they were going to slow down and talk to her. The group kept moving. She lit her cigarette. Looking back, the young man said, "I'll see you in class tomorrow." Ah, he was in her math class. Could not remember his name, though. She heard them talking. *Those eyes* were the only thing she understood. She grinned. She should learn more Arabic. One of the boys punched her classmate on the shoulder and they disappeared around a corner.

Her eyes kept reverting back to a sprig of grass between the sidewalk slabs. It looked out of place. She wanted to pick it since she felt some strange affinity to it. Just as she was about to bend down, she heard Régine calling.

As usual Régine showed up first. Fatima was habitually

late. Régine was dressed to the nines, *en tailleur Chanel* as the Lebanese would say, which surprised Janet. She assumed Régine wanted to look older to impress the woman. Maybe Régine was not as confident as she appeared.

"Are you ready?" Régine asked, stepping partly toward Janet. She searched through her handbag, stood feet slightly apart, her weight unbalanced.

"Yes, sure. Are you?"

"Yes, of course. Done this lots of times." She lit a Marlboro, her hands trembling slightly, exhaled loudly.

"I don't believe in the stuff anyway."

"You'll see. She's good."

When the dark-red Rambler stopped in front of the girls, Régine quickly threw the cigarette on the ground and stamped it out. Fatima got out of her father's car. Régine had to stoop, look through the car's passenger window, to greet Fatima's father.

The girls waited until the car turned the corner before all three of them opened their purses and took out cigarettes. Régine flagged a taxi. When Janet looked down, she noticed the sprig of grass had been sheared by Régine's high-heel.

———————

The fortune-teller's house was in Zi'a' el-Blatt, a neighborhood Janet had never been to. Like other houses on the street, it was old, Lebanese old. Régine knocked on the oversized door and the girls waited. And waited. Janet noticed the ubiquitous turquoise hand, palm outward, dangling from a chain at the top of the door. After a while a woman opened the door.

"We're looking for Sitt Noha," Régine said.

"Well, you found her. Come on in, girls." Her manner was not cheerful, nor crude, neither welcoming nor antagonistic.

However, Janet knew Régine and Fatima would already feel slighted. The fortune-teller had not shown enough respect.

Sitt Noha led them through the foyer into the main room of the house. Janet had yet to see a house like this. Her friends all had modern apartments, whereas this house showed nothing belonging to the twentieth century. The floors were all smoothed stones with intricately painted Islamic designs. A huge Persian carpet dominated the room. Other carpets were hung on the walls. The seats were contiguous cushions on low benches against the walls, circling the entire room. Sitt Noha picked up a plate of food from the top of a low hexagonal brass table and took it into the kitchen. She was obviously in the middle of having lunch. "You girls make yourselves at home," she said as she left the room.

Janet was enthralled by the room. This was the exotic Middle East she had come for. The gilded mirror on the wall, the antique chandelier, the oil lamps that were obviously functional rather than decorative, the finely detailed backgammon board, open, on one of the cushions—apparently a game had been interrupted.

"I can't believe she was having lunch in the living room," Régine said, "and she knew we were coming." She sat rigid, starched, back straight. She pouted, looking more about to cry than angry.

Janet stared at a turquoise rosary on the seat next to her. It was not made for human hands, the beads much too big, for a giant's hands. The ashtrays on the table in front of her were silver, shaped in the form of pineapples. Why pineapples? She found that amusing. She sat cross-legged on the cushion. She lit a cigarette.

"And my mother likes her," Fatima said. "I wonder if my mother comes here or asks her to come to our house. I can't see my mom here."

Janet hoped after she had been in Lebanon a while, she would be able to understand the conventions better. Sitt Noha was from a lower class than the girls so she should have shown more respect. On the other hand, she was much older so she did not have to. They were her clients, about to pay, so she should have. It was so confusing. How Régine and Fatima figured out what was appropriate was beyond her. At least she had begun to know intuitively when they felt slighted.

She stared out one of the Turkish windows across the room, into the garden, dominated by a black oak and an orange tree, side by side.

"And she's so fat," Régine said.

Although Sitt Noha was overweight, Janet did not think she was that fat. Sitt Noha probably weighed less than Régine's mother. What Régine was actually commenting on was Sitt Noha's apparent lack of concern with her weight, her lack of any attempt to cover it up.

Sitt Noha walked back into the room, had changed from her housedress into another, dark purple with gold stitching. Janet had to grin. She was sure Régine and Fatima would scorn the new housedress and mock it, but Janet thought it was charming. The housedress made Sitt Noha look like a giant decorated aubergine.

Sitt Noha had a toothpick in her mouth. Tomato paste stained the corners of her lips. She moved a low ottoman right in front of the girls and sat down, knees apart, her hands between them, packing up loose folds of the housedress.

She yelled, at the top of her lungs, "Where is the coffee, Asma?" The girls jumped, startled.

"What can I do for you, my daughters?" she asked in Arabic. All Janet understood was *my daughters*.

"We're here for fortune-telling," Régine said. "Like I said

on the phone, our friend here is all the way from America. She doesn't speak Arabic very well." Neither did Régine, who was having substantial problems constructing a complete Arabic sentence. Having grown up in a French-speaking household, she, like many Lebanese, had trouble with her mother tongue. "But I can translate for her."

"And you two don't want me to tell you anything? You're not looking for husbands?" Sitt Noha pulled her disheveled hair back, forming a loose ponytail with a rubber band.

"We want to, but we're here for the American." Janet was not following the conversation well, but she did notice Régine and Fatima move slightly forward.

"We want everything," Fatima said. "We can pay."

"Can you actually tell what our husbands will look like?" Régine asked, breathing noisily, her eyes sparkling.

"When you called," Sitt Noha said, "I thought you were the foreigner."

"No," Régine said. "I'm Lebanese, from Beirut. She's the American."

"You said your name was Régime. What kind of name is that?" Janet understood the French word for *diet* and tried hard to stifle her laugh.

"It's Régine, with an *n*," Régine replied, moving back into the cushions. She fidgeted with her handbag.

"Why would your mother call you that? Did she know you were going to grow up fat? She must be a fortune-teller too."

"No, no. It's Régine, not Régime. It means queen."

Sitt Noha was oblivious to Régine's irritation. A little girl, no more than ten years old, dressed in a similar aubergine housedress, came in carrying a silver tray with a pot of coffee. She gave each of the girls a cup. Janet shook her head, but Sitt Noha insisted. She kept moving the toothpick from one side of her mouth to the other. Janet could not take her eyes off it.

"Drink, drink," Sitt Noha said in English, gesturing with both her hands. She followed that with an aspirating sound as she brought an imaginary cup to her mouth with one hand, while the other held the imaginary saucer steady. "Drink."

"You must drink it," Fatima admonished, "or she won't be able to read your fortune correctly. She must have a coffee cup."

"Can't she do it without my drinking coffee?"

"She probably can but the coffee cup finalizes everything." Fatima drank from her coffee cup, modeling the acceptable behavior to her friend. "She reads the patterns of the coffee sediments left in your cup, the dregs."

"That's disgusting."

Sitt Noha shook her head, appearing to have understood the conversation. "Tell the girl one must suffer to know one's future. Tell her to drink up." She adjusted the ottoman beneath her, bunched up her housedress once more and, not so discreetly, scratched herself.

Sitt Noha turned Janet's cup right side up. "Not ready," she said in English, turning it over again. She turned Régine's cup. "Almost ready." Régine smiled in anticipation.

"I can see a husband already," Sitt Noha said.

"Really?" Régine was twittering. "Is he tall?"

"Tall? Yes, he's tall. Not too tall. He's handsome. Black hair and a mustache. Ah, he's an engineer. He will fall in love with you. I see that. There are problems."

"What problems?"

"Your parents won't approve. They don't want you to marry him."

"Why? Why? Is he from a poor family? He's an engineer. They have to approve."

"I'm not sure. It's not clear yet because the coffee hasn't settled. See this line. Look here. This shows how much he loves you. This here shows problems."

"I must know why. They must approve. I don't want to elope. I want a big church wedding and a big reception. Like my sister."

"Ah, there you go. It says here there will be no church wedding. He's a Muslim."

"I can't convert."

"You will."

"Are you sure he's not a Druze? He'd be the one who would have to convert if he's a Druze. Tell me he's Druze."

"No. He's not Druze."

"Oh, my god," Régine exclaimed. "Don't tell me he's . . ." She could not even finish the sentence. Even Fatima gasped.

"No," said Sitt Noha. "He's not a Shi'ite. He's a Sunni, from Beirut."

"Oh, thank god."

"Hey, maybe I know him," Fatima said. "You know what. Maybe it's my cousin Nabil. He's studying engineering at USC right now. He's tall with black hair and a mustache. Maybe it's him."

"Can you tell his name?" Régine asked Sitt Noha.

"No, not the whole name. It starts with an *N* though. See here."

"Oh, my god. It *is* an *N*."

"Oh, my god. It's Nabil. You're going to marry my cousin Nabil. We'll be relatives. Like sisters."

"Is he handsome?"

"He's incredibly handsome," Fatima gasped. "You have to watch out because every girl will be after him."

"But he'll be in love with me."

"True, but after you marry him, girls will still go after him because he's handsome and smart."

"Don't worry about that," Sitt Noha said. "When it's time, come see me. I'll teach you what to do and he'll never be able to get it up for another woman."

The girls began giggling again.

———————

Sitt Noha stared at Janet's cup. She twirled it gently. "The coffee refuses to settle," she said. "Her future does not want to be completely written. You tell her that, Régime."

"What does that mean?" Janet asked. "How can my future be written?"

"All future is written," Sitt Noha said. "We just have to know how to read it."

"How come if all future is written, mine isn't? Ask her that."

"Her future is partially written, not all of it. I can read some of it, but the rest is yet to be written. That's because she's a girl with a strong personality."

"That's bad?"

"There's no good or bad coffee. It's just coffee. Nothing you can do about what is written."

"So you're saying I can write my future?"

"Not sure if it is you who will write it. It can be someone else. You'll marry into a strong family. Stronger than you."

"I'm not going to get married anytime soon. Ask her about my Middle Eastern history professor and why he hates me."

———————

"You will marry a Lebanese man from an old family. He's a doctor. You'll get very sick. This man will save your life. He'll save you from certain death and fall in love with you. He will sell his soul for you."

"That's so romantic," Régine said. "Don't you think that's wonderful?"

"I don't want to get married. I'm still too young to settle down. Anyway, what's so romantic about getting sick and almost dying?"

"Tell her that her husband will save her," Sitt Noha said. She chewed on her toothpick, moved it from side to side. "She'll get married soon. She'll have three children. Two girls and a boy. The boy will come last. He'll be the jewel of her life. He'll look as beautiful as her. The boy will be her gift to the world."

"That's perfect, Janet," Régine added. "Two girls and a boy. That's a wonderful family. Aren't you happy?"

"I don't want a family yet."

"Hold on." The toothpick snapped between Sitt Noha's teeth. "Tell her I see trouble. Tell her I see trouble, but she can avert it. Tell her she has to change. Tell her the man comes from a strong family. They will swallow her. She can't resist. Tell her she has to change, become lighter, learn to float. She'll no longer be able to be herself, she will become part of a larger whole. She can't move independently, she has to move with the family's river. She'll become the family. She can't change that. The family swallows. It's difficult for her. She's beautiful. She's strong. She is American. They don't understand family over there. She has to adapt, she must learn to accept. She will change. Tell her she'll drown if she tries to swim. She must not fight. The two worlds will clash and she's not strong enough to fight. She should give up and float. Tell her the son will carry her. He'll know how to float between two worlds someday. He'll be the bridge. Tell her she has to learn to float not swim. You tell her that. You tell her all of it."

"I don't have to worry about that. I'm not getting married anytime soon. Ask her if she knows anything about my Middle Eastern history professor. Why does he hate me?"

"Tell her for an extra five Lebanese pounds, I can teach her how to make a curse, which will get her teacher off her back. Or else."

ON RUNNING

Why runners make lousy communists. In a word, *individuality*. It's the one characteristic all runners, as different as they are, seem to share . . . Stick with it. Push yourself. Keep running. And you'll never lose that wonderful sense of individuality you now enjoy. Right, comrade?

The first time I saw the advertisement for running shoes, I cut it out and push-pinned it above my desk. That was in 1984 (it appeared at the Los Angeles Olympic games) and I was considering divorcing my second husband.

That wonderful sense of individuality.

I always tried to walk a path unbeaten by others, to touch the untouched. I moved from the land of conformism to the land of individualism. I moved from a country that ostracized its nonconformists to one more tolerant and more hypocritical. I moved from Lebanon to the United States.

*　　　*　　　*

The myth of the rugged individualist is integral to the American psyche. Most Americans, native and naturalized, consider themselves admirers, or at least indulgent, of individualists. I was no exception. It was only recently that I had begun to recognize the hypocrisy. As an American once wrote: Except in a few well-publicized instances (enough to lend credence to the iconography painted on the walls of the media), the rigorous practice of rugged individualism usually leads to poverty, ostracism and disgrace. The rugged individualist is too often mistaken for the misfit, the maverick, the spoilsport, the sore thumb.

*　　　*　　　*

I am the daughter of a Lebanese man and an American woman, a fairly brief marriage. My mother, in a burst of independence, arrived in Lebanon to study at the American University of Beirut. She was a free spirit, did what she pleased. Like many foreigners who landed on Lebanese shores with dreams of conquest, she was swallowed whole. She fell in love with my father, got married, and had to subdue any sense of individuality she may have had in order to fit in, to conform to what was expected of her. I say *may have had* because at times I wonder whether there is such a thing as a sense of individuality. Is it all a façade covering a deep need to belong? Are we simply pack animals desperately trying to pretend we are not?

*　　　*　　　*

Americans landed in Beirut in droves, getting off their cruise ships and TWA flights, wanting a taste of the Middle East without actually having to soil their shoes. Beirut obliged. It gave them a taste all right, but only a taste. The city hid its Arabic soul and presented the world a Western veneer. *Life* described Beirut as "a kind of Las Vegas-Riviera-St. Moritz flavored with spices of Araby." But not too spicy.

They bought trinkets in the cute *souqs* built especially for them, but they spent their big money buying Christian Dior gowns in downtown stores. They bought hookahs and backgammon tables as proof of their having been in Arabia, as vindication. They visited quaint Arabic restaurants, but their main meals were the imported steaks and lobsters at the *cafés trottoire*.

We are special, they said. We are different. When they went to the Ba'albak festival, they chose to see Ella Fitzgerald, never Umm Kalthoum.

*   *   *

So did I. I hated Umm Kalthoum. I wanted to identify with only my American half. I wanted to be special. I could not envision how to be Lebanese and keep any sense of individuality. Lebanese culture was all consuming. Only recently have I begun to realize that like my city, my American patina covers an Arab soul. These days I avoid Umm Kalthoum, but not because I hate her. I avoid her because every time I hear that Egyptian bitch, I cry hysterically.

*   *   *

I have been blessed with many curses in my life, not the least of which was being born half Lebanese and half American. Throughout my life, these contradictory parts battled endlessly, clashed, never coming to a satisfactory conclusion. I shuffled ad nauseam between the need to assert my individuality and the need to belong to my clan, being terrified of loneliness and terrorized of losing myself in relationships. I was the black sheep of my family, yet an essential part of it.

*   *   *

CHAPTER ONE

Faint

For in the prophet Habbakuk in the Christian Old Testament/the Neviim in the Jewish Holy Scripts it is written:

"For the violence done to Lebanon shall sweep over you, the havoc done to its beasts shall break your own spirit, because of bloodshed and violence done to the land, to the city and all its inhabitants."

On rainy days in San Francisco everything seems mortal. Everyone stays home and the color of death is everywhere. The city was having an unusual autumn storm after a cold summer. I walked up to the counter and ordered my *macchiato*. I loved the café because of its outdoor seating, but the weather forced me inside. Muzak blared from the decrepit speakers, the sounds of scratchy Enya, or maybe it was Celine Dion's *Titanic* song. I took my coffee back to my seat. The café was much too gloomy on a gray morning.

There were only four people including me, each sitting in a corner. I had chosen the west corner. Two preppie gay men faced each other diagonally across the room, giving each other *les doux yeux*. Most probably horny waiters. Across the room from me sat a pale, youngish woman, straight black hair and layers of black cloth. A Goth, she had piercings protruding from all over her face, wore black lipstick and heavy black eyeliner. I wondered if she used makeup to make herself so white. She had a tarot deck spread out on the table in front of her. I had seen her reading the cards a number of times before, but for some reason she gave me the creeps today. I slugged down my coffee and left.

No one else walked the street. Few cars. A four-wheel-drive Toyota stopped ten yards in front me. A red umbrella emerged from the Toyota, followed by a young man in jeans. Just as he closed the door, the sky was filled with a bright light and the sound of an explosion. The man shrieked a high C and ducked behind the Toyota, his umbrella lowered, rain dotting his beige suede jacket. San Franciscans were not used to thunderstorms. The lightning must have hit somewhere close. It rained harder. I looked up at the sky, saw more lightning. The thunder that followed was deafening. I felt myself getting dizzy, realized I was dropping slowly before I blacked out.

I woke up in a darkened, unfamiliar room. I recognized the light and panicked. The daylight seeped in from windows closed with louvered shutters. Only in Beirut. I did not dare move. I was lying on the floor sideways, my face resting on a pile of newspapers. Someone must have put me there. I stared at the unfamiliar water stains on the wall, one mushroom cloud and a map of Italy. Where was I? I had to do something. I sat up and looked around me trying to gauge the room. I was in an old Beiruti house.

The sound of a shot rang out, shaking me out of my stupor. My head moved at a dizzying speed. I had to take in everything, figure out if I was in danger. I have been through this before. Instinct took over.

The walls were sandstone, not effective at impeding bullets. What floor was I on? I should look out the window. I heard another shot. Then another. A staccato burst. The boys were building up. It was going to be fierce. The shots were intermittent, a funny rhythm, a five over four, not a disco beat. Dave Brubeck would have been proud. On the wall next to me stood a large bookcase. I did not want to be underneath it if the books fell. I stood up. The thunderstorm from hell erupted.

Machine gun fire from every direction. Cannons, rockets, missiles detonated at the same time, enough to wake the dead. I should concentrate. I used to be able to figure out who was fighting whom by differentiating the sounds of gunfire, used to be able to tell Belgian missiles from Russian rockets. Where was I? I must look outside.

I opened the door slightly and put my head out. An old staircase, light coming through broken windows. Another door, slightly ajar, facing me. And nothing above me. Through the door, in the other apartment, I could see a family huddled together, like a flock of frightened birds. Are you all right? I yelled. They paid me no notice. Where am I? I asked. No reply. I looked through the broken windows. I was on the second floor. I should move down. I began to step out. A bullet whizzed by. I shut the door in panic, ran to the corner and cowered, held my knees to my chest and waited. I will survive this, I said to myself. I have before and will again. Must distract my mind. How did I get here? Where was my family?

I looked at the bookshelf. The books were all in English, all American authors, all romance novels. I stared in awe when I realized the bookshelf contained every book Danielle Steel had written. In hardcover no less. At least I think it was every book she had written. I could not be sure, but at the same time, I was certain she could not have written more books than were available on that bookshelf.

Two hours went by. No sounds. The fighters were taking a break. The most dangerous time. I heard the sound of dripping water coming from another room. Chinese water torture. Drip. Drip. A couple more minutes to make sure and then I would stand up and check. I heard the high shrieking meows of a threatened cat coming from outside. I got up from my corner and walked slowly to the window. I opened the shutter slowly and peeked outside. I did not know whether I had been in the neighborhood before. I might have, but I did not recognize it in this state. All the shutters of every house were closed. Down in the street three dogs, looking like they had been starved for days, cornered an orange cat against a wall. Even from a distance, I saw the cat's hairs standing up. The dogs moved slowly around the cat, snarling, waiting to attack. They got closer, pulled back, approached again from a different angle. The cat's wail was terrifying. A shot rang out and one of the dogs fell down, his head exploded, panoply of red. Another shot and another. All three dogs lay dead. The cat had not moved yet. It looked around and then bolted. The fourth shot got the running cat.

"Good shot," screamed a voice in Arabic, coming from way down on my right.

"Allah is great," came the reply from way down on my left.

Would they start shooting at each other again now?

I slowly closed the shutter, but not slowly enough. A bullet came through, right next to where my arm was. My body recalled the heat of gunfire and reacted instantly. I stood still to avoid the ricochet. The bullet hit the floor, jumped up, went left, hit the wall, bounced back and lodged itself in one of the books in the bookshelf. Indoors, bullets never traveled in a straight line. I did not worry about a second bullet. The first was just a warning. If the sniper had wanted me dead, I would have been.

I looked at the bookshelf. I saw the Danielle Steel book that was shot. It began to bleed. Blood dripped from it slowly. Drip. Drip.

I fainted.

I woke up in a car. It took me a minute to realize it was my ex-husband's second car, the blue Volvo he loaned me every time I visited Beirut. I was holding on to the steering wheel, but the engine was not running. I looked in the rearview mirror and noted that my cheek had ink on it, as if I had slept on a newspaper, yet there was no paper in the car. I could read the writing in the mirror, it flipped a text already flipped. In Arabic, the text said something about the son of a politician, asking is any offspring innocent in a guilty family.

I looked around me. I was in Never Never Land, the green line of Beirut, not too far from Martyrs' Square. I must have taken a wrong turn. Destruction was all around, but so was greenery. Trees and bushes sprouted from unrecognizable buildings. A jungle attempting to reclaim its glorious past from its concrete counterpart.

In the distance atop a hill of rubble, I saw the silhouette of a young boy, with a machine gun growing from his hip. I began to shake. I realized it was ironic I was not afraid of the gun as much as I was of the boy's silhouette. Some memories are hard to release. He began walking toward me. I tried the ignition, but the car would not start. The only sound that could be heard was the false starts of the Volvo. The engine caught. I stepped on the gas. The car lurched forward, toward the approaching boy, and died. I tried again. Another false start. The engine caught again and died before I could step on the gas.

The boy tapped gently on my window. I lowered it, trying hard not to stare at his face that seemed to have suddenly erupted in a rash of pimples and choral cystic acne. He was smiling gently. I smiled back, nervously.

"Are you all right?" he asked me.

"Yes, I think so. I seem to be lost and my car won't start."

"Do you want me to look at it?"

"Do you know anything about cars?" I asked. Behind the pimples, his face was cherubic, high and full cheekbones. He looked innocent, or at least trustworthy.

"I know some. My dad was a mechanic. Let me look. Open the hood."

I pulled the latch and just as he lifted the hood, I heard gunfire. The boy showed his head from behind the hood. "Uh oh," he said, still smiling. "We should get out of here. It's going to get messy."

"Where to?" I asked. "Where can I go?"

"Come with me. I know a shelter."

I got out of the car gingerly. He walked in front, too slow it seemed to me. I caught up with him and tried to move him along. He would not hurry up. I heard men shouting from one of the pockmarked buildings. Some men shouted back from below. I could not understand what was being said. We arrived at a building, getting there from the side. There was a hole at ground level, caused initially by a shell, but enlarged by men for easier access. The boy stepped into the building, and I followed bending my head as I entered. The smell of burned refuse, decaying flesh, excrement, and urine greeted me.

"You'll get used to it in a minute," he said. "The nausea passes."

A kerosene lamp lit the windowless room. A thick layer of dust covered everything, a small table, four rickety chairs. A couple of M16s and three hookahs stood in a corner next to a television set whose screen had been shattered by bullets. A guitar stand, without the instrument, occupied another corner; under it lay a dead rat. An exquisite backgammon board lay open on the table.

"Do you play?" the youth asked as he sat on one of the chairs.

"I don't think I should," I replied. "I'm too anxious and I don't have my Xanax. I don't seem to have my handbag."

"That's okay. They won't take long. The shooting will go on for ten minutes or so and then they'll stop. Everybody is exhausted."

"Why are they fighting?"

"Who can remember anymore? Habit, I guess. Nobody knows anything else. They start shooting, forgetting why. They stop. They start in a different way. They stop again. Try a different attack. They can't seem to be able to finish a battle. It's endless."

"Can't someone get them to stop?"

He shrugged. I guess the question was too silly. I sat on one of the chairs. My heels were killing me. "Why aren't you fighting?" I asked.

"Because my father died."

"You were fighting for him?"

"Oh, no," he said. He took out a deck of cards from his

pocket and began laying out a solitaire game. "My father did not want me to fight at all."

"I don't understand," I said. "If he didn't want you to fight, why did you stop fighting after he died?"

He looked up at me and gave me an angelic smile, white teeth and all. "Because I'm the bad son. I didn't want to be like him. I didn't want to stand around while they took everything away from me. I took up the gun. He said he had no son anymore. I was free for a while or I thought I was. But now he's dead. I don't have to be unlike him."

"You can fix cars?"

"Yes." He sighed, the smile disappearing. "I'm good at it too. Just like he was. I can't run far enough."

The battle outside was going full blast. We were hearing every type of weapon. I hoped the boy was right and it would be over soon.

"Are we safe here?" I asked. "I mean a shell came through here once already."

"A shell never hits anywhere twice."

"That's lightning. That rule doesn't apply to shells."

"Oh, well. Is anywhere safe?"

On cue, the battle stopped. More men shouted. I looked through the hole in the wall, but I could not see anything.

"Shall I fix your car now?" he asked.

"Yes. I should get out of here. It's not safe."

He stood up and came toward me. He held my hand as he went through the hole. I followed, the harsh sunlight blinding me. I took a deep breath. The cleaner air was disorienting. I could smell cordite and smoke. I tried to breathe again, but felt myself blacking out. I looked at the boy before I lost consciousness.

*   *   *

I wake up to the barely audible voice of Bernard Shaw reciting the news on CNN. I had slept slouched at my desk. My neck is sore. I stretch it backward, then bend it down and rotate my head sideways to release the crick.

Fish swim languidly across my laptop's screen. A red fish eats a blue fish and swims away. Blue fish swallows the red fish. Fish come and go without any discernible purpose. Rain slaps my bay windows, water streaking along thin paths on the glass. I look outside, a dreary, stormy day in San Francisco. Without moving from my desk, I click the remote and mute the television blather. I run my hand along the edge of my mahogany desk.

I consider taking a plate with a piece of half-eaten buttered toast back to the kitchen.

Lightning flashes outside, momentarily brightening my study. I look around at the walls. I am no longer sure I can live with the butter yellow color. Maybe I can paint the trim something other than white. One of my paintings hangs on the wall, a strong one, one of my chosen. Cadmium red bars on titanium white background. The second lowest bar on the right is not a perfect rectangle, which tilts the whole painting. Few people realize that. The eye always fills in the imperfections. Eleven perfect rectangles; the twelfth must be as well. Maybe that is why I feel irritable. I should hang the painting in another room, or repaint the rectangle, or repaint the walls a peach and not butter yellow. I should paint peaceful paintings.

The pigeons sheltered above my window, under my roof, flap their wings in unison. I hear movements, an apparent jockeying for positions. Then softer, and the cooing recommences. This is their home now, I think. Shoo, Fly, Don't bother me. They coo softly, settle in.

I can paint the walls a robin's egg blue.

I drag my forefinger across the computer touchpad to eliminate the carnivorous fish. Out pops my manuscript. My manuscript. Mine. I tense, feel a knot building in my right shoulder. I feel about to faint.

I stand up and put on my coat. I will walk across the street for a coffee, something to ease the tension. I stretch my back.

1- Inversion

Sarah woke up late, on an early August Sunday in San Francisco, had slept much longer than was necessary. She rose out of bed, stumbled slowly into the bathroom, swaying as if drunk, trying to disentangle her brain from the cobwebs of sleep. She looked out the window, was not surprised to find a heavy, wet fog. Summer in San Francisco. She still felt groggy. She slapped her face, shook her head vigorously from side to side, and sat on the toilet. She noticed the empty toilet roll dispenser. She thought she had gotten a new roll yesterday. She was almost sure of it. She remembered the roll was on the small table in the corridor. She was bringing it into the bathroom when the phone rang. She must learn to complete her projects. She used facial tissues. She stood up, annoyed with herself for being so easily distracted. She would go directly and fill the dispenser.

As she passed by the mirror, she stopped. Her reflection looked good today. Her features were soft, as were her brown eyes. She felt relieved. She put her head outside the bathroom door and yelled, "Are you up?"

From the kitchen, "Of course, I'm up. I don't need ten hours of sleep."

"Maybe you should try it. I look wonderful this morning."

"Go back to sleep then."

"No, no. Come see and bring me a cup of coffee, please!"

Kamal turned the corner into the corridor, carrying a steaming mug of coffee. He was already dressed, ready to go. "I think you should be the one bringing me coffee. I'm on vacation, a guest here."

"Shut up and get your butt over here!" He slowed down, began sauntering. She had to admit she loved the way he walked. She thought her son was handsome, with his dark, long hair, and brown eyes. She was thankful again that he did not take after his father in looks. He pretended he was moving in slow motion, every step taking an eternity.

"Get in here," Sarah said when he was close enough for her to grab. She took the coffee from him and kissed him. "Look at your mother. Doesn't she look wonderful this morning?"

She held him, made him stand next to her facing the mirror. "You look the same as yesterday," he said.

"Ah, what do you know? You're not even looking. You'll always miss the finer things in life."

"*This* is one of the finer things in life? I worry about you, Mom. Staring at yourself in the mirror? Hey, looks like there's water damage here."

"Where?" she gasped, her hands going quickly to her face.

He bent down to look at the wall next to the bathtub. "You should fix this," he said. He was right. She should have fixed that five years ago when she first noticed it.

He stood up and walked out of the bathroom. "Well, what's the point of looking wonderful if you're going to spend the morning having breakfast with homosexuals?"

She yelled at his departing form, "Your uncle doesn't have breakfast, he has brunch." Pleased with herself, she began to get ready. Happy.

. . .

Sarah went into the hardware store. "Your uncle asked us to get him a pitcher. He broke his." Kamal followed, dragging his feet. On her way to kitchenware, she stopped in front of an ugly fake plant, bright plastic fuchsias dangling from dusty synthetic leaves in a tattered woven pot. Sarah began tearing. Her hand covered her mouth and she wept silently. She knelt on one knee to look closer.

"It is awful, isn't it?" a man asked her.

Sarah glanced up at him in surprise and quickly wiped her tears away. "It's terrible." She tried a weak smile.

He hesitated. "I'm sorry. Are you okay?" He ran his hand though his hair, raking it back.

"Oh, yes. This thing just reminded me of someone."

The man looked both ways, tying to gauge if anyone was watching, then with wrists on hips, arms akimbo, he whispered, "Well, you know what, hon? If this thing reminds you of him, believe me, you're better off without him. I mean, come on, a plastic fuchsia?"

She giggled.

"Anyway," he went on, "like I always say, 'And this too shall pass.'"

She stood up, noticed her son was standing back observing, bemused.

The man, no longer looking at her, but up at the ceiling, sighed. "And sometimes it doesn't pass, which is why I'm on Paxil."

"Paxil?" Sarah asked. "Doesn't it make you sleepy? I couldn't deal with it. I was sleeping all day. I prefer Zoloft."

"Zoloft works for you?"

"Oh, yes. Quite well. I love it." She looked at her son, who pursed his lips, trying not to laugh. "Thanks so much, dear," she told the man as she grabbed her son by the arm and began moving away. "You've been a great help."

Sarah dragged her son along the aisle. She could not help but chuckle with him. "No, I don't always discuss my medications with strangers," she said. "So don't you start."

"You attract homosexuals."

Kamal seemed distracted as they walked. She put her arm in his. "Do you still think of him?" he asked her.

He still wanted to be her confidant. Her ex-husband told her a couple of years earlier that Kamal had ceased to confide in him. Would he still confide in her? One benefit of her son growing up thousands of miles away was that he did not have to rebel against her, or so it seemed.

"Do I still think of whom? David? Not often. Every now and then something will remind me of him, like that stupid fake plant, but for the most part I no longer do. It has been so long."

"But why do you even bother?" He asked this sternly, looking at her. She noticed the left corner of his mouth twitch momentarily, and then go slack.

"I don't know. I guess I just loved him."

"But you loved a lot of people. You always say you loved Dad."

"I still do. It's different, that's all." She slowed down. They were getting close to her brother's house, and she wanted to enjoy this walk a little more. "Who is your girlfriend?" she asked hesitantly, careful not to let her eagerness show. She ran her finger across his cheek.

"Well, if you know I have a girlfriend, then I'm sure you know who she is. Dad must have told you."

"Well, why the subterfuge?"

"Because it's nobody's business."

"Oh, my. This is serious." She watched him begin to redden, even his ears changed color. "Is this love I see before me?"

"Cut it out."

"So is it true what your father said, that your lips and hers seem to be sewn together?"

"Glued together. The metaphor is glued together, not sewn."

"I can use whatever metaphor I like. I'm the writer."

"You wish."

"Oh, my, my, my. This *is* serious." She could not help smiling. She had heard about what was going on, but had not expected to find him so smitten. "This is love. I can see why you'd have a fight with your dad over her."

"Is that what he told you?" He shook his head in consternation. "He told you the fight was about her? He didn't tell you about FreeCell, I assume."

"FreeCell?"

"The computer solitaire game. That's what all politicians in Lebanon do. They drink coffee and play FreeCell. Dad doesn't let anybody use his computer. You know why? He doesn't want to fuck up his FreeCell ratio. Can you believe that? I sat and played the dumb game and I lost. I broke his record of eighteen straight games. He freaked. He started screaming I should leave his FreeCell alone."

She started laughing again. "That wasn't about FreeCell, you know."

"Don't start with psychoanalysis, Mom. Please. FreeCell isn't a metaphor for his penis. I don't care about his FreeCell or his penis."

By the time they reached the door, she was convulsing with laughter, wiping tears from her eyes.

Sarah's half-brother, Ramzi, lived with his lover in an old Victorian across the hill from her flat. The house, like everything in their life, was meticulously kept. The garden, which was small even by San Francisco standards, had a tropical motif. In the northwest corner stood a miniature fountain, shaped like a giant seashell, with water spouting from the mouth of an "authentic" black-lava Tiki god with red, faux-ruby eyes. In the northeast corner sat a hot tub, barely seating two, built to look like a miniature volcano, including a lava flow fit to scale. The plants were mainly giant birds of paradise, ferns, and even a new mutation of a banana tree, which produced inedible fruit full of seeds.

The brunch was in the tiny gazebo dominating the center of the garden. Sarah sat on the chair—the color of all the patio furniture was forest green, which was also the color of the gazebo—and felt dew seeping through her skirt.

"You know, Sarah," Peter said when Ramzi was back with the drinks, "it's always disconcerting to see you with your son."

"Why's that?" Sarah asked.

"Simply thinking of you as a mother is disconcerting."

"Thanks, Peter," she said. "I can always rely on you to say just the right thing to make me feel better."

"No, I'm sorry," Peter said. "I didn't mean it in a bad way. I just meant it's difficult to see you as a mother since you never seemed to have developed any competence at being an adult."

"Fuck you," she hissed at him. "You're such a stupid ass-hole sometimes."

"And she didn't mean *that* in a bad way," added Kamal.

"Now, now." Ramzi squeezed himself next to Peter. "Let's talk about more important things. What's this thing I hear about you being in love?"

Kamal stared at his mother. "I can't believe you," he said. "Don't you have anything better to talk about?"

"Your mother wasn't the one who told me," Ramzi said. "I think the first to mention it was my mother. When I talked to your father, he told me as well. Then both my other sisters told me. Come to think of it, only Sarah hasn't told me."

"That's because Sarah has better things to talk about." Sarah gave her son a raspberry, beginning to feel the two mimosas. "If I wanted to talk about you, my dear, I would have told everyone how you were having an affair with Mrs. Hatem last summer."

"I can't believe you said that," her son yelled.

"Did you say Mrs.?" Peter asked in mock seriousness.

"Oh, settle down, Kamal," Ramzi said. "Did you think we wouldn't know?"

"Everybody knows," his mother said, sipping her drink slowly. Kamal looked more and more glum. "You're part of the family. You can't escape no matter how hard you try. Trust me. I tried."

Ramzi glanced at his sister, a look of concern. "Was that a little bitter?" he asked. "You doing all right?"

"I'm fine. It's not bitterness as much as confusion. I was just wondering how I could've been so gullible. I've been thinking about it all recently. I mean here I am, the black sheep of the family, yet I'm still part of it. I tried separating from the family all my life, only to find out it's not possible, not in my family. So I become the black sheep without any of the advantages of being one, just the disadvantages. It doesn't seem fair!"

"How do you mean?" asked Ramzi.

"So, Kamal," interrupted Peter, "what do you think of our summer weather?"

Sarah stood up and stretched. She walked over to the volcanic hot tub. "You want to go in," Ramzi said, standing right behind her. She smiled.

"No," she replied softly. She sat down on the edge of the volcano, above the lava, and faced her brother. "I just wanted to get away from your boyfriend. He treats me with a certain condescension, which I do not like. It has to stop."

"I know." He stood in front of her, slightly embarrassed, hands in pockets. "Don't think it's personal. He just has trouble with my family, and with his for that matter. He's terrified of anything coming between us."

"Well, tell him if he doesn't stop, something *will* come between you. I will fucking kick his butt back to Minnesota and he'll never see you again."

"Look, I'm sorry. He doesn't realize he's doing it. I'll talk to him. I promise. Anyway, I'm interested in what you were saying about being part of the family. I'd like to hear what you have to say sometime." He bent over and kissed her.

"Hey, Mom," Kamal called, turning around in his chair. "Did you watch the women's World Cup?"

"Of course, I did," Sarah replied. "I loved it."

"Hey, your mother was way ahead of her time," Ramzi added. "She was damn good too. I can vouch for that. She was better than anybody on those teams."

"I wouldn't go that far."

"In any case, your mother cried during the whole final," Ramzi said.

"Well, that's not saying much," Kamal replied. "She cried in the hardware store on the way over."

"You did? What about?" Ramzi held her hand.

"Nothing important. Something silly reminded me of David."

"Oh, come on. Are you still thinking of that jerk?" Ramzi turned away, looked up at the sky.

"You have to tell her," Peter said, straightening his collar and adjusting his shirt. "It's better if she knows."

"Shut up," Ramzi yelled.

"Tell me what? What should I know?"

"I didn't want to tell you this, but we met David's lover."

"Oh, God. Is she beautiful?"

"*He. He* is beautiful." He fidgeted, his hands came together, fingers interlocked. A half-smile appeared on his lips.

Sarah laughed. "Get real. We're talking David here."

"It's true, darling," Peter said. He walked over to her. "David is gay. Or bisexual or whatever they call themselves these days. We met him and his lover of ten years. They're an openly gay couple. David cheats on him with women. He's just an asshole."

"But he was married." Sarah could not hide the shock.

"Yes. His lover told us the whole story. His wife caught the two together *flagrante delicto* and divorced him. David came out of the closet and moved in with his lover."

"But he's supposed to be getting married."

"He's a liar, Sarah," Ramzi said. "He's lied to you from the start, about everything. You know, in his perverse way, he probably loved you, which is why he hung around for so long. Who knows? But that's why he didn't want to go out anywhere with you."

"Are you sure it was David?"

"Honey, I'm sure. David Troubridge. None other. He recognized us. We were talking to his lover first and all of a sudden David showed up. He could have died right there on the spot. He was stuttering. I wanted to leave that poor bastard alone, but Peter here couldn't."

"Oh, you'd have been so proud of me," Peter told her. "I threw one of your tantrums. Ha! I told his lover, loudly, I might add, I'd never want to be seen with a closet heterosexual. I told him I know we've come a long way, but this city was not yet ready for a closet hetero. Then I told his lover we were leaving because his asshole of a boyfriend fucked and then dumped my sister-in-law. You should've seen his face. David could have croaked right there, but you could tell his lover had no clue. Well, now he does."

"You went out with a homosexual for four years, Mom?" Kamal now completed the foursome around the volcano.

She turned around toward the hot tub, pressed the air-jet button, and dunked her whole head in the water. She heard distorted giggling from above. She lifted her head out of the volcano and faced the others.

"Feeling better?" her brother asked.

"I'm awake now, I think," she said. She flicked her hair, ensuring that everyone got at least a little wet. Her son tried to get out of the way, laughing.

"I wonder if someone can drown in our volcano," Ramzi said.

"Tell it to me again. You saw David?"

ONE

On a rusty swing set in the garden of my father's ancestral mountain home we sat, my stepmother, Saniya, my sister Amal, and I, between them. The red cushions were tattered, the swing's canopy chafed thin, no longer an adequate protection against the sun. The metal springs clanked whenever the swing moved, which was not often. It was a lazy afternoon.

"You should get another swing set," I suggested. "I'm surprised Father has kept this."

Saniya sighed. "I don't know," she said. "No one but us uses it. I don't think your father has been out here in over ten years." She looked straight ahead, at the runways of Beirut's airport, apparently thinking of something. "It holds many memories. I don't want to get rid of it." She paused, smiled. "We made love on it once."

Amal laughed. I could not help but smile. "You should have told us before we sat on it," I joked.

"Janet used to love this swing," Amal said.

I quickly glanced at Saniya to note her reaction. Nothing. She was still smiling genuinely. After thirty-five years of marriage, she was no longer bothered by the mention of my father's first wife.

"She's the one who bought it," Saniya said. "She chose this

bright red color." She looked at me, smiling wickedly. "It matches the color of your hair."

"It does not. My hair isn't that bright."

"Almost!"

"She used to sit where I'm sitting," Amal said. "This was her corner. Funny what we remember."

I did not remember my mother from her days in Lebanon. I was too young when she left. When I moved to New York in 1980, I was able to get to know her, but my Janet was nothing like the Janet the rest of my family knew. My Janet was bitter, a defeated woman.

"Sarah's right," Amal said, glancing at a group of sparrows flocking to the giant holm oak on her left. White butterflies hovered ahead of us, some floating, some flitting about nervously. "You should get another swing set or at least reupholster this. The color is all wrong. Nostalgia shouldn't interfere with taste."

"I don't want to get rid of it," Saniya replied. "It's a testimonial, a reminder of how things used to be, or how I imagined them to be."

Amal's eyebrows were raised, but she did not say anything. It took me a minute to decipher what Saniya said. I could not keep quiet though. "Are you saying you no longer make love?" I asked.

"We haven't made love for a long time," she said. "Not since the hysterectomy. It was rare before, but stopped completely after."

I felt Amal shift next to me. I knew what she was thinking. She and I had had that discussion before, but I was unsure whether she would bring the subject up. Her innate reticence would prevent her from doing so, yet her deep feelings about it made her antsy. She gave me a knowing look, then turned and stared ahead at a tranquil view of Beirut.

"You shouldn't have let him do a hysterectomy," she said. Deep feelings won. I smiled to myself, proud of her.

Him was my father, an ob-gyn.

"It was necessary," Saniya said. We both waited, thinking she would elaborate.

"I don't think so," Amal went on. "Mild spotting is not a good enough reason for a hysterectomy."

"There was a change in my pap smear."

"So what?" Amal asked. "Did he try to figure out what was going on? Did he ask for a second opinion. Hell no. Let's just cut. If it needed to be done, you should have had someone else do it. Dr. Baddour would have been good."

"Your father is a good doctor."

"A good doctor does not perform a hysterectomy on his wife."

"He did one on his mother."

"I rest my case."

"You're putting too much into this," Saniya said. She took her cup of Turkish coffee from the rusty stand attached to the swing. She sipped slowly. "I'm not sure I would've wanted anyone else to do it. He delivered all of you. It's not a big thing."

The birds in the tree were getting louder. Amal looked up. "I think this family is one big mess," she said.

"It's my family," Saniya replied.

CHAPTER ONE

A Day in New York

I woke up with a hangover. Thousands of tiny ants marched in step between my temples, having come through my mouth and dried their feet on my tongue.

I did not recognize where I was. Some hotel room. Why didn't they put Alka-Seltzer in every room instead of Gideon's? Dina was sleeping next to me. Slowly, it dawned on me. New York hotel. Friday, January 20. The complete fiasco, otherwise known as the opening reception of my first, and probably last, New York exhibit was last night. I covered my head with a pillow and moaned.

I got out of bed, careful not to wake Dina, who looked peaceful and serene lying on the bed. I would not have survived the night before had she not been with me. She deserved better than my mood today. I tiptoed to the bathroom and closed the door. I looked at myself in the mirror and jumped back. God, I looked awful. I opened my pillbox, took out two Tylenols and one Xanax, popped them in my mouth. I drank a whole glass of water, refilled it and drank again. My mouth was still dry. I turned the hot water on. I desperately needed a shower.

The water felt refreshing. I placed my head under the spray, closing my eyes, wishing I could cleanse myself. I wondered why I was not feeling as bad as I should after last night.

Maybe the reception was too surreal, maybe I drank enough to subvert any real feeling.

I opened my eyes to reach for the soap and saw a large spider at the edge of the tub, small body with long, spindly legs. It was struggling hard to get out of the tub, but drops of water were getting in its way. I was sure the steam was not making it feel safe either. I wanted to help it, but did not know how since I was wet. I turned my back to it to block the water and help it climb out. I soaped myself, thinking the spider had to save itself. Usually, I used a tissue to move spiders out of the way. I was fond of them.

My first boyfriend, Fadi, had to study the Koran like all dutiful Muslim boys. I remember him telling me a story once about one of the adventures of the prophet Muhammad. When the prophet was running away from infidels who were trying to kill him, an angel told him to hide in a cave. Once the prophet went in, a spider built a large web covering the entrance and a dove laid eggs within the web. When the infidels arrived at the cave's mouth, they decided no one could have entered without disturbing the web and the eggs. The prophet was saved. Ever since I heard that story, I liked spiders.

The phone rang. I turned the water off and reached for the bathroom phone, hoping to get it before Dina woke up. I said hello and heard its echo from Dina in the bedroom.

"Oh, good. I got both of you." My stepmother, Saniya, was on the phone, calling from Beirut. "Tell me everything. How was it?"

"Disaster," I moaned on the phone.

"Wonderful," Dina said.

"That's about what I'd have expected you two to say," Saniya said. I could hear her chuckle on the phone.

"Don't listen to her," I said, sitting down on the edge of the tub. "It was an unmitigated catastrophe. There was a fistfight, for crying out loud. Guys were punching each other at my opening. How can that be wonderful?"

"Did you know the men?" Saniya asked.

"No, she didn't know them," Dina added. "They were just guys who walked in off the street. It wasn't a big deal. The show looked fabulous, Saniya. It was gorgeous. You'd have been proud of her."

"What do you mean no big deal? People were slugging each other at the opening. How can that not be a big deal?" I wanted to get out of the bathroom and slug Dina myself.

"Let's just say her paintings had an extreme effect on viewers," Dina added. "The show elicited visceral reactions. Emotions were flying all over the place." Saniya began giggling at the other end. I was jealous that my stepmother and my best friend got along so well.

The evening *was* a disaster. Dina and I left our hotel at five-thirty. We took the subway from Seventy-second Street and got off at Fourteenth to avoid the midtown crush and then frantically searched for a cab to take us down to SoHo. We arrived too early. The reception was from six till eight. One of the gallery assistants was still sweeping the floor.

The gallery had three rooms with three different exhibits. Mine was in the main room. In the smaller gallery there was a group exhibit of New York artists, both paintings and sculptures. In the smallest room was a conceptual exhibit by a Russian émigré.

By six o'clock, no one had arrived. The wine, however, was on the table. There were, count them, six *jugs* of cheap white wine. The only other thing to drink was tap water in pitchers. The gallery had gone all out. The owner must have spent all of twenty dollars.

By six-fifteen, strange-looking men started arriving. The elevator door would open, and a couple of haggard, wretched-looking men would pour out. They did not look at my paintings, but walked straight to the smaller gallery where the wine was. The other artists from the group show soon followed, every one of them dressed in black, looking pretentious and self-important. They too began to drink. Everybody congregated in the small room, and no one was looking at my paintings. I went to the table to get myself a glass of wine, but almost gagged when I tasted it. It was fructose-laced vinegar. I threw the plastic cup in the wastebasket only to be glared at by two of the men for wasting precious liquid.

I ran back to Dina and whispered. "They're winos. These guys are here for the free wine."

"Sure looks like it," she said, amused.

Thankfully, some friends from my college days in New York arrived. They loved my paintings and we were distracted for a while. The other gallery was full, everybody hanging around the wine table, when a fistfight broke out. One of the winos punched another. The punchee gulped down what was left in his glass and jumped the puncher. They dragged each other around the small gallery, each man using a headlock on the other. One of the artists, a skinny, acne-faced, effeminate young man, jumped up and down, screaming hysterically, "Watch out for my sculpture," a traffic-department wooden sawhorse covered with sheepskin. He tried to direct the combatants away from his chef d'oeuvre without daring to get within reach of them. The owner of the gallery did not budge from his seat. Finally, a couple of the other winos separated the two. One guy, a South Asian, took the man who lost the fight out of the gallery. For the next hour, until the wine ran out, the South Asian came up to the gallery and left with two glasses of wine every ten minutes.

None of my friends stayed for more than a couple of minutes. I could not blame them. I wanted to leave my own opening. Two drunks, probably homeless, stood in front of one my paintings. One said to the other in a loud and quivering voice, "These are awesome paintings. They keep moving." He was barely able to keep himself standing, swaying from side to side.

"See." Dina nudged me. "They get it." She was taking everything a little too lightly.

"They're moving because you're drunk," the second man said, slurring his words. He could handle his alcohol much better than his friend. "There's color interplay here, but I don't think you're sober enough to see it. These paintings are *informed* by Mondrian as well as by the hard-edged abstract school that came out of Los Angeles. I think they'd have worked better if they weren't all so uniform."

Dina cracked up. I wanted to kill them. I actually moved in their direction to give them a piece of my mind, but Dina held me back.

"Only in New York," she said. "Let it go and enjoy it. This is only the reception. As you can see, no one who loves art will show up tonight."

A group of Russians, friends of the conceptual artist from the smallest gallery, went out the fire-exit door carrying their own bottles of vodka, wanting to smoke. Shortly thereafter, they began singing Soviet anthems. We could hear the singing clearly, though muffled, coming from behind the wall. The first drunk looked at his friend. "These paintings are singing now," he said.

"That's really weird," his friend replied.

I freaked. I wanted to leave right then. The two walked back to the table and realized the wine was all gone. Within a couple of minutes, the gallery emptied. All that remained were a couple of artists, the gallery owner, and Russian songs. I walked out fuming, went to a bar and got drunk. To add insult to injury, my own mother, my only relative who lived in New York, did not show up at my reception.

I was telling the whole story to Saniya, with Dina doing color commentary on the other phone, when I felt the Xanax kick in. It was timely: I began to see the ridiculousness of the whole thing.

"The show will get good reviews," Dina told Saniya. "The opening won't influence that."

"I'd better hang up," Saniya said. "I'm sure everyone will want to call and find out what happened."

She was right. The instant we hung up the phone, it rang again. It was my sister Amal from Beirut. I let Dina talk to her and tell her the whole story, while I dried my hair. I remembered the spider and checked the tub to see if it was still there. Didn't see it. I looked around and nothing. I figured it must have died and was swept down the drain. All of a sudden it occurred to me to look at my butt. There the poor spider was, squished, looking like an intriguing tattoo on my ass.

I came back to the room wearing the hotel's bathrobe.

"That looks nice," Dina said. She sat on the edge of the bed. "We should filch it."

I put my hands to my face, screamed a high note, but not too loudly. "Who are you and how did you get in here?" I had to shout that every time I saw her without makeup. It was our ritual.

"Shut the fuck up." That too was part of the ritual. She stood up and went into the bathroom.

The phone rang. It was my half-brother, Ramzi, calling from San Francisco. He wanted to know everything. He was taking care of my cat and plants and told me I owned, without a doubt, the stupidest cat in the world.

The phone rang again. It was my half-sister Majida from Beirut. I had to tell her the same story. I was feeling fine and

I told the whole story as one long joke. I could hear her and her husband laughing across the line.

By the time my ex-husband Joe called from Dallas, I had the story down. I was laughing hysterically with him on the phone. My ex-husband Omar called from Beirut. Ditto. We laughed so hard, Dina came out of the bathroom and handed me tissues to dry my eyes.

"Did everybody call?" Dina asked, while getting dressed. "Let's go out for coffee."

"Not everybody," I said dejected. "Neither Lamia nor David called."

"And neither one of those two will. Get dressed."

"David might call."

She shook her head in exasperation. "You two are breaking up," she said.

"Well, my husbands called. Why not him?"

"Because they are decent human beings and they care about you, which he doesn't. Get off your ass and get dressed."

The phone rang on cue. I reached for it and gave Dina a raspberry. It was Margot, her lover. I could have died. Dina took the phone from me, snapped her fingers for me to get dressed.

At eleven o'clock we found ourselves walking across Central Park, a habitual walk. When I lived in New York, I had an apartment in the same neighborhood, the Upper West Side, and I used to cross the park once or twice a week to visit my mother, who lived on the East Side. I realized I wanted to confront her. I had not expected her to show up to the reception even though she had promised she would. Nonetheless, I found myself disappointed at her confirming my expectations.

We entered my mother's building and Jonathan, the concierge, came running toward us, more like lumbering, since he was corpulent. "Ms. Sarah, I've been trying to find you," he said anxiously. He had a look of concern, which was not uncommon for him since my mother was not an easy tenant. "I didn't know where you were staying."

"My mother does," I said. "Is there something wrong?"

He looked unsure about what to do, which disquieted me. His expression went from afraid to nervous to sad to tragic to worried, trying to settle on an emotion. "I have some bad news," he said. He paused, hesitated. "I don't know how to say this. I'm so sorry. Your mother is dead."

Before I could say anything, I felt Dina hold my hand. I wanted to say something, but my mouth seemed sewed shut. Different feelings welled up within me, yet the predominant one was shock.

"When? How? What happened?" That was Dina. I squeezed her hand to make sure it was still there.

"Yesterday. She called down at noon asking for a car in the evening. She wanted to go to Ms. Sarah's opening. When the car came, she wouldn't answer her phone. Clark went up to see if she was okay and found her dead in the bathtub. She had killed herself."

I began to feel faint.

"I tried to find you, Ms. Sarah. The police have been here. So has her attorney. She left everything to an artist colony in Maine. I called her brother and he didn't want anything to do with her. We're wondering what do with her stuff, Ms. Sarah. I don't think it's right that strangers take her personal stuff. We had no one to call, Ms. Sarah. She had no one else."

I heard the words he was saying, but did not exactly grasp them. They floated about, revolving around my head, it seemed. I was lost, dizzy.

"The attorney wishes to speak to you, Ms. Sarah," he went on. "He says you can take all her personal material, but please don't take anything expensive because, technically, it all belongs to the colony. They'll sell everything. But you should go through her possessions."

I must have nodded or given him some sign he interpreted as acquiescence because we were walking toward the elevator. I followed, terrified of what I might find upstairs. My mother could not still be up there. I wondered who would have dealt with the corpse. How did she kill herself? So many questions, but being mute, I could ask nothing.

"We cleaned everything once the police left," Jonathan said as he let us in the apartment. "After they removed Mrs. Nour el-Din, we had to clean the bathroom."

It took a minute to register. He was leaving, closing the door when I heard myself shout, much louder than I should have, "Jonathan!"

He reentered quickly, frightened.

"What did you call my mother?" I asked, quieter, but firm.

He looked confused. "Mrs. Nour el-Din."

"She didn't go by Janet Foster."

"No, ma'am. Janet Nour el-Din."

I plopped down on the couch. Dina sat next to me. Jonathan let himself out quietly. We sat silently on the couch for over an hour.

"Why would she keep her name?" I asked. "She hated our family." I lay back on the sofa, looked up at the ceiling. "Why keep reminding yourself of past pains?"

"Sometimes you're so naïve," Dina replied. I looked at her, eyebrows raised. "She was as much a Nour el-Din as any of you. Just because she was ostracized doesn't mean she's not part of the equation. Think about it."

"I don't get it."

I got up and walked to the desk in her office. I wanted to make sure. I went through her papers. All her bills were for

Nour el-Din. I became increasingly frantic as I searched. I wanted to find something, but was not sure what.

"Help me look for her artwork," I said excitedly. "I have never seen anything of hers."

I opened the closets in the office. There was nothing there. We went to the bedroom. Nothing. I searched the closets and dressers. There was only one room left. I looked in and there was a drafting table. On the table were some brushes and tubes of gouache. I felt my face flush and a feeling of relief overcame me. My mother always talked about being a painter, yet no one had seen a single painting. In the back of my mind, I wondered whether she even owned any paints. I searched the room and found no paintings.

"Look here," Dina said, pointing at some papers stacked underneath a heavy book of impressionist paintings. There were only ten of them, all of them seemed abandoned after a couple of strokes. Some were left in mid-stroke. So many false starts. I began to cry.

Dina pulled out a framed piece. It was a *Time* magazine cover. Saddam Hussein's photographically darkened face dominated the cover. My mother had painted little hearts in red gouache all around his face. Some of the hearts had silver arrows running through them. It was signed Janet Nour-el Din in the bottom right-hand corner.

"What's this about?" I asked.

"She had the hots for Saddam?"

"I don't get it."

"I know a woman up in Boston, a kindergarten teacher, who thinks Saddam is amazingly sexy."

I rummaged through the papers. No more paintings. "We should go. I don't want anything. I don't think I can take this much longer."

"Are you sure? You might regret it later."

I looked around. "I don't know what to take," I said.

"Pictures," Dina said. "There must be pictures."

"Yes." I ran to the bedroom. I had a feeling they would be next to her bed and I was right. In the drawer of her nightstand. Only four, but they were all of our family. With her in every picture. There was one of my father, in which he looked so joyful, full of life, holding my mother. She looked serene, but he was ecstatic, a man who had conquered the world. I was flabbergasted. In all the years I had known my father, I had never seen him look like that. I put the pictures in my handbag.

I walked back to the living room. The day before, my mother had sat on the chair in the corner. She had looked radiant, in a long, billowing green dress. Her red hair reflected the sun. She inhaled her cigarette voraciously. "Look at this," she said to me, handing me an old kaleidoscope. "Isn't it beautiful?"

I looked though the lens. "It's just a regular kaleidoscope," I said.

"No, it isn't. I bought it yesterday at an antique store. It's beautiful. I love how it comes together."

I looked again. I didn't know what antique store she had bought it at, but I had a feeling she must have overpaid. "Yes," I had said. "It's lovely."

On the table, next to the corner chair, lay the kaleidoscope. I took it and left.

Starbucks as Metaphor

"Here I am, the wretched city, lying in ruins, my citizens dead . . . you who pass me bewail my fate, and shed a tear in honor of Berytus that is no more."
—UNKNOWN SIXTH-CENTURY POET

1.

The Kent billboard says *Evolve* in six languages. Hardly recognizable, Beirut has changed much in the last seven months, billboards obscuring brisk construction of high-rises, bright-colored ads exhorting me to listen to avant-garde Lebanese radio stations, to switch cell phone services, to attend the absolute Millennium event. Beirut at the turn of the century. A relic remains, Bruce Willis announcing he is the last man standing, an ad for a film that had played in Beirut at least three years earlier. A short, pockmarked building flickers briefly on my right. A mosque's crescent moon on a tall steeple glides by.

We speed along the new highway connecting the airport to the center of town. The trip now takes only ten minutes. My ex-husband sits next to me in the sumptuous backseat of the Mercedes. Black everywhere, his suit, my dress, the car's leather.

"You don't have to go directly to the hospital," he says, holding my hand gently. "He's no longer in any danger. Why don't we unload the bags at home and you can unwind?"

"No, I'd rather go to the hospital."

He has been reassuring me for the last twenty-four hours, his call at home, my call from Charles de Gaulle, but I know from experience he can easily lie to me over a phone if he wants to. Face to face, he cannot. I know his every nuance. He faces me with his easy smile, not the camera-ready smile, pencil thin, no teeth showing, heavy eyebrows crunching in the middle of his brow. He is relaxed, not performing; himself, not the politician.

Like most Lebanese, the driver considers the newly painted white lines a mere suggestion and drives in the middle of the road. I look out the window at the other cars, getting close to the city's center, traffic slightly heavier. I remember being driven on this stretch of road by my father when I was younger, in his brown Oldsmobile, a happy drive because we would go to a supermarket-cum-department store the entire family loved. The building is still there, but it is abandoned, a malnourished edifice, the new highway no longer leading to it. In that department store, I rode my first escalator. I could not have been more than four or five. My sister Amal and I went up and down those escalators a thousand and one times while our parents shopped. Every now and then, we watched a yokel stare at the moving machinery, wondering fearfully how to get on. Amal and I would smile confidentially, cunning sophisticates in the land of greenhorns. All of a sudden, I hear the car's siren go off, shocking me out of my languid reverie. The driver wants the other cars out of the way. My ex-husband is a member of parliament and he always has the right of way.

"My God, Sarah," Omar says suddenly. "How do you keep in such good shape?" He openly ogles my crossed legs and short skirt.

2.

The afternoon light's yellow dominates the fluorescent bulbs' blue, warm shadows overpowering the cool, long prevailing over short shadows. A horde of people sit in the sterile waiting room of the cardiology unit, most of them family members I have not seen in ages. My stepmother, Saniya, entertains, chatting with everybody, further evidence my dad's condition is not as serious as first feared. Her face brightens on seeing me. My sister Majida rushes up to me, giggling. "You're here," she says. "He's okay. The diuretics finally worked. The water is out of his lungs."

"I'm glad you came," Saniya says, leading me arm in arm toward my father's room. "I wanted to call and tell you he's okay and you didn't have to come, but you'd already left. He's being discharged tomorrow."

"It's quite all right. Now the whole family can spend the New Year together for the first time in I don't know how long."

"The Millennium, not just the New Year," she says, laughing.

My father sits propped up by many pillows on the angled hospital bed. Around him sit my sister Amal, my brother, Ramzi, and two men who introduce themselves as acquaintances of my father, there only because duty requires their appearance.

"Ah," my father yells, "the princess is finally here." His pleasure reflects more than my arrival. This has been his third brush with death in the past two years. "She'll only show up if I'm dying."

I bend over and kiss him, noticing how much he has aged. My father's face has always been asymmetrical, but lately it is exaggerated. His left eye is lower than his right, and now his left cheek is slack. His face gaunt. The mustache, his ever-present trademark, is shaved. When he smiles, I see nothing of the man I know.

To the side, I notice Saniya's foldup bed. My father can never sleep if she is not in the same room.

"I knew this was a hoax." I sit down on a blue plastic chair facing him, feel my rear end sinking slowly. "You wanted me to come here because you didn't know how to celebrate the Millennium without me, but were too embarrassed to ask directly. Do you think I'm naïve? *Please come, Sarah. Your dad's sick and wants to see you.* My ass. You guys were bored stiff and needed some excitement. Well, here I am."

"Well," my father snaps, "when are you moving back?"

"Soon," I lie.

3.

We stand outside, Amal and I, seeing Omar off. He lights another cigarette. "Here, before I forget," he says, handing me a cell phone, smaller, more complicated than the one he gave me during my last visit. He pats his pockets, a tick he has had since I have known him, and raises his hand, signaling his driver, who drives down the hill toward us. "I do have to go. I'll send you your car this evening."

The car draws up at the curb. I kiss his cheek before he climbs into it. "Thank you."

"Talk to your son, will you?"

"I'm not talking to him about his tattoo. He already told me about it and is trying to convince me to get one." I smile.

"Not the tattoo," he says. "I don't care about that. It's his bad taste in clothes. All these garish colors all of a sudden. He wore bright red pants last night and some awful green paisley shirt from the seventies. It's embarrassing."

Amal takes me by the arm as the car speeds away. "Let's take a walk and grab some coffee." I lay my head on her earth-tone angora sweater. She sure loves her angoras.

4.

When I was five, my father took Amal and me to see *Mary Poppins* at the Strand Cinema on Hamra Street. My sister

Lamia preferred to stay in her room as usual. While Julie Andrews sang "With a Spoonful of Sugar" and luscious colors poured out of the medicine bottle, a spark ignited near the screen and the whole theater went dark, an impenetrable black. Someone screamed, "Fire!" Everyone panicked and rushed for the sole exit. My father spoke calmly, telling us to hold on to each other. He loudly admonished the stampeding crowd. "Be careful of the children." Louder. "It's only a short. Calm down, everyone." Amal and I were suddenly separated from him. I heard him call our names, over and over, but his voice grew faint. He was being pushed toward the exit. Amal squeezed my hand. I held hers with both of mine, terrified. I felt myself being pushed behind. I pressed myself against her back, held onto each of her arms, onto the angora sleeves. I placed my head on the back of her sweater, relying on her to lead me out, to save me. "Don't push me," she yelled at someone. She kicked a man's shin. "Let us through," she screamed as she maneuvered us between anonymous thighs and hips. She stomped on toes. I thought the unkempt hair of her blue angora would be the first thing to catch fire as I buried my face deeper. Up the stairs and into the light, my father's voice grew stronger. The crowd thinned after the bottlenecked stairs. Amal moved us confidently toward my father. Down on one knee, he hugged us.

"We kicked ass," I said, regaining my voice.

They both laughed.

5.

Starbucks on Hamra Street looks like its counterparts in America, the faux-modernist murals, the pimply-faced teenagers behind the counter, the logoed coffee mugs. It is swamped, Beirut's latest *in* place, to see and be seen, clamorous, the noise of chatter exceeded only by the ringing of cell phones. When Starbucks flung its gates open, Beirut's elite returned to Hamra Street after an absence of more than twenty-five years. The Mercedeses and BMWs reappeared, cautiously claiming parking spaces that once belonged exclusively to them.

"One grande low-fat latte and one cappuccino for here," the cashier announces. She writes something down on two cups and passes them to the boy working the espresso machine. The boy repeats the order earnestly, a diligent echo.

"How may I help you?" the cashier asks the woman in full-designer regalia, suit, pumps, jewelry, and sunglasses. The cashier speaks English with a horrible attempt at an American twang. The woman does not look at her, but at the floor.

"Where did you get these tiles?" the woman asks, in English with a Lebanese accent. She holds her Prada handbag, brown with clear plastic handles, close to her. The woman repeats the question, deliberately, as if talking to someone mentally handicapped, still not looking at the girl. The girl looks at her co-cashier, who shrugs her shoulder. The espresso boy arches his eyebrows.

"She's asking about the floor," Amal says in Arabic. Both woman and girl stare at us.

6.

We sat on a hooker-green sofa, on the basement floor. Starbucks is large, covering over two floors as well as the sidewalk. Multiple rooms and sections surround a huge fireplace.

"Why do you let him get to you?" Amal asked between sips of coffee. Everything about her appearance whispered comfort. Her clothes were elegant, yet unthreatening, a dark cream dress and a burnt-sienna sweater. Her black hair was braided and pinned. Unobtrusive makeup on a soft face, her eyes tender. None of the stress of my father's hospitalization seemed to have affected her.

"I don't know, but I'm getting better. Now it takes me about five minutes to revert to being a little girl. It used to be instantaneous. I'm constantly torn between trying to please him and wanting to hurt him. I'm going to be forty in a few months and he still treats me like a child."

"It's because he doesn't see you that often. If you lived here, he'd get tired of it." She chuckled. "At least he'll stop asking you to move back. He used to get on my case all the time, but he doesn't much these days. I miss that."

I moved my coffee cup back, as if to throw it at her. She pretended to duck, laughing.

"He loves you," she added. "He wants you near him. We all do."

"I can't move back for many reasons," I said, slightly unsettled. I hated having to repeatedly enunciate my reasons for not wanting to live in Beirut.

"Name one."

"Okay, you know what I hate? I hate the fact that in all of Lebanon, one can't find a box of tissues that dispenses one tissue at a time. No matter what brand I get, I always have to pull three or four at a time to get one. Doesn't that bug you?"

"Get serious."

"Here's another. Last time I was here, Omar took me to his gym. It was so luxurious. They had the newest machines but no one really used them. Everybody used the Jacuzzi and that was it. But my god, what a Jacuzzi! It can fit a hundred people easily. It had fountains in the middle. There's a bed in the damn Jacuzzi. Twenty people can lie on it. No joke."

"What has that got to do with anything?"

"This country is just appearances."

"And America isn't?"

"Yes," I said, unable to control my grin, "but in America, tissue boxes dispense one tissue at a time."

She giggled. "You're terrible. You keep saying that as a

family we don't talk, that we try to bury our problems, yet every time I try to talk to you, you start making jokes and really bad ones too. You no longer have any good reasons for staying in America, do you?"

"My life is there. I have nothing here anymore."

She smirked. "And fuck you too."

"You know what I mean."

"No, I don't really. We'd love to have you here. I need you. Your son needs you."

"Beirut holds terrible memories for me," I said slowly, measured.

"Stand in line. Come back and deal with them."

"Can we talk about this some other time? I just arrived. I promise I'll think about it and we'll talk another time."

"Okay, I'll hold you to that." She took another sip of coffee. "And you're wrong. There are many tissue boxes that dispense just one. You're just getting the cheap brands." She smiled mischievously.

"Come here," she said. She reached over, hugged me. "Welcome back," she whispered in my ear. She kept holding me close. I squeezed her tighter, swallowed by her warmth, my shoulders relaxing. I felt caffeinated faces registering our inappropriate behavior. Across the room, the eyes of a framed Latino coffee-picker smiled at me. I smiled feebly back at him. Next to the photo was another of a red cup filled with black coffee on a yellow-and-blue plaid table cover.

7.

My father, who had an unhealthy addiction to Chuck Norris's *Walker, Texas Ranger*, lay in bed staring up at the television. Majida and Saniya watched the episode, but I could not. I was able to tune out the dialogue but could not do the same with the show's music.

My father had black, expressive eyes that wore a look of reproach as if I had committed an inexpiable sin, accusing me, not of something, but of everything. When I was younger, they were magical eyes, frightening, brimming with both promise and menace, both anxiety and wonder. They shone with an intoxicating, mesmerizing energy that both repelled and attracted me.

In the cheerless hospital room, as he watched *Texas Ranger*, I saw his distracted eyes, still beautiful, no longer threatening, neither dangerous, nor auspicious.

8.

"Pizza Hut delivers," my half-sister, Majida, said. "Or we can have Chinese. I'm up for anything."

"Why don't you girls go home?" Saniya stood up and stretched. "We're doing fine here." She took my father's gray-blue food tray and placed it outside the room. On the tall night-stand beside my father's bed were two oranges, a red apple, an off-white phone, a box of tissues, a plastic bottle, and a half-full glass of water.

"I want to see the end of the show," Majida said.

My father's breathing was flabby and shallow, with a slight gurgling sound like the soft hookah aspiration of a young boy. "At least until the fight," he said. *Walker* always ended with Chuck Norris and his black sidekick beating up on the bad guys, followed by commercials, and then the final joke, where the regulars of the show convened to shoot the breeze. My father watched the fight, but turned the television off before the joke, which he never found funny.

"Why don't you go home?" I said, looking at Saniya. "I'll spend the night. You take a break." Both my parents looked at me quizzically, as if I had spoken in Latin. "I'm serious. I'd like to stay here for the night. You go home and rest."

"He's being discharged tomorrow," Saniya said. "We can all sleep in our own beds then. You go home and see your son."

"Be quiet, both of you," my father snapped. He turned the volume up with the remote control; his hand had a slight tremor. Chuck and chum punched, kicked, and karate-chopped six bad guys, cowboy hats burst in every direction.

9.

Saniya, in blue sweats and tennis shoes, pushed her arms against the wall outside the room, curved her back and stretched her calves. She looked like a Sunday jogger getting ready for a run.

"Are you sure about this?" she asked, softly.

"It'll give us time to talk."

"He's going to sleep soon. I don't see how you can talk much. You'll be able to see him as often as you wish when he's back home."

In the room across from us, Pavarotti sang on television with Ricky Martin and Mariah Carey, a pre-Millennium concert.

"I rarely spend time alone with him," I said. "I'd like to tonight. Even if he's sleeping."

"Come, walk with me. I need the exercise." We walked slowly down the corridor, arms entwined, looking discreetly into each room, evaluating each family's story. "Where's your son?"

"He called me from McDonald's half an hour ago. He's going out dancing tonight. I won't see him till tomorrow morning." She was cozy, warm, and comforting.

"You should talk to him about eating too much junk food."

She stopped when we got to the waiting room, looked outside at a giant green laser dueling the dark sky.

"That's Beirut 2000," she said. "CNN says Beirut is the third best place to be for the Millennium, after Paris and Cairo. Everybody has been celebrating for days and it'll go on afterward too. James Brown is coming."

"I guess I'll have to miss that."

She smiled, cleared her throat. "Is there something you want to tell me?"

"It'll be fine," I assured her. "There's nothing specific I want to talk to him about. I won't upset him. I just want to be with him."

"I'll get my stuff."

10.

While I was visiting Beirut years ago, my son, my father, my ex-husband, and I went to see *The Unbearable Lightness of Being*. The war had recently ended, a few old movie theaters had reopened, running on large generators.

"It's been years since I've seen a movie in a theater," Omar said. Once the film began he worried, considered it inappropriate for Kamal, who slept between opening and closing credits while his father fretted. I sat confused, unable to understand the film, yet enraptured by Daniel Day Lewis and Juliet Binoche.

"Well," my father said, walking out of the theater, "at least they got the unbearable part right."

11.

"Close the door," my father said as he leaned across to the nightstand and withdrew a cigarette and a box of matches from the drawer.

"What are you doing?" I asked and moved quickly toward

him after closing the door. "You can't smoke in here. Give that to me. You're not even supposed to be smoking."

I put out my hand, he crossed his arms, hid the offending cigarette behind his underarm.

"Give it to me," I said.

He shook his head. "Let a dying man smoke in peace."

"I'll call the nurse."

"Who do you think gave this to me?"

I sat on the bed, perplexed. He smiled, realized he had won, and lit up. He took a short drag, his wrinkled, quivering hand covering his mouth.

"When did you start again?"

"I never stopped," he said, smiling sheepishly. "Don't worry. I'll smoke only half."

Blue smoke curled from the tip, spiraled outward, rising toward the fluorescent lights. He looked at the chair next to his bed, Saniya's usual seat.

"I'm surprised she lets you smoke."

"She doesn't know. No one knows."

"She knows."

"I don't smoke in front of anyone. They all nag too much." He grinned impishly, arched his left eyebrow. He took a last drag and extinguished the cigarette in the half-empty glass on the nightstand.

"Here," he said, handing me the glass. "Get rid of the evidence."

I went into the bathroom, heard him say, "I'm the great deceiver."

Chapter One

Mark Twain said there are five kinds of actresses: bad actresses, fair actresses, good actresses, great actresses—and then there is Sarah Bernhardt. To paraphrase him slightly, there are five kinds of stories: bad stories, fair stories, good stories, great stories—and then there are Sarah Bernhardt stories.

I was brought up on all kinds of stories, but my favorites were the ones about Sarah Bernhardt. Those stories shaped and molded me. When I examine my life, I am amazed at how much they penetrate every aspect of it.

My grandfather named me for the great Sarah Bernhardt. Like so many men before him, the aforementioned Mark Twain, D. H. Lawrence, Marcel Proust, Henry James, Victor Hugo, and none other than Sigmund Freud (to name only a few), my grandfather was immoderately smitten by The Divine Sarah.

After having already named two girls, my parents had not prepared a name for a third. My father had a name for a boy. He was not to use it. I was born with a little tuft of red hair, direct from my American mother. When my grandfather saw me for the first time, noting the red wisp, he greeted me with, "Welcome to the world, my little Sarah."

My destiny was written.

• • •

I have begun to see my grandfather again, in the most inappropriate places. He has been gone for over twenty-five years, but now I feel him more clearly than ever. I see him with his white hair, the slight comma across his forehead, the black-framed, Clark Kent glasses, the dark tie and pressed white shirt—short sleeves in warm or hot weather, but still a dark tie. I see him in my living room when I am alone, usually sitting across from me, smiling, happy, a smile which, if worn by someone else, I would have considered patronizing and condescending. For lately when I am with him, I am not the anxious, strange, and morbid adult, not my habitual self, but the child he taught to love the world.

I was running from my nemesis, my sister Lamia, across the hallway in our apartment in Beirut. Lamia, a heavy sleeper, had been napping on her bed, deathlike, looking solemn. I talked to her but she would not wake. I breathed on her face but she would not wake. I lit a candle, waited anxious seconds, tilted it, and allowed a tear of wax to drop onto her forehead. She woke. She screamed. I screamed. She lunged at me. I eluded her and ran across the hallway, screaming and laughing, she, screaming and threatening.

My stepmother came out of the kitchen to see what the racket was. I had reached the foyer when the door opened. My grandfather came in and scooped me up in one motion— he lived in a cavernous apartment two buildings down from ours and never knocked or rang the bell when he dropped in. He lifted me up in the air. I yelled with joy. Lamia stopped in her tracks, her eyes boring viciously into us.

"What's my little troublemaker been up to?"

"Nothing," I said. "I didn't do anything."

My stepmother, pregnant, about to deliver her first child, stepped into the foyer. She moved slowly, purposefully. She looked at my sister Lamia standing rigid, tiny fists balled up, eyebrows bunched together, nitroglycerine about to explode. "What happened, Lamia?" my stepmother asked.

Lamia kept staring at me. Her fiery eyes should have burned me to cinders. She rarely responded quickly or rashly, always deliberately. "Nothing," she said loudly. "Nothing happened." She turned around and stormed off to her room. If there was one person she despised more than me, it was my stepmother, the usurper. She could not complain to my grandfather. She hated him because he loved me. She could not even complain to our father, whom she blamed for making our mother vanish into thin air.

"I'll take care of this rambunctious little scamp," my grandfather said, carrying me into the living room.

"Please, don't fill her head with wicked stories." My stepmother's requests fell on inattentive ears. She walked back to the kitchen, looking as if she had already lost a major battle.

My grandfather sat in his dark ultramarine chair—even though he had a home of his own, he had an armchair (with its own taboret) in our house, which no one was allowed to sit on. I sat on his lap and played with his white hair, sparse, smooth to the touch. He jiggled, adjusted himself to a comfortable position.

"The great Sarah Bernhardt was just like you. She was a troublemaker, always a scamp. Even when she grew up, she was known for her winsome, sweet, playful ways. But when she was a little girl like you, she caused a lot of trouble. Just like you. At school, oh boy. She was a firecracker. She drove the nuns crazy. Big troublemaker. She could curse with the best of them, make the nuns blush every time she came up with a doozie."

"I bet I can curse better than her. Your mother's vagina is plugged with a thousand donkey dicks."

My grandfather roared, his head jerking back, his glasses almost falling off the tip of his nose. "That's a good one."

"Yes. My dad says I have a tongue like a sailor on leave."

"And your dad's right."

"The nuns liked Sarah, right? They all liked her because she was special."

"You bet. Even though she was a troublemaker and was hysterical most of the time, they knew she was a good girl. She was a star. Everybody could tell that. And stars are quite passionate. She had uncontrollable passions. At school with the nuns, she also became devout because she was extremely passionate. She wanted to be a nun."

"But she didn't, right?"

"Right. Because she grew up and she was smart. Remember, Jesus is only for children and people who never get smart. And anyway, she became passionate about the theater. She had her first play with the nuns at Grandchamp. How old was she?"

"She was thirteen."

"That's right. She was thirteen. At first, the stupid nuns didn't put her in the play. They didn't think she could do it. This big archbishop was coming to the school."

"The guy in a dress."

"Yes. The fat guy in a dress came to the school and they staged a play for him. But Sarah was not in the play. She watched and watched all the rehearsals. She didn't want just any role. She wanted the lead role. She knew she could be the star. Then when the guy in the dress came and he sat down to watch the play . . ."

"He lifted his dress to sit."

"That's right. He lifted his dress to sit. The girl who was

supposed to be the star got scared. She started crying. Stupid girl. The girl said she was too scared to go on stage in front of people. She was shaking and crying. The nuns didn't know what to do."

"So Sarah said she'd do it."

"Yes. She came out of nowhere and said she could do it. Sarah said she knew the role. She had memorized it. So the nuns didn't have a choice. They let Sarah be the star."

"And she was great."

"Always. She was the Divine Sarah. She came on stage and the guy in the dress cried and cried like a little girl because Sarah was so good. Now, people from all over the world, from Brazil, from China, from Africa, they all go to Grandchamp just to see the school where the great Sarah went on stage for the first time. Nobody remembers the stupid nuns or the guy in the dress. They just want to see where the Great One began. It's a pilgrimage. You know what a pilgrimage is?"

"Yes. Like Mecca."

"Yes. Like the silly Muslims who go to Mecca and walk in white dresses."

I still hear him to this day. I hear his sonorous tones when I take walks. I hear his silly laugh when a crow caws. I hear his collusive whispers in the passing breeze. *Don't tell your stepmother. She can't know about this.* He had a heavy Druze accent, stressing his *Q*s. Whenever I hear a mountain Druze speak, I am reminded of him.

"Tell me about the time she fell in the fire."

We were at his house, in the family room, a room covered with books and bookshelves, and the little wall space not covered was painted a striking yellow-green. I sat on his lap as usual.

"Her mother sent her to live with a nurse in Brittany, in the northwest of France. Her mother was a bad woman. She didn't want Sarah around when she was seeing all those men. So she kept sending Sarah away to live with other people. Her mother hated Sarah because she knew Sarah was a star of the greatest magnitude and her mother was envious because when Sarah was around, nobody looked at Sarah's mother. Poor Sarah. All her life she tried and tried to make her mother love her, but she couldn't. Her mother couldn't love her because she loved all those men. Sarah liked Brittany because she stayed on a farm and she played all day with a lot of animals and the animals loved her. Why did the animals love her?"

"Because she was the great Sarah and everybody loved her."

"That's right. And when she grew up she had lots of animals she loved and they loved her back. What kind of animals did she have?"

"She had lots of dogs and cats and a cheetah."

"That's right. And more too."

"An alligator from America. Ali Gaga. Not Ali Baba. And a parrot. His name is Bizibouzou. And a monkey called Darwin."

"That's right. So one day, while her nurse was in the garden gathering potatoes, and the nurse's husband was drunk in bed, sleeping, baby Sarah was sitting in her highchair watching the beautiful fire in the hearth. She unfastened the little tray in front of the chair and now there was nothing in front of her. All of a sudden . . ."

"Baby Sarah fell into the fire."

"When she screamed, the nurse's husband was quick. He

ran and snatched Sarah up and he dunked her in a pail of milk and then he covered her with butter. All the peasants came from all over Brittany to give Sarah butter to heal her burns. Then a week later, her mother came with her man and she brought doctors too. And then Sarah's aunts, the bad women, they came too with their men. They kept saying, 'Poor Sarah. Poor little Sarah,' but then they got bored and left and didn't take poor Sarah with them even though she begged her mother to take her. And she cried and cried and poor Sarah was all alone without her mother."

"Poor little Sarah."

One time, my stepmother, Saniya, came into the kitchen and found me naked, having covered my whole body in butter, both salted and unsalted.

These days, I also hear my mother cursing him, calling him all kinds of names. She has been dead for some years now, but I hear her curse the son of a bitch—her favorite name for my grandfather—for the things he put her through. "He worked and worked until your father was forced to divorce me." My mother cursed him till the day she died. "He was evil, evil incarnate. Everybody thought he was the nicest man, but the things he did, the things he said."

On the terrace of my grandfather's summer house in the mountains sat my grandfather, my grandmother, my father, stepmother, uncles and aunts. Under the grape arbor, which provided shade all the way from the terrace to the driveway, protecting the cars from the despotic sun. I stared at the grapes, my mouth watering. They were still sour, a ways from being ripe, what we called *hosrom*. These were my favorites—eating the sour grapes with salt was a veritable taste explosion. While the adults were chatting, I climbed the pergola until I reached the vines and began moving slowly across the arbor, suspended high in the air, hanging on with one hand at a time.

"Oh, my god." My stepmother jumped up, ran and stood right underneath me with her hands held up to catch me. "Sarah Nour el-Din. Get down here this instant."

"I want to get some grapes."

"What are you doing up there, Sarah?" My father asked me this while I hung ten feet from the ground. I noticed he still sat in his seat. My grandfather was chuckling.

"Let go, Sarah," my stepmother said. "I'll catch you."

"I want to get some grapes."

"I'll get you some. We get them by using a ladder, not by climbing the vines. I don't want you to hurt yourself. Now, just let go."

"You look like a little monkey, my little Sarah," my grandfather said.

I let go and dropped into my stepmother's arms. "Don't you ever do that again," my stepmother chided. "You can get killed. Girls don't climb trees."

"Are you going to get me some grapes?"

She shook her head in despair, still unsure what to do with me. "Okay. I'll get some for everybody."

By the time she came back with the ladder and a pair of shears, I was in my grandfather's lap. I knew the story he would tell. I had climbed the pergola. I was called down. There was only one story he could tell now: The Prince of Believers.

"Who was the boy that climbed trees?" he asked me.

"The Egyptian boy."

"What was his name?"

I racked my brain, but could not remember. I knew the story, but the medieval Arabic names were completely foreign to me. "The Caliph," I said.

"He was the Caliph, but that was not his name. A caliph is like a prince. It's not a name. Don't worry, my little one. I'm sure even your father and uncles don't know his name. That's because they don't care where they came from."

"I know his name," my father interjected.

"Al-Hakim bi-Amrillah," one of my uncles said.

"See. I told you they wouldn't know because they don't pay attention. Not like you. His name was al-Mansour. He was only eleven. This was a long, long time ago in Egypt. During the great Fatimid dynasty. The Caliph was going from Egypt to Syria to fight the bad Byzantines who wanted to come and take over our lands and make us all Christians. So the Caliph stopped in Bilbays because he felt sick. He knew he was going to die. He felt bad because unlike those Christian emperors who sat in their castles and told people what to do, our Caliph was going to join his army and fight alongside his men, but now he knew he wasn't going to make it. So he lay in bed and he called al-Mansour, who was playing outside. The little boy came and he saw the Caliph in bed. The Caliph called him over and kissed him and hugged him like this. And everybody was there and saw the Caliph hug him. And then he told the boy, 'Go out and play. I will be all right now. I know you'll be a good Caliph.' So everyone knew that al-Mansour was going to be the next Caliph."

"And he was a star."

"That's right. So the little boy went out to play. After a little while, an intendant from the court, whose name was Barjawan, came out looking for the little boy. He looked and he looked, but he couldn't find him. All of a sudden, he heard the voice of al-Mansour saying, 'Hello, Barjawan.' Barjawan still couldn't see our boy. So the boy said, 'I'm up here.' And Barjawan looked up and saw al-Mansour playing in a sycamore tree. Barjawan said, 'Please come down from the tree, your highness. The Caliph has gone to heaven. You are now the Prince of Believers.' And the new Caliph came down from the tree. Everybody saw that he was an emissary from God. Then they all returned to Cairo, which the Fatimid had built. And the boy Caliph walked in front of everybody and all the people came out to see. The people realized at the same time that they loved the boy Caliph. He sat on a throne of pure gold. All the people came to pay their respects. They saw a confident Caliph with piercing eyes that could see the truth. They saw a beautiful boy with the face of a wise and learned man. They saw that the new Caliph was touched by God and his angels. The boy looked at them all and smiled upon his people. They felt his grace. And he said, 'My name is now al-Hakim bi-Amrillah.' You know what that means?"

"The ruler by God's command."

"Yes. And even though he was only a little boy, he became the greatest Caliph of all time. He was the star. He was generous and just, wise and judicious. Three months after becoming Caliph, he sent missionaries to herald the coming of a new age, which was to start when the time was ripe. In this new age, truth will be revealed and the knowledge of God was to be disclosed. That was the Call."

"The Call for the Druze."

"It was years later when the time was ripe and the Druze were born. Al-Hakim bi-Amrillah was older and even wiser. But even when he was a little boy, all the people could see he was special. That boy is the reason we are all here."

"So I am the Prince of Believers."

"You're the Princess of Believers."

"You keep putting these strange tales in her head," my stepmother said, as she placed the large straw tray filled to overflowing with bunches of the sour white grapes on the table in front of all of us.

It was spring, in May, some years ago. I was visiting my sister Amal at her apartment in Beirut. A lazy afternoon, her kids playing in the den, while she and I lounged on a huge sofa. We sat facing each other, massaging each other's feet, a favorite pastime of ours since we were children.

"I don't understand why he loved you so," she said wistfully, reminiscing.

"Neither do I, but I am grateful he did."

"Are you? If you were Hitler's favorite child, would you be grateful for his love? I'm not sure I would be."

"He was not Hitler. I know most of you remember him differently than I do, but he was not evil. Grandfather was just quirky. He was not a bad person."

"He was a Machiavellian asshole, prejudiced as hell, xenophobic and bigoted. You just don't remember him well. With you, he was all kindness and warmth; with the rest of us, he was a manipulative bastard."

"He wasn't that bad. He just didn't care for you as much as he did for me. I can't explain why he cared for me so much, but he wasn't bad with you. He just ignored you."

"You're so naïve sometimes. He was a misogynist. He hated all us girls. He thought all women were whores. He beat Grandmother up on a regular basis. You were just too young to remember. In any case, what he did to our stepmother alone is enough."

"What we all did. We were all unkind to Saniya when she arrived."

"We took our cues from him."

"We took our cues from Father."

"Nope. Father was willing to forgive Saniya's inadequacies. After all, he picked her. He chose an uneducated peasant girl for a wife. He knew what he was doing. It was Grandfather who started the attacks. He turned all of us into the jeering audience. You should talk to her sometime and listen to her stories about him. It'll give you goose bumps. He was a horrid man. He even told Lamia to her face that she would never find a husband unless she had plastic surgery. He hated women."

"He loved Sarah Bernhardt."

"He did not. He loved the myth, the unattainable myth of what a woman is. He had no clue who Bernhardt was. He apotheosized her. Her mother he called a whore, but according to him, Sarah lived *la vie galante*. Fuck that. She started out as a prostitute, like her mother, like her aunts. No metaphors, no euphemisms. She had to be a prostitute like her mother. There was no other way a woman could survive. But your grandfather probably thought she died a virgin. At least he wanted to believe so. *She was born a star.* Bullshit. Like any star in any age, she made it by sleeping her way to the top."

"I can't think badly of him, though. He meant so much to me."

"I know that. It's a good thing for you he died when he did. If he had waited until you reached puberty, he would have turned against you."

"I'm not sure about that."

"I am," she said emphatically. "Do you ever wonder why he always told you the story of the Prince of Believers, but not the story of Sarah?"

"He always told stories of Sarah. What are you talking about?"

"Not Bernhardt, dummy. Sarah, the first woman sent out
on the Druze Call. You don't even know what I'm talking
about, do you? You don't know who your real namesake is?"

"No idea at all."

"Al-Muqtana sent a messenger to Wadit-Taym to recon-
firm the vows of the followers of a heretic called Sukayn.
They tortured and killed the messenger. Al-Muqtana decided
to send a woman messenger because she would not meet the
same fate. Since the new faith felt that men and women
were equal in the eyes of God, he sent the most faithful, a
woman by the name of Sarah. You didn't know that, huh?
She led a congregation that included her own father. *Her own
father.* Can you imagine what an amazing woman she must
have been? She was unbelievably successful. She reconfirmed
the vows of most of the followers, men and women. I loved the
fact that your grandfather used to say that the boy was the
reason we are all here. Sarah was the reason we are here. We
are the direct descendants of the people she converted. Don't
you find it strange that he would not mention her? He preferred to fill your head with stories of the Divine Sarah, but
not the Druze Sarah."

I was in bed, sleeping over at my grandfather's house. He
tucked me in and began another story. "A long, long time ago,
all the Christians in the world got together and decided to
invade our country. As always, they couldn't stand the fact
that not all the world was Christian like them. So they got
together and decided they wanted to liberate our country
from the infidels, which meant us. They wanted to liberate
us from ourselves. They called themselves the Crusaders.
When the Crusaders started coming, we fought them all over
this country. But they kept coming and coming like ants and

we kept beating them and beating them. One day this big ship of Crusaders landed in Sidon. They didn't know what to do because all the crusaders were losing everywhere. So there was this young Crusader who was smart and evil and he had lots of plans. His name was Richard Nixon. Nobody liked him because everybody thought he was up to no good, but they always listened to him because he was smart. So Nixon looked around when the Crusaders landed and he decided he knew why they always lost. It was because all the seashore was flat and the mountains were so close that we always won because we attacked them from up high. So Nixon told the Crusaders they had to climb the first hill and build a fortress and they had to do it quickly before we arrived. The Crusaders listened to him because they knew that Nixon was devious. They climbed the hill and started building the fortress. They built and they built, they cut down trees, our cedar trees which were ten thousand years old. That's why we have fewer than one hundred cedar trees left. It was all because of Nixon. They used wood and they moved rocks, and then they got tired when the night came. They were almost done so they thought they would finish it the next day. Well, at night, our birds and animals got together and they decided they didn't like these foreigners coming over here and cutting down our trees. So while the Crusaders slept, the birds flew over and began taking each piece of wood and each stone, the donkeys put the heavy stuff on their backs, the foxes directed traffic, the rabbits dug holes under the walls so they would come tumbling down. The birds and animals worked until daybreak when everything that Nixon built was broken down on the ground. When the Crusaders woke up, they saw that all the work they did had been in vain. Nixon stood up and told them all was not lost. He told them they had to start all over again before the infidel army came. He told them they would win the war but all they needed now was a little more effort. So the stupid Crusaders began building the fortress again. They worked and they worked until they got so tired and it was night and there was only a little bit left to do so they went to sleep and decided they would finish it the next day. Again, that night, the birds and animals came and they were laughing. The birds laughed as they carried the wood. The donkeys laughed as they carried the stones. The rabbits laughed as they dug holes. The foxes and the turtles laughed. Because the Crusaders were stupid. When the Crusaders woke up the next day they saw again that the work they had done had been in vain. So Nixon got them to start working again. Same thing happened the next day and the next. Our army arrived one day from the mountains. The general looked down at the Crusaders and started to laugh. He said those stupid Christians think they can stop us with a small fortress like that. They won't finish it in time anyway so we'll attack them tomorrow after getting a good night's sleep. The Crusaders did not see our army so they worked and they worked until night came and they got tired and went to sleep. The next day, when our army woke up, they saw that there was no fort at all. They saw the Crusaders begin to build the fortress again. The army wanted to attack, but the general said no. He said the army should wait until tomorrow because the stupid Crusaders were getting tired of building and they would never finish it anyway. They would attack them tomorrow when the Crusaders first woke up. So they went to sleep and when they woke up, the general saw that there was nothing there again. He laughed and he laughed when he saw Nixon telling the Crusaders they should build the fortress again. So the army sat down and watched the stupid Crusaders build the fortress again and again and again. Years

It took me years to accept the truth. When I finally heard what my grandfather told my mother at my birth, I was converted.

"The Americans are so stupid," he told me. "They all grow up in barns. They're cow people. Even now, they all have money and things, but they still are stupid. When Sarah went to America, the Americans loved her because she was the greatest star in the world. But they didn't understand her at all. Sarah was a hard worker. In America, she was doing play after play and she was extremely tired. One time, she got so tired in the middle of the first act of a play, she fainted. The director brought down the curtains to see if she was all right. Being the trooper that she was, when she woke up she wanted to go on with the play. She said she was ready. They raised the curtain, but there was no one in the audience. Thinking the play was over, those dummies had left. The stupid Americans didn't understand a thing."

Amal was right about one thing. My grandfather told me so many stories of Sarah Bernhardt, of her awe-inspiring acting, her wonderful sculpture, her devilish tantrums and hysterical rages. He talked of her beauty and charm, of her eyes that borrowed color from the changing light. He talked of having met her as a young boy of eleven and her kindness toward him. He talked of her presence on stage, the brilliance of her personality. He could not stop talking about her infatuation with death, her sleeping in caskets. How she was the only actress in history to have been a success as both Hamlet and Ophelia. He never talked about Damala, the gorgeous, abusive Greek she gave herself to. That I had to find out on my own, how obsessed she became with the man twelve years her junior, their tumultuous marriage, how she let a man with no talent convince her to let him become her lead actor. He never told the story of the Prince de Ligne, the Belgian who seduced her when she was still a young girl, who showed her a different life only to withdraw when she told him she was pregnant. He never mentioned all the men she toyed with, who were so in love with her she kept them on a leash for her entertainment. He never said anything about her pattern of falling in love only with men who could not love her back.

He never once mentioned her son, not how he was born out of wedlock, not how much she loved him.

"She was so skinny at a time when girls were fat," he told me as I sat on his lap. "You could see her collarbone, just like yours."

"She's just like me."

He traced the jutting collarbone. "You have exactly the same collarbone, deep and capacious. I'm going to start drinking my soup from here." He bent down wanting to lick my neck and I laughed like crazy.

I was visiting my mother in her New York apartment. She lay back on her divan, enigmatic and morose. She was in a talkative mood for a change.

"Your grandfather was an evil man," she said without any hint of emotion. "He made my life miserable. Whenever no one was around, he would whisper things like, 'You may think you have him because you spread your legs, but all vaginas go sour after a while.' He even called a couple of times and I picked up the phone and bang, he'd call me a whore or a slut. What could I do? I tried telling your father, but he didn't believe me. There was no one I could talk to. He did not relent, kept going after me again and again. You know, when I heard your father remarried, I was so hurt at first. I wanted his new wife dead. But then I thought, you know, there's no worse fate I could wish on someone than having that devil for a father-in-law."

"He did treat her very badly."

"The worst was after each of my deliveries. Did I ever tell you what he told me after you were born? He and his fucking wife were in the hospital room with me. Your father was in the waiting room playing host with all the visitors. Your grandfather picked you up and said, 'You know, Janet, I love this girl so much. Do you know why?' Like an idiot, I asked, 'Why?' And he said, 'I love her so much because she's the reason I am going to be able to return you to your fucking country.' "

CHAPTER ONE

Our novel opens with the sound of running water. We are unable to discern clearly at first because we are at a distance. We feel a cold, the cold of low temperatures not that of harsh weather. The visuals are unclear. It is hard to see for everywhere there is white. Snow covers the ground, the trees, every stationary thing. As we get closer, we realize the sound is a waterfall. The sound is concentrated, bowl-shaped. Within ten feet of the waterfall, it is deafening, yet one step farther quiet creeps in.

Hovering above the waterfall, we see that the river is about thirty feet wide. The fall is manmade. No. That is not exactly accurate. The fall is man-aided. The drop has been evened out, but the rocks and the spasmodic fits of water at the bottom show that nature has not been completely vanquished. The white of the water is slightly more colorful, less virginal, than the white of the snow covering the rocks.

It is March in a small town in New Hampshire.

Our river runs through the center of the sleepy town, houses and small buildings on each side. We hear the sound of a miniature snowplow driving along the sidewalk. The street has already been done. Even though the sky is a dazzling blue, not many pedestrians are out. Only one woman steps off the sidewalk onto the road to let the plow through. She smiles at the driver, who stops.

"Hello, John," she says cheerfully. She is of hardy New England stock, short, no more than five-two or so, we can guess one hundred and sixty pounds, but we can't be completely sure because of the dumpy gray overcoat she wears. A woolen cap covers her relatively small head, which makes it difficult to figure out her hair color, but we can assume, with some confidence, that it is gray, for she does not seem like the kind of woman who would bother with hair coloring.

"Mornin', Mary. Turned out a lovely day, hasn't it?" John sits behind a large bushy mustache and the handlebars of the snowplow. He seems eternally happy, plowing being the perfect job for him, dreaming of motorcycle racing.

"Ah, yeh. They say there won't be another storm for three days."

"That's what they say."

"Did you see that coat there?" Mary asks, pointing at a couple down below the road watching the waterfall.

"Must be from Boston."

"Must be. Well, I'd better be getting along. You have a good day, John."

There you go. We have now been introduced to the coat and the woman wearing it.

If we look down at where sturdy Mary pointed, we see two women below the road, along the promenade, leaning across the metal railing, watching the waterfall. Right away we can tell they are not local, but we are also sure they are not Bostonians either. The coat alone should have been enough of a clue. It is fake fur, ankle-length, hyacinthine, and seems to highlight the woman's lovely curves as opposed to obfuscating them. She wears purple high-heeled boots with matching mittens. Her hair (we note the absence of any hat, more prima facie evidence she is not local) is a lustrous blue-black, wavy and abundant, dropping an inch past her shoulders. We are observing her from the back, still, almost statuesque, watching the raging waters do battle with the implacable rocks.

The woman standing to her right seems jittery in comparison, shifting her weight from one foot to the other. She moves her head sideways to glance at her companion, as if gauging the other's feelings. We can tell from the appearance of the woman on the right that she is slightly perturbed. She wears a small black skullcap that barely covers her head. The cap is obviously no match for the temperature. She also wears a parka, which makes her look like the Michelin man, with a warm hood that is not being used. It hangs loosely on her back, barely held on by one button, like a relic about to be discarded. Her hair is recently cut, a short boyish crop, dyed an unnatural red. Her hands are parked in her parka. She has obviously forgotten her gloves.

We can't hear much of their conversation yet; the sound of running water overpowers everything. Let us try and move closer so we can eavesdrop. We begin to hear a conversation already in progress. The hyacinth woman says, "His hair was still soldered with brilliantine. It was still black-black. I couldn't believe it. My mother actually dyed the hair of the corpse and then used a ton of brilliantine like she did every morning while he was still alive. I walk into the room and the bastard looks like he's twenty years younger except he doesn't look anything like himself, all sallow and pallid. My mother had him lying on the bed, his head on the pillow, his arms folded on his chest, exactly like he looked all the time when he was resting and I wasn't allowed to disturb him. It was right out of the *Twilight Zone*. Kept waiting to hear the music in the background. So here I am, just arrived, everybody berating me for being late as if I could have taken the Concorde to Beirut or something, and my mother takes me in to see him and he looks like he's been waiting for me. It was sick. My mother says I can touch him if I want. Well, the only thing I wanted to touch was his hair. I don't know what came over me. I wanted to muss up his hair."

"Actually," the red-haired woman says, "I've always wanted to do that myself. Not sure why."

"Me too. But I couldn't do it while he was alive and now here he lay dead in front of me. So I tried and you know what? I couldn't do it. That damn brilliantine was so stuck it felt like I was trying to break up cement. It remained like a bowling ball. All I did was break his hair into compact strips, but it sure didn't move. Even at the end he frustrates me. Too bad he's dead because he could have explained all this to me."

"Brilliantine is never just brilliantine."

"No," the hyacinth woman says with a giggle, "nothing is ever just what it is." She smiles for the first time. Her companion joins her in smiling, happy to be of some use. Hyacinth woman puts her arm through her friend's, moves closer and lays her head on her friend's shoulder.

Now, what can we gather from this glimpse into these two women's lives? We have a slightly clearer picture. First, let us name them, for we cannot keep calling them the hyacinth and the red-haired woman. The former we shall call Dina and the latter, Sarah, good Lebanese names. It is fairly obvious from the snippet of conversation we overheard that Dina has just attended her father's funeral, which must have happened in Beirut. It seems Sarah is here to comfort her. We can tell from the last physical interaction, the laying of the head on the other's shoulder, that they are close, probably old friends. What else? Well, they spoke without much of a discernible accent— discernible foreign accent, that is. That means they have probably been living in America for a while, probably arrived at a fairly young age, not children, but young adults. Dina does seem to have a noticeable Boston twang to her words, so maybe Snowplow John, with his quick assessment, was not far off after all.

Dina delivered her speech impassively, not removing her gaze from the waters until the end. Her face is heavily made up, even the purple eye shadow applied with thought to match the outfit. Whatever is troubling her is not apparent to the inexperienced eye. She seems serene, content with her life. Yet Sarah's face shows a concern for her friend that eases slightly only when Dina smiles.

Let us find out more.

Sarah walks over to the stone bench and sits down. She seems slightly more at ease, but not much. She takes off the cap, scratches her head, and puts the cap back on. "I should have been there," she says. "You should have let me come."

"No. I was fine. It wouldn't have mattered."

"It would have. I should've been there for you."

"Oh, come on," Dina says, still somewhat impassively. "My mother would have had a conniption. She would've been on me the whole time. If you wanted to help me, your not coming was a great help."

"Hey, thanks."

"You know what I mean. My mother still thinks you turned me into a lesbian. She hates your guts. You ruined me, admit it. You led me down this road of sin and left me there. It's your fault I'm a fallen woman."

"If only I could talk to your mother. Listen, can't I just talk to her? Next time I'm in Beirut, I can just go over and talk to her."

Dina sits down next to her friend. "Get real," she says seriously. "Do you think you'd be able to get through to her? Do you think you can say anything I haven't? She remembers what you were like. We slept together in the same bed many times. Ergo, you're the lesbian and you converted me. It's simple."

"Your mother's fucked up."

Dina smacks the back of Sarah's head playfully. "Earth to Sarah. What do you think I've been saying all these years?"

"I should've been there. For you."

"It was almost as if you were there. Your whole family showed up. All of them. That was so wonderful. Even your ex-husband was there with your son. I was so grateful. I think we should plan on getting you two remarried."

"And his wife?"

"Details, details. We can easily get rid of that little ninny."

"Kidnap her and force her to wear something other than Armani. That'll kill her on the spot, don't you think?"

"He still loves you dearly."

"I know. And I love him. It just didn't work out, that's all. We still talk three or four times a week. Sometimes I wonder what could have been, but it never would have worked out. We always wanted different things. In a way, we're closer now than we've ever been. We have no need to change each other."

"We still should get rid of that little ninny."

"And get him a better haircut."

"And make him stop smoking."

"And get him out of politics."

Sarah and Dina have their arms entangled again. Sitting on the bench, Sarah looks quizzically at her friend, still wonders if Dina remains troubled. A questioning expression keeps reappearing on Sarah's face.

"Your father was there. I was surprised. He offered me his condolences. Surprised the hell out of me."

"It shouldn't have. He's a stickler for rituals. He was just doing his duty."

"He still hates my guts."

"Yours hated mine."

"Your mother was wonderful."

"My stepmother?"

"Yes. She's extraordinary. I love that woman."

"She always loved you. From the beginning."

"She took me out to lunch a couple of times. It seems every time I see her, I gain more respect for her. Do you realize she's the only one who asks how Margot is doing? For everyone else the relationship doesn't exist. Twenty years together and my mother doesn't want to know anything, but your mother cares enough to ask. Maybe she should adopt me."

"If she did, you'd be set financially."

"Yeah, and who would've believed that?"

The women have been sitting silent for a while. Sarah wants to interrupt the interlude, but is unsure how to proceed. She is examining Dina's face in an attempt to read the secrets hidden there. She finally breaks in: "Why are we here?"

"I wanted to be out of Boston," Dina answers.

"Yes, but why here? Why didn't you just visit me in San Francisco?"

"I didn't want to be *that* far out of Boston!"

"Why not New York?"

"I like it here. Always have. I can think here. It's so beautiful."

We can see Sarah is not fully satisfied with the answers. She hesitates, trying to figure out the best way in. "Are you worried about work?"

"Work? No. I took a leave of absence from the firm. I can come back whenever I feel ready. They've been quite supportive. Speaking of work, I designed a cabin in the woods about two miles north of here. We should go up and visit. You can see what my early work looks like."

Sarah shakes her head. "I know what your early work looks like. I know all your work. Remember?"

"I meant in person. We can see the cabin for real instead of blueprints. Self-exposure in the woods instead of on paper." Dina grins seductively at her friend, which only causes Sarah to shake her head even more.

"Where's Margot?" Sarah asks pointedly.

"She's at home."

"Did you have a fight?"

"Yes."

"Big one?"

"Yes. Big one."

"Really big one?"

"Biggest one we've ever had." Dina disentangles herself, stands up, and moves closer to the railing. She absentmindedly runs her gloved hand over the metal, removing the snow from the guardrail.

"I see. And you left?" Sarah shuffles her feet, stares intently at her friend.

"Packed a small bag."

"Does she know?"

"She'll find out tonight."

"Just like that?"

"She told me to go to hell."

"And here you are."

"This isn't hell," Dina exclaims. She turns around smiling, her arms gesturing to encompass everything around her. "Look. This is beautiful. This is closer to heaven. My kind of heaven at least."

"This is hell. Did you notice all the churches?"

"There's a great vintage clothing shop."

"Used clothing. Used, not vintage."

"No, no. Vintage. Believe me, what they have in that store should be in a museum. It's vintage."

"Are you going to call her?"

"No."

"You're going to let her suffer not knowing where the fuck you are?"

"Yes."

"Aren't you being childish?"

"Sarah Nour el-Din. Let's not talk about being childish, shall we?"

"I'm just repeating what you say to me."

"I know."

"Call her."

"Fuck no."

"Call her."

"No way. She called me a baby."

"You're acting like one."

"I'm not calling."

"I will if you won't."

"You die if you do."

"This is so unlike you. I can't believe you will stay here when she'll be worried sick when she gets home tonight."

"Tough."

"No, no. Hold on a second." Sarah looks energized, as if finally comprehending. "I know you, Dina Ballout. Margot knows you're here."

"Nope, she doesn't. I just packed and left. Didn't tell her anything."

"She's been here. She knows about this forsaken place. She must know about this place. She probably knows exactly where to find you."

"She has been here." Dina says this, pretending noncha-
lance.

"You've been here together."

"We come here every year."

"This is where you met?"

"Right here."

Dina stands staring at the water. She cries softly. Sarah
comes over and hugs her. "She'll be here," Sarah says.

"Well, she'd better drive over tonight or I'll break her
fucking legs."

"I know her. She'll be here. She'll figure it out."

"Well, I packed my thermal underwear so she knows I did-
n't go to Florida!"

"That's a good clue." They both giggle.

"Hey, no one can accuse me of not planning ahead. And I
packed the espresso maker. She knows the swill they serve for
coffee here."

"Great idea. Let's get some coffee. I'm freezing."

We see them walk up the embankment, arm in arm. And
this is as good a place to end our first chapter as any.

Introduction

I sat down in front of the television with my first quart of Ben & Jerry's ice cream (the first, Chunky Monkey; the second, Cherry Garcia). I was confused, slightly blue. I flipped channels as I stuffed my face. Ice cream worked better for me than any antidepressant or mood enhancer.

I was having trouble writing my memoir, not being able to figure out how to attack it. I had tried different methods, but the memoir parried back expertly. When I was a little girl, I used to watch a cartoon called *Touché Turtle*, the name of a fencing turtle musketeer whose sidekick was a talking dog called Dum-Dum. Every time I tried something new with my memoir, I felt the memoir become Touché Turtle, fighting me all the way. "Touché," the turtle would say every time it stabbed me, which was fairly often. At the end of each frustrating writing session, I would hear the damn turtle's farewell call, "Touché away," complete with closing credit music. I sat in front of my television devouring ice cream, healing my saber wounds before I attempted to enter the fray again.

I settled on a PBS nature documentary about lions in Africa. There was Red, the dominant male of the pride, getting older and barely holding on to his position within the pride. Juna was the best hunter, and the pride began to follow her lead while hunting. It was exquisite to see the pride on a hunt, the interminable wait, the coordinated movements, as if they were one organism, such murderous poetry in motion.

A lioness called Pinky delivered three delightful cubs, Bucka, Monk, and Ginny. Ginny turned out to be the cutest cub of them all, playful and cuddly.

Time passed. One of the younger males, Lewis, matured and decided to leave the pride and make his own way. Bucka, Monk, and Ginny were about four months old. It was a joy to watch and I was lost in a whole new world. I loved the interactions and relationships. I enjoyed the friendship between Pinky and Lisa, who seemed inseparable. I loved the communal rearing of the young.

A new lion appeared on the horizon, Corey, in his prime, beautiful, strong, and obviously up to no good. He stood on a hill and roared. Old Red, now alert, roared back. But even from the roars, you could tell the fight was over before it even began. Old Red was done for. I felt sad for him, but hey, that was life. The old had to go at some point. Old Red left the pride after a token fight. Corey was the new leader, but then that son of a bitch did something that shocked me.

Corey walked over to where my babies, Bucka, Monk, and Ginny, lay shivering with fright and began to kill them one by one. He started with Bucka, while Monk and Ginny cowered at his feet. He lifted Bucka by his neck, shook his head ferociously until the cub's neck snapped, and flipped the corpse away. He then picked up Monk while Ginny stayed where she was, waiting her turn for annihilation. By the time he killed Ginny, I no longer recognized myself. The announcers were pedantically explaining the logic of Corey's behavior, while I sat open-mouthed, shocked, unable to hear anything. I sweated, felt porous, like my body was made of clay not yet fired. I was afraid if I moved even an inch, one of my limbs would fall off.

On the screen, the pride was adjusting to life with Corey. Slowly, I began to grapple with what had happened. Individuals came and went, but the pride was what survived. Always. I had identified with each lion or lioness as a separate entity. I had thought I knew about lions because I saw Ginny as a cute and cuddly cub.

If I wanted to know about *lion*, I had to look at the entire pride. I had to look at it not as a single organism per se, but as a new unit much larger than the sum of its parts. Red was *lion*; Lewis, the lion who left the pride, was *lion*; Lisa was *lion*; Corey was *lion*; and my baby, Ginny, whose life was snuffed out to ensure Corey's new lineage, was *lion*. I could not begin to fathom what being a lion was if I only looked at each lion individually, or even at the relationships between the lions. All of them together, not all of them individually summed up, but all of them as a dynamic organism, were the species; all were the word *lion*.

I had tried to write my memoir by telling an imaginary reader to listen to my story. Come learn about me, I said. I have a great story to tell you because I have led an interesting life. Come meet me. But how can I expect readers to know who I am if I do not tell them about my family, my friends, the relationships in my life? Who am I if not where I fit in the world, where I fit in the lives of the people dear to me? I have to explain how the individual participated in the larger organism, to show how I fit into this larger whole. So instead of telling the reader, Come meet me, I have to say something else.

Come meet my family.

Come meet my friends.

Come here, I say.

Come meet my pride

ACKNOWLEDGMENTS

I used many books as reference or inspiration: *Lebanon: Death of a Country* by Sandra Mackey; *Pity the Nation* by Robert Fisk; *The Druze Faith* by Sami Makarem; *Civil War in Lebanon, 1975–92* by Edgar O'Ballance; *Crucial Bonds: Marriage Among the Lebanese Druze* by Nura Alamuddin and Paul Starr; *The Divine Sarah* by Arthur Gold and Robert Fizdale; *The House Gun* by Nadine Gordimer; and, of course, *If on a Winter's Night a Traveler* by Italo Calvino.

Raya Alameddine offered her impeccable French. Asa DeMatteo, despite his skewed priorities, offered his convoluted English. The writer Suleiman Alamuddin generously offered many historical tidbits, chief among them the story of the Druze Sarah. Nicole Aragi remains God's gift to writers. I owe a debt of gratitude to Barbara Dimmick, Hana Alamuddin, Karim Heneine, Debra Meadows, Michael Denneny, Ashraf Othman, and my editor, Alane Salierno Mason.

I wish to thank the staff of the MacDowell Colony.

I am blessed to have the endless support, guidance, generosity, and patience of my family. I thank them.